The Assassin
El Paso

Jim West

Copyright by Aurora Publications

The mounted cowboy over the state of Texas is the trademark of Aurora Publications.

This is a work of fiction. Names, characters, places, and incidents either are product of the author's imagination or are used fictitiously, and any resemblance to any actual persons, living or dead, events, or locales is entirely coincidental.

My special thanks go to my longer than time itself friend, John Fleenor, whose satirical wit keeps me straight. Thank you, John.

ISBN
Hardcover: 978-1-964289-94-6
Paperback: 978-1-964289-93-9

Other Books by Jim West

DNAlien
DNAlien II
DNAlien III
Genocide by GMO
Living Within a Strange Mind Vol. I
Living Within a Strange Mind Vol II
The Making of an Assassin Atlanta
The Assassin Baltimore
The Assassin Chicago
The Assassin Denver

Prologue

"American Airlines 2144, contact Fort Worth Center 127.7," the FAA Departure controller directed.

"Fort Worth on 27.7," Jim Lashley answered, keying the microphone on his controller column as he entered the frequency into the secondary head of his radio.

After waiting for a second to make sure no one else was on the frequency, Jim said, "Fort Worth, American 2144 with you out of 7 for 10."

"Roger, American 2144, radar contact, climb and maintain Flight Level 230, turn right heading 270 and proceed direct Abilene when able," the controller directed.

"Up to 230, heading 270, direct Abilene when able," Jim answered as he saw Captain Kirby set the new altitude and heading into the control panel. "Any ride reports?"

"Smooth," the controller answered before answering another flight, checking on to the frequency.

Jim sat back, watching Ray entering Abilene into the GPS navigation system, and mentally verified that everything looked normal.

Ray coupled the GPS to the autopilot and said, "Direct to Abilene and up to 230. You got the aircraft and radios, Jim. I'm going to make a quick announcement to the folks in back."

"I've got the aircraft," Jim answered as Ray removed the handset from the pedestal between their seats.

As he rechecked the autopilot to ensure that it was climbing correctly and was navigating to the assigned location on the departure, he listened to Ray go through his standard spiel to the passengers about how glad he was that they were flying American, telling them that it should be a smooth flight as he turned off the seatbelt sign, and reminded them to please keep their seatbelt on when in their seats, and ended by saying that he would do everything possible to get them to El Paso on time.

After hanging up the handset, Ray said, "I've got the jet. Anything new from Fort Worth Center?"

"You've got the jet," Jim answered. "Nothing new. Still assigned Abilene and 230."

"Good," Ray told him. "Still plan on hanging out at the hotel this evening, or would you like to meet with the Flight Attendants for dinner?"

"Actually, I'm meeting an old Air Force buddy for dinner this evening," Jim answered. "We were together in Vietnam, and I haven't seen him since then."

"What's he do now?" Ray asked as they approached 18,000 feet altitude, or Flight Level 180.

"Some corporate job," Jim answered as he changed his altimeter to the standard setting of 29.92 and watched Ray changing his. "Not really sure what he does, something in security, I think."

"American 2144, contact Fort Worth on 118.7", the controller directed as they passed 20 thousand feet.

"Fort Worth on 18.7," Jim answered, entering the new frequency.

"Fort Worth, American 2144, with you approaching Flight Level 230, direct Abilene," Jim said as soon as he changed the radio.

"Roger American 2144, continue to Flight Level 320, now cleared direct Lifft for the Sammr Three arrival to El Paso," the controller directed.

"On up to 320, direct Lifft for the Sammr Three to El Paso," Jim answered as Ray changed the autopilot to correspond to the new altitude assignment and the navigation system to take them direct to their new waypoint for the arrival.

"I figured you Marines, especially you guys that went to Vietnam, would have more contact," Ray said as he finished verifying the autopilot was performing as directed.

"Not always," Jim answered as he turned on his overhead speaker and removed his earpiece. Taking the hand microphone from its holder and hanging it on the sliding window latch handle, he continued, "Some of us do, but most of us just lose contact over the years."

"I know what you mean," Ray said, taking his earpiece out and turning up the volume of his overhead speaker. "I've kept track of one or two of all the guys I flew with before I left the Air Force. But most of them have more or less disappeared."

"Yep," Jim confirmed, nodding. "I occasionally hear from someone; I'm pretty much clueless about most of them."

"There are a few here at American that I sort of knew from the Air Force," Ray acknowledged. "But it's rare if I happen to run into them at the airport, and other than a few words if we're in Operations together, I don't have a clue about their lives."

Jim gave a short laugh and said, "After being so close during the service, especially when I was a mud grunt in Vietnam, I would have bet we'd always stay in touch. But life moves on."

"That it does," Ray agreed, looking out at the flat plains of central Texas. "Best friends back in high school, forgotten in college. Best friends in college, forgotten after graduation. Best friends in pilot training, never seen after reassignment."

"Even some of my friends here at American have been forgotten when they are transferred to Chicago, Miami, or New York," Jim replied as he thought about what was really going to happen after he got to El Paso.

The company he worked for, Muddy Water, was the domestic enforcement division of Black Water. Black Water had contracted with the US government to solve an issue that the government had been unable to manage due to the restrictions placed on law enforcement agencies across the country. From the local or city level up to the highest agencies of the federal government, the problem of gang violence wasn't being controlled by the law enforcement agencies that were tasked with the safety of the ordinary citizens of the country. In particular, Mara Salvatrucha, more commonly known as MS-13, was growing at an alarming rate.

And their signature method of dealing with their victims, either rival gangs or people who merely looked at one of them the wrong way, was using the machete. This was a throwback to the weapon of choice in their home country of El Salvador.

Tonight would hopefully end the year-long planning and month-long execution of the company's tasking. The goal was mainly to remove the top 50 members of each cell, or cliques as they were called, in each major city across the US where they were operating. And the same went for the other countries where MS-13 was operating. Except their sister organization that carried out Black Water international contracts, known as Dark Water, was running that concurrent operation.

Page Left Blank Intentionally

Chapter 1

Jim Lashley was drinking his second cup of coffee while watching the local news as he debated what he would do while his wife Jennifer was at work. He had gotten back from his scheduled trip yesterday evening late and he and Jennifer had stayed up later than normal catching up on what had happened since he had left four days ago.

Although both he and Jennifer were accustomed to a somewhat erratic work schedule since he had become a pilot with American Airlines after retiring from the Marines, it was still a disruption to their lives when his schedule changed from month to month or sometimes from week to week. Although Jennifer maintained her nine-to-five job, she sacrificed her time off when necessary to fit his constantly changing hours at home. Just as he was deciding that it would probably be a good day to mow the yard, the phone rang.

"Hello," Jim said as he rose from his chair to take his empty coffee cup to the kitchen.

"Good morning," retired Marine General Gene Barker told him. "What's on your agenda for the day?"

"Good morning, sir," Jim answered, smiling. "Just a few domestic chores, I guess. But I'm guessing that was actually a rhetorical question more than a genuine interest in my daily activities."

"Not so," Gene replied, chuckling. "I'm always interested in what you do on your unlimited days off."

"I wish I had unlimited days off," Jim told him as he put his cup in the sink. "Although, even if I did, I'm pretty sure you'd have something of the utmost importance to national security that you needed my sage advice and wisdom to solve. And there would go another of my unlimited days off."

"Why, Jim, how could you even think such a thing?" Gene joked. "Is it so inconceivable that an old fellow Marine pilot would want to have a friendly visit? Just a few moments of your busy day to reminisce about bygone days?"

"Not inconceivable, but certainly unlikely," Jim retorted, smiling. "But, giving you the benefit of the doubt, what pleasantries would you care to discuss?"

"Well, actually, it's more of a discussion of an upcoming contract," Gene admitted. "But I'd still like to think of it as a chance to reacquaint ourselves. You know, just to catch up."

"Oh yeah," Jim countered. "Reacquaint. Catch up on everything that's happened since the last time I saw you. That was what, two weeks ago?"

"What's time for except man's devised system of measuring the periods between things he's done or things to come?" Gene asked. "However, in this case, it's something more in the category of things to come."

"In that case, I'm assuming that you can't discuss it over the phone and want me to come to Virginia to share my views," Jim said.

"Maybe, or probably, later," Gene told him. "But, for now, I'd like to take you to lunch and give you a bird's eye view of the situation and what the objective is."

"Lunch is certainly doable," Jim replied, walking back into the living room. "What time did you have in mind?"

"Let's say about five minutes," Gene answered. "That's about how long it will take me to get there. If you can be ready that fast."

"I should have known," Jim said, shaking his head. "I don't think you ever call a day or two ahead of time. And you're usually only a block or two away when you do call. One of these days, you'll fly down here unexpectedly, and I'll not be available."

"A chance I'll have to take, I guess," Gene told him. "But this time, I just got lucky. And I'm pulling into your driveway as we speak. Do I need to come inside and wait, or are you ready?"

"I'll be out as soon as I hang up," Jim told him as he turned off the TV. "I'm on my way."

Locking the door and pulling it shut as he walked out, Jim noticed the usual Lincoln Town Car Gene preferred when he had to drive himself. Stepping to the passenger side, he again observed the dark tint of the windows as he opened the door.

"Thanks for being so prompt," Gene said as Jim slid into the leather seat. "Where would you like to go for lunch?"

"Since you know me so well, why don't you make the decision?" Jim answered as Gene backed out of the driveway.

"Venice Pizza it is then," Gene told him, smiling as he accelerated down the street. "One of these days, you need to broaden your interest in dining facilities. I'd bet that 99 times out of 100, you pick that place."

"Well, it has great food, and it's close," Jim said as Gene drove the well-known route to the restaurant. "And we usually have complete privacy in the back dining room, and I'm pretty sure we couldn't have that if we went to What-a-Burger."

"I do like What-a-Burger. One of the best chain burger joints in the world," Gene commented as he left the residential neighborhood. "But you're correct about the privacy part. And those folks at Venice have always been very accommodating. Regardless of how many of us show up. And to emphasize the food, it is good. And it's been a long time since I had some really good lasagna."

"That almost sounds like you planned this," Jim replied as they approached the restaurant. "Not that I'm complaining, but if you'd let me know ahead of time, I'm pretty sure Jennifer would have enjoyed lunch with you as well."

"And I always enjoy her company," Gene said as they pulled into the parking lot. "But, in this instance, I'm pretty sure she doesn't need to hear our conversation."

"Let me guess," Jim said as they exited the car. "Black Water has been given another contract that is short on details and even shorter on time to accomplish something that the entire US government can't handle."

"Close," Gene answered as they walked into the restaurant. "But the reason they gave us the contract is they know we can handle it. Which, by the way, is why we're paying you such a generous salary to supplement the meager amount American Airlines pays its pilots."

"Good morning, gentlemen," Billy, the owner of Venice Pizza, said as they entered. "Let me guess, you want a table in the rear, two iced teas with lemon, and probably the lasagna."

Gene looked at Jim, shaking his head, and repeated, "I keep telling you to broaden your dining choices. It seems that everyone here knows what you want without asking."

"He didn't mention the rolls," Jim joked as they took their seats. "I particularly like the rolls. With plenty of butter."

"And they'll be right out," Billy said with a smile. "As will your tea. "And I'll make sure you aren't disturbed while you eat."

"Thank you, sir," Gene said nodding. "I'm sure Jim appreciates your most outstanding service. As do I."

Chapter 2

"Okay, what's the mission this time?" Jim asked as Billy walked away. "And when do we start?"

"What do you know about MS-13?" Gene asked, sitting back in his chair.

"Not a lot," Jim admitted, leaning forward and putting his elbows on the table. "As far as I have heard, they're a rather brutal gang. Another one of those 'Blood in, Blood out' gangs. Mainly out in California, I think. Fond of mutilating their victims by hacking them up with a machete, if I'm not mistaken."

"All true," Gene said. "But they're no longer just in California. They've pretty much gained a substantial foothold across much of the United States as well as Central America."

"What's their primary goal?" Jim asked as one of the waitresses came in with a tray of bread and a bowl full of butter along with their tea.

"Let's do a little history first," Gene said, selecting one of the rolls. "Then we'll come to the present, as well as what we envision as their future.

First off, the gang is more formally known as Mara Salvatrucha," Gene said. "They started out in Los Angeles by refugees fleeing the civil war in El Salvador. Their primary objective was to protect themselves from the Latino gangs, such as the 18th Street gang, that controlled much of the area.

They became international as members were caught and subsequently deported," Gene continued. "Mainly back to Central and South America. That is part of the reason Black Water got involved. Because our government doesn't have jurisdiction in those countries and can't send in the military, they chose us as a solution."

"Why do we care what's happening in those countries?" Jim asked, smearing butter across the warm roll. "I'm sure most of them have more efficient ways of dealing with gangs than are possible here."

"That's partially correct," Gene admitted. "They do have more leeway in how they deal with criminals than we do with our, let's say, a castrated judicial system where the criminal has more rights than the victim. But, until we get complete control of our borders, they keep coming back and bringing more recruits with them."

"What's our approach?" Jim asked as he visualized machete-wielding gangs roaming the neighborhoods.

"Sort of like we did in Chicago, but on a more global scale," Gene answered as the waitress came into the room with their meals.

"You're referring to eliminating the top tier of their leadership," Jim surmised as she left the room.

"It goes much deeper than that," Gene said taking a fork full of the steaming lasagna. "MS-13 is more organized, especially in El Salvador, and has many more cells, or cliques as they are known here."

"So, how many operations will we be running?" Jim asked as he used his roll to break the string of cheese that ran from his fork to the dish of lasagna.

"Hundreds," Gene answered. "And that's just here in the US. Dark Water will be running as many, if not more, across the nations to our south."

"You've got to be joking," Jim said, looking surprised. "How do you plan on resolving the leadership issue, if that's what you're talking about, in one operation?"

"As I said, there are hundreds of operations," Gene explained. "Since you're only involved with the domestic side, we won't look into the international issues. But there are hundreds of cells, and our tasking involves every one of them, so it's going to be a massive undertaking."

"I'm guessing this is larger than any operation I've been involved with," Jim replied as the enormity of the operation became evident. "And how much time do we have to plan this minor little operation?"

"Believe it or not, the company, including Dark Water and Muddy Water, has been working on this for over a year now," Gene answered. "The intelligence gathering has been phenomenal. Of course, Black Water does have access to the enormous resources of not only all of our intelligence facilities, but those of the other nations."

"Even so, how many field agents are going to be needed?" Jim asked. "I can't imagine the number of people you'd need to remove just the top person of each cell or clique in one night."

"You're correct," Gene clarified. "We couldn't possibly put together enough people to do it overnight. It's going to be tough to do it in the month we have gamed the operation. If we were only talking about Los Angeles, we could do it much like we did in Chicago. But with MS-13 spread across much of the country, especially in Washington DC, Maryland, Virginia, and New York, a month is considered the shortest amount of time we'll need."

"What's the organizational structure here?" Jim asked.

"In some ways, it's rather complex," Gene answered. "For instance, each cell has its territory and operates somewhat autonomously from the other cells. However, since there are several cells in the larger cities, such as Los Angeles or Washington DC, there needs to be an overarching program to ensure that turf wars don't disrupt the overall organization."

"You said that they were highly organized in El Salvador," Jim replied. "Is it the same here in the US?"

"We've determined that it's loose connections everywhere except in Los Angeles," Gene answered. "Since they were the initial location, they've become more highly organized. The other cities have mainly cells operating in certain neighborhoods independently. However, all of them are answerable to the central organization that remains in El Salvador."

"I'm guessing that letting Dark Water handle the central organization won't solve the problem," Jim said.

"No, it may even exacerbate the problem," Gene answered. "If each clique were to become autonomous outside of Los Angeles, there could possibly be turf wars unlike we've ever seen."

"How many members are there in the central organization?" Jim asked.

"The Council of Nine," Gene answered. "At least there were initially nine members in El Salvador. They were responsible for the gang's strategies and financial issues, appointing members to be clique leaders and retaining final authority over any areas of dispute. It's possible that there are more members now that MS-13 has become more international. But we're only concerning ourselves with the domestic side of the contract."

"Not to drift off the subject," Jim said, smiling. "But, do you know where else you'll find the 'Council of Nine'?"

Gene leaned back and shook his head, answering, "Probably not, since you seem to have thousands of bits of minutia floating around inside your head that the normal person would have long forgotten. But enlighten me."

"In the beginning, according to UFO-ologists and Greek mythology, Zeus and eight other deities came to earth over 25 thousand years ago," Jim started. "They came to earth and created the first human female, Pandora. She was given what were called 'seductive gifts' by each of the nine.

She was then given as a gift herself to Epimetheus," he continued. "It was then she opened a large sealed jar and released evil upon all mankind."

"The story of Pandora's box," Gene replied, nodding. "We've all heard the story about how curiosity caused the world's problems. And just how does that relate to our discussion?"

"It doesn't," Jim admitted. "I said it was off the subject. I just thought about it when you mentioned the Council of Nine."

"Is that all of it?" Gene asked, shaking his head.

"Except that there's India's legend of the Society of Nine or nine unknown men who wrote books that are in some secret library in India or Tibet," Jim answered smiling. "And then there're the nine worlds in Norse mythology. I could go on about the 'Lab-9', a paranormal research facility that supposedly has been in contact with the Council of Nine."

"No, I think we've dug deep enough into the discussion of nine of anything," Gene told him. "Right now, I feel as if I've opened Pandora's box. I should know better than to let you drift off into one of your parallel universe things. I guess I've got to learn to control my curiosity, too."

Chapter 3

"Now that we've finished discussions of any nine related issues, other than the MS-13 Council of Nine, can we return to the relevant subject?" Gene asked when their waitress had left after checking on them.

"Certainly," Jim answered, smiling. "Of course, that means you'll never learn about what's behind the phrase, 'dressed to the nines' or 'the whole nine yards,' but if that's a loss you're willing to bear, let's continue."

Looking at the ceiling and shaking his head, Gene finally said, "A loss I'll gladly bear if we can wrap this up within the next hour."

Looking back at Jim, he continued, "We, Black Water, Dark Water, and Muddy Water, are planning a meeting at the Black Water headquarters in Quantico next week. I know your schedule, and we've worked around the other participants' schedules to make sure we can get everyone together then. At least the top players for each of the locations."

"How many locations are you looking at?" Jim asked.

"Just five," Gene answered. "Even though they've spread across at least 22 states, we're concentrating on these areas because of both the number of gang members and the levels of violence."

"I'm guessing that Los Angeles is one of them," Jim volunteered.

"Of course," Gene told him, nodding. "The other areas we are targeting are Long Island, New York, Fairfax County, Virginia, Montgomery County, Maryland, and El Paso, Texas."

"What about Chicago?" Jim asked, surprised at its exclusion.

"MS-13 doesn't have much of a presence up there," Gene answered. "I've been briefed by the head of the Chicago Gang Task Force, and they believe that the presence of the other gangs up there, and there are approximately 59 gangs with over 100,000 members, have kept them out."

"I guess that's a good thing," Jim acknowledged. "What little I've read about MS-13, I'd prefer to have one of the other generic gangs in my area. Probably two of them, and let them fight each other."

"It would be nice if there weren't any, but that's certainly a pipe dream," Gene told him, nodding.

"Did our operation in Chicago regarding the Gangster Disciples, Vice Lords, and the others have any impact on what's going on up there?" Jim asked.

"Some," Gene admitted. "The gangs are still there but operating at a substantially lower rate. Killings are down, the drug trafficking has been reduced, and several other indicators of lowered activity have been noted."

"Did it shift to St Louis as we thought?" Jim asked.

"It's still a little early to say for sure, but that's the initial reaction we've heard from the law enforcement people there," Gene answered. "And they aren't exactly jubilant about it."

"I imagine not," Jim said, finishing his lasagna. "But everybody knew it was going to happen when we removed all those gang leaders in Chicago. The drug distribution problem doesn't just disappear. It'll either move or be absorbed into another gang's operation."

"Unfortunately, as long as there's a demand, there'll always be a supply," Gene added. "The war on drugs will never end. And with the inclusion of the opioids, especially the prescription issue, it's a bigger than ever problem."

"What area are you looking at for me?" Jim finally asked after thinking about the areas Gene had mentioned.

"El Paso," Gene answered.

"Why there?" Jim asked. "I sort of thought that you'd send me to Los Angeles since we have a shit load of flights there every day, and that'd make it easier."

"We looked at that," Gene admitted. "But we have a lot of people there. We picked El Paso because American has daily flights from DFW, and we know you'll be able to bid on one of the trips that have at least two overnights there every week. And you'll be there five trips next month when you get the bid."

"How very convenient," Jim commented, looking at Gene. "I don't suppose Black Water had any input into having exactly what you need for this little operation, did they?"

"Of course not," Gene answered, pushing his plate away. "We looked at previous schedules from all the bases that American has and for the airlines where we have other agents. And we selected El Paso for you because the schedule just happened to work out. The same as with the other agents and locations."

"It just seems that Black Water has an extraordinarily high level of coincidences when it comes to their needs," Jim replied. "No matter what my schedule needs to be to fit their requirements, something always happens that favors the company. Lo and behold, I'm rescheduled to fly the exact trips that benefit their plans. Yeah, there are a lot of coincidences."

"Regardless of that, and I'm sure that they really are coincidences, we need to get everyone together this weekend and make sure we have everything covered for next month," Gene told him.

"How many people will I be working with in El Paso?" Jim asked as the waitress came to refill their glasses of tea.

"About 50," Gene answered as soon as the waitress left. "But, there's one in particular that will be with you instead of in the field."

"Fifty, that's a lot of people to keep track of," Jim said. "What sort of communications equipment will we have, and how will they know where their targets are?"

"That brings us to a special assistant you'll have while you're in El Paso," Gene answered. "But, let's discuss the equipment first. The communication equipment is an upgraded version of the gear you used in Chicago. This one uses hands-free, voice-activated transmission technology but doesn't have the usual background noise, such as breathing. Every member of your team will be on the same frequency and will hear every transmission from you or other members."

"That could turn into a real quagmire of noise if you get four or five people talking at once," Jim observed.

"That's one of the unique qualities of this new system," Gene explained. "If there's an incoming call, each individual microphone is canceled until there's blank air.

If you're calling any one of the members, or if any of them are making a transmission, none of the other sets will interrupt," he continued. "Once the 'current' transmission ends, the first set that made a call gets priority, and all the others are blocked."

"What if I need to override them?" Jim asked. "There are times when I may need to give an order or something that should override any of theirs."

"That's taken care of," Gene explained. "All of the sets are married to yours. If you make a call, let's call it keying your microphone; it overrides their sets. There's another set that your assistant will be using that also overrides any set except yours."

"I guess that means my assistant will be with me all of the time," Jim ventured.

"More like you'll be with her," Gene told him, smiling. "She's more or less the key to your other question, knowing where the targets are. She's actually the one that developed the computer systems the tracking systems are using."

"So, she can track hundreds of targets at a time?" Jim asked.

"Not just the targets but our operatives as well," Gene answered. "I wish we'd had this system available when we were in Vietnam. If we'd had it at the time, it would have saved thousands of lives."

"I'm guessing that she's using satellite systems," Jim said. "Global Positioning Satellites were something that would have been very convenient for bombing as well. A hell of a step up from the inertial navigation system."

"You should have been around for the dead reckoning," Gene said, smiling. "The emphasis was more on the dead than the reckoning. It was sort of like measuring with a micrometer, marking with a grease pencil, and cutting with an axe. More or less got you in the ballpark, but in the end, it was TLAR, or That Looks About Right."

"I guess we've made some improvements in killing people over the years," Jim added. "So, what does this lady do that makes her other than the normal computer nerd?"

"We'll discuss that later," Gene answered as the waitress brought their check. "But you'll find this story very interesting."

"How long will I need to be there?" Jim asked as Gene picked up the check and left a tip on the table.

"Just Saturday should cover it," Gene answered as they headed for the cashier. "And since I know you're flying Monday, we can take a little time Sunday morning to wrap it up if necessary."

"What days are you looking at?" Jim asked as they walked to the car.

"I'll send the jet to pick you and Jennifer up Friday afternoon," Gene answered. "We'll meet Saturday and Sunday morning, if need be, and the plane will take you back Sunday afternoon."

"I'm sure she'll be happy to go," Jim told him as they drove away. "I still say you should go a little easy on the private jet thing. As you know, she's getting to think that it's her private jet."

Chapter 4

After Gene dropped him off at his house, Jim started researching MS-13 on his computer. The amount of material was monumental. And the scope of their operations here in the United States was much larger and wide spread than he had imagined.

One of the things that really caught his attention was that MS-13 would recruit young boys from Central America who had entered the US illegally and were extremely vulnerable due to being isolated, with little resources or connections to their new community to take care of them once they made it to one of the cities.

In some instances, MS-13 would include potential gang members in their operations, where they were paid to smuggle illegal aliens across the border. That benefited the gang in two ways: money and more members.

And the problem is not reserved for the large cities. Many rural communities have experienced an influx of gang members. Here, there aren't sufficient funds allocated to fighting gangs or the violence they bring as much as the larger cities where gang violence has been an issue for years.

Add in the brutality, and the reason for the sudden need to eradicate the gang both within the United States and internationally becomes apparent. When individuals come into the communities and hack teenagers to death simply for not following a gang member's orders, the people demand action.

Unfortunately, a combination of lack of funds, especially in the smaller towns, inadequate police training regarding gang activity, and the increasing number of sanctuary cities has led to a rapidly growing problem across the nation.

Glancing at the time, he had just closed the window on the research and was looking at his upcoming schedule when he heard Jennifer come in.

Seeing that he would have to fly again on Monday, the upcoming trip tomorrow would give him just enough time to get back from Quantico Sunday evening and repack for the three-day trip the next day.

"Back here," he called out as he looked at the next trip and shook his head at how little time he would have at home with his commitment to General Barker and the ever-pressing schedule flying for American Airlines.

"Hey, handsome," Jennifer said as she stepped into the unused bedroom Jim had converted into his office. "Anything exciting happen today?"

"Gene stopped by," Jim said as Jennifer looked over his shoulder at his flying schedule. "How about you?"

"Nothing new," she answered, turning to leave the room. "What did the General want? Just a good ole' boy lunch or some insurmountable problem that only you two can solve?"

"A little of both," Jim told her as he shut down the computer and stood. "But the biggest thing is that he's sending the jet down tomorrow afternoon to take us up to Virginia if you would like to go."

"Tomorrow?" Jennifer asked, turning quickly to face Jim. "Why such short notice? I mean, I really need to get my hair done, and I'm not sure I have anything nice to wear. It would be nice if he could give me at least a week's notice. I don't think that's too much to ask."

"Well, I guess I can call him in the morning and tell him that I'll be coming alone," Jim told her, smiling. "I'm sure he'll understand. Maybe they'll reschedule everything for next week. Oh, I guess that won't work because I'll be flying."

"Don't be such a smart ass," Jennifer said, shaking her head. "You know what I mean."

"Yes, I do," Jim told her. "And after all these years, you know that Gene does what he needs to do and tries to make accommodations that include you if at all possible. And that includes sending his personal jet."

"I know he does," Jennifer said, putting her arms around Jim's neck. "And I really do appreciate it. And I know how close you two are and that he could always leave me out of any plans. But I also know that he knows how difficult it would be for you if he did leave me home while you boys do your Marine stuff. So, let's just call it a truce, and I'll pretend I'm happy to drop everything, and you boys can pretend you've made every sacrifice possible to include me."

Finally kissing him on the cheek, she continued, "Now that it's settled, what time do we leave, when do we get back, and where are we staying? I hope it's that Inn where we stayed last time."

"I don't know the answer to the where, but we need to be at Love Field as soon as you can get off work tomorrow, and we're coming back Sunday afternoon," Jim answered. "So, I'm betting that we'll be somewhere closer to the base this time."

Chapter 5

The next morning, after Jennifer had left for work, Jim was continuing his research on MS 13 when the phone rang. "Good morning," he answered, looking at the web MS 13 had woven across America.

"Good morning, Jim," Gene told him. "Everything ready for the trip up here this evening?"

"I guess," Jim answered. "Jennifer's at work, and I'm guessing she's planning on leaving early so she can sort out her wardrobe. Other than that, and her complaint about insufficient notice, we're ready."

"Good," Gene told him. "I just wanted to let you know that there will be an additional passenger coming with you. The jet will pick her up at the old Carswell AFB, now NAS/JRB Ft. Worth."

"Will she be on the plane, or will we get her after we're aboard?" Jim asked.

"They'll pick her up first," Gene answered. "The stop for you guys will be about 5:30, and the plane won't need to refuel since they'll do it at NAS/JRB."

"Sounds good," Jim acknowledged. "Anything I need to know about her?"

"That's part of the reason for the call, to give you a little background," Gene answered. "She's part of the team I've assembled for you in El Paso."

"So, she's Muddy Water," Jim offered.

"Not really," Gene replied. "She's connected to Black Water, on loan for this operation."

"What's her function?" Jim asked.

"She's the computer geek we discussed the other day," Gene told him. "Although she's going to be with you in El Paso, she and her staff will be providing information to each of the teams both here and in the other countries."

"Sounds like she'll have her hands full," Jim said, nodding. "I'm guessing she'll be reporting back to Quantico during the operation."

"Yes and no," Gene answered. "She's more or less yours, but she will interface with Black Water Headquarters regarding any issues with the Dark Water teams down south."

"That sort of surprises me," Jim told him. "I'd have thought that she would be up there if she's working with Headquarters."

"We've got enough computer folks up here," Gene said. "This is sort of a unique operation, and we're using some, let's call them hired help. She falls into that category."

"Sort of freelance," Jim stated, wondering about working with people outside the organization.

"Sort of," Gene admitted. "But she doesn't really have the option of not working on any operation where Black Water needs her particular set of skills."

"Just what are those unique skills that you don't already have up there?" Jim asked, getting interested. "And what do you have on her that would prevent her from refusing an operation?"

"I can't get into everything on this line," Gene answered to remind Jim that the phone wasn't secure to discuss classified material. "But I'll sort of tell you how she came to us, which will give you a hint of Black Water's hold on her."

"This has got to be interesting," Jim said as he headed for the kitchen to refill his now barely warm coffee.

"It seems that a little while back, someone managed to hack into some very secure government servers," Gene started. "And I'm talking about some supposedly *unhackable* servers, according to our nation's top computer folks."

"And I'm betting that this lady is that someone," Jim said. "And I'm going to guess that Black Water found her instead of the usual governmental offices like the FBI or the CIA."

"You are correct, sir," Gene answered, chuckling. "Those agencies, and others such as the NSA, spent an ungodly amount of man hours and dollars without ever getting a whiff of who was running through their systems with impunity. It was like a mosquito fart in a hurricane, not a whiff."

"And our geeks found this geek," Jim replied. "I guess that makes our geeks the best."

"Nope," Gene corrected him. "Our geeks don't hold a candle to this lady."

"How the hell did they catch her?" Jim asked incredulously.

"With a little outside-the-box thinking, which most governmental employees seem to abhor, and an amazing amount of luck," Gene answered.

"The only thing they, the government folks, ever found was that her 'handle' was Bracer, Gene continued. "And that wasn't difficult. But they could never tie it to anyone or any computer or anything else that might lead them to her."

"So, they tried every letter combination to discover a name, and it all failed," Jim offered.

"I'm sure they tried everything known to man," Gene replied. "All to no avail."

"So, did the term Bracer have anything to do with her name?" Jim asked.

"Sort of," Gene acknowledged. "It was from a set of vanity tags from years ago."

"Vanity tags?" Jim asked. "Like me having '62 Vette' for the license plates on my car?"

"Pretty much," Gene answered.

"I'd have thought that our esteemed governmental folks would have run Bracer through every computer file in the land," Jim said. "And I'm sure each state has a registry of every license plate on file."

"That they did, and there're plenty of vanity plates in the system," Gene answered. "But it came up with zilch."

"This has got to be good," Jim told him. "Who figured it out?"

"Let's start with the government giving us everything they had done and all of the results," Gene answered. "Our guys reran every program, plus some that aren't quite legal, and still came up with nothing.

Then, one of the guys thought about how slow some of the more, let's call them backwoods towns or counties, were in inputting the data from their old paperwork into their computer system."

With that in mind, we, or Black Water, sent teams out to some of the most isolated towns across America. They went to every courthouse or automotive registration facility in every state."

"I can only imagine what that costs," Jim said, shaking his head. "But I can only imagine what Black Water charged the taxpayer, known as Uncle Sam."

"I can guarantee that it was a hefty sum, but I'll also tell you that it was cheap compared to the damage that could've been done if we hadn't found this lady," Gene acknowledged.

"I bet," Jim agreed. "Especially if she's as good as I'm starting to suspect, she could shut down the entire government. Or, blackmail every Senator or Congressman who ever sent a text or email of a somewhat risqué nature."

"She literally had the ability to interrupt any communication between the military, the governments of every nation, or any system that relied on any computer program," Gene admitted. "The only saving grace was she wasn't interested in any of that."

"Wow!" Jim exclaimed. "Where did this lady learn her trade? She must have a PhD in cosmic computer science."

"Never went to college," Gene answered. "Never had a computer class that we can tell."

"You're telling me she's self-taught?" Jim asked.

"That is the fact," Gene answered. "She told us that all she did was get interested in computers and start reading anything available. Taught herself computer code. If the term 'idiot savant' has any meaning, it means her. There isn't a record of her ever attending any class. Maybe that's why she succeeded where most other computer specialists failed. She didn't know any of the usual methods of hacking into computers that the schools teach. She developed her own system."

"Unbelievable," Jim said. "So, since she's so computer savvy, how'd she miss the vanity tag thing?"

"Dumb luck on our part," Gene answered. "She admitted that she had searched the auto registration just like the others. Since she didn't find anything, and she definitely knew that she had used Bracer, she didn't go door to door, so to speak, to where she had used the tags."

"So, someone from Black Water goes to some Podunk town, talks to some county employee about vanity tags, and he spills the beans," Jim replied.

"Something like that," Gene confirmed. "In this little country town named Cleburne, in Johnson County, Texas, there just happened to be a gentleman who had been with the auto registration department for over 20 years.

When our guy approached him to look at any records of vehicle registration that hadn't been entered into the computer system, the man asked what he was looking for. Then, when our guy says we're looking for any tags with the term Bracer, the guy sort of smiles and says he thinks he knows who used those tags."

"How far back were these tags used?" Jim asked.

"About 20 years," Gene answered. "Now, what was really the stroke of luck was that the guy knew the lady who had used the tags."

"No shit?" Jim asked, laughing. "What, did he go to school with her or something?"

"Exactly," Gene answered. "And you'll get a kick out of this. The lady was a rodeo rider. A barrel racer, to be exact."

"Hence the Bracer tags on her car, or more likely, her pickup," Jim offered.

"Her horse trailer," Gene corrected. "The tag guy was the one who processed her request for the vanity trailer tag.

Those tags were never entered into the computer system because they were no longer in use when they started transferring the data. But the real reason he remembered her was that he'd had a crush on her when they went to school together."

"Boy, if he knew that he'd just turned in a most wanted criminal, who just happened to be an old flame, he'd probably go hang himself," Jim said.

"He actually never knew what we were looking for," Gene told him. "When our guy saw the records and had her information, he told him that we were looking for a man who had been using the name as an alias to marry several women across the USA."

"Ah yes, the old polygamist ploy," Jim said, laughing. "So, a former lover rats out the lady who jilted him. That's classic."

"I never said they were lovers," Gene corrected him. "Merely that the guy had a crush on her in high school. And we never told her how we found her. So, none of this ever happened as far as any discussion with her during this operation."

"Got it," Jim said. "I'm not sure if I can keep from smiling when I meet her, but I wish I knew the auto registration guy's name. I'd love to see the look on her face if I happened to mention it."

"And you'll never know it," Gene told him. "For that exact reason. For now, just call her Debbie."

"How about if I call her Debbie Bracer?" Jim asked, smiling to himself.

"How about if you just call her Debbie, as I asked? And her last name is Walker," Gene told him. "I'll see you this evening."

Chapter 6

As soon as Jennifer got home and changed into jeans and a sweatshirt, Jim started loading bags for the trip to Love Field to meet the jet. As he finished, Jennifer came out carrying another small bag and tossed it in the rear seat.

"I thought you had everything you needed in the other bags?" Jim asked as they got in the car.

"Just a couple of last-minute things I thought of at work this morning," she answered, smiling.

"Oh yeah," Jim said as they headed for the airport. "There's another lady going to be on the flight today."

"What?" Jennifer asked, turning to look at Jim. "Why didn't you tell me this? I would have worn something different. Something nicer."

"What you're wearing is perfectly fine," Jim told her. "This isn't some fashion exhibit. And I'll bet she's probably dressed the same as you are."

"I don't care how she's dressed," Jennifer replied. "I just don't want her to see how I'm dressed and disapprove. Let's go back, and I'll change."

"We don't have time to go back," Jim explained, shaking his head. "It's just someone else on the plane, just as if we were on American; who cares how somebody back in seat 33 D is dressed."

"But this is a private jet," she argued. "We should dress better than someone back in coach on a commercial flight."

"This is a company plane," Jim reminded her. "It's not our private jet. And she's apparently an employee of the company. So, please, let's drop it and just enjoy the flight and the weekend."

"Fine," Jennifer huffed as she turned to look out the passenger window. "You guys will never understand how important it is to women to dress for the occasion."

"Probably not," Jim agreed as they neared the airport. "If I could live my life in Wranglers and a T-shirt, I'd be happy."

"That's why you'll never understand," she argued. "Women are different. We see each other more critically than you guys see each other."

"Probably so," Jim acknowledged as they entered the parking lot for the General Aviation area. "We men tend to look at the other man, not what he's wearing."

"That's not true," she retorted as they parked. "I don't know how many times I've heard you make some remark about someone's hat or belt buckle."

"Only when it's some dude from New Jersey that's trying to look like a cowboy while he's here visiting," Jim said as he gathered their bags. "Some crappy-ass cheap hat and a shiny concho hat band that probably costs more than the hat. And the dumbass even put that on wrong."

"See, you do notice other men's clothes," Jennifer said as they entered the lobby.

"You're right," Jim said as he saw their airplane sitting just outside. "Can we argue fashion later? Our plane's waiting, and I'm sure the lady traveling with us probably doesn't care about my opinion regarding western wear."

"Mr. Lashley," a man standing at the desk said as he hung up the phone. "I'm John, and I'll be your Captain for the flight to Quantico this evening."

"Hi, John," Jim said, shaking his hand. "Please just call me Jim, and this is my wife, Jennifer."

"Good to meet you, Jim. And you too, Jennifer," John said, reaching for their bags. "I'll take those out for you if you'd like."

"Not necessary," Jim answered as they headed out to the airplane. "How's the weather for the flight?"

"Excellent," John answered, holding the door open for them to go outside. "Should be smooth with a fairly nice tailwind."

"Great," Jim said as they neared the airplane. "I understand there's another lady on board."

"Yes," John said as another man came from the back of the airplane. "We picked her up at the old Carswell base about an hour ago. And the guy coming around the airplane is our copilot Boo."

"Boo?" Jim asked. "Is that his real name, or were his parents scared when they first saw him?"

John laughed and said, "I hadn't thought of that, but no, he's Albanian, and I can't even begin to pronounce his real name. It's Buka something. Nice guy. Flew for the Albanian Air Force before coming here."

"What did he fly?" Jim asked, watching him approach.

"The Chengdu F-7," John answered. "It's sort of a version of the Soviet MIG 21, but built by the Chinese."

"I know the MIG 21," Jim said. "All too well."

"Mr. Lashley," Boo said as he met them at the bottom of the stairs to the airplane. "Can I take your bags for you?"

"I'll take them up," Jim said, shaking his hand. "I'm sure you have more important things to do than toss bags."

"Not really," Boo answered. "Please, let me at least take the bag the lady is carrying."

"That's so nice of you," Jennifer said, handing him her bag. "I'm Jennifer, and it's a pleasure to meet you."

"You as well," Boo said, taking her bag and heading up into the airplane. "I'll see you guys on board after we get airborne."

"Please, go on up," John said as Boo cleared the stairs. "I'll introduce you to the other passenger if you'd like."

"Not necessary," Jim said as Jennifer climbed into the plane. "I've been briefed on her, and we'll take care of the introductions."

"Sure thing," John replied, following him up the stairs. "Just take a seat, and I'll get back to you guys when we're ready to taxi."

"Hi," Jim said as he reached the seat beside Jennifer across from Debbie. "I'm Jim, and this is my wife, Jennifer."

"We just met," she told him, nodding at Jennifer as she held out her hand. "I'm Debbie."

"Nice to meet you, Debbie," Jim said, buckling his seatbelt. "How was the flight from Ft Worth?"

"Short," came the quick answer.

"I imagine so," Jim said, smiling. "I'm sort of surprised that the company didn't ask us to meet the plane there or you to come here."

"That would have made more sense," Debbie agreed. "Except that my contract requires them to come to Ft Worth, and I'm assuming that you have the same requirement about where you get picked up."

"Not really," Jim told her as he heard the engines starting. "But it's normal for us to be picked up here since it's the closest to where I live."

"Please make sure you're seated with your seatbelts on," John said over the speaker system. "It's a quick taxi, and we'll be taking off in about 5 minutes."

Jim glanced at Jennifer and Debbie as the plane began to accelerate to make sure their seatbelts were on. "Wonder how this is going to go?" he thought to himself as they sped toward the runway. "So far, she seems rather blunt."

Chapter 7

Fifteen minutes later, John announced that they were passing ten thousand feet and they were free to move about. As Jim unbuckled his seatbelt, he asked, "Would either of you care for something to drink? I'm going to the rear to get something for myself."

"Just water," Jennifer answered, glancing at Debbie.

"I'd like a Dr. Pepper if they have one," Debbie told him.

"I'll be right back," Jim said, rising.

"Okay, one water," he said as he returned and took his seat. "And one Dr. Pepper."

"Thanks," Debbie said, taking the can from Jim. "How long have you worked for the company?"

"Jim doesn't work for the company," Jennifer told her. "He's just friends with General Barker, and we go up to Quantico sometimes when he wants Jim's advice on something."

Debbie took a quick look at Jim as he sat back with a small frown and a slight shake of his head. "Oh," she replied.

"I guess I just thought that since it's a company plane, everyone worked for the company."

"Jim's a pilot with American Airlines," Jennifer offered. "He and the General met when Jim was a Marine in Vietnam. They've been friends ever since."

"So, this is mostly a social trip for you guys?" Debbie asked, looking from Jim to Jennifer.

"Mostly," Jennifer answered. "What do you do?"

"I'm a computer consultant," Debbie told her as she sat back, watching Jim's expression. "I contract with various companies for advice on their computer systems. Mainly in computer security."

"That's interesting," Jennifer said, smiling at her. "How did you get into that field?"

"I've had an interest in computers since I was a kid," Debbie answered. "Especially when it comes to how computers have taken over everyone's life."

"What do you mean, taken over?" Jennifer asked.

"For example, do you use the internet, like Google, AOL, or send email?" Debbie explained. "Of course you do. Almost everyone does. And there are new sites called social media, like Six Degrees or Open Diary, where people tell every aspect of their lives. This is going to be a gold mine for hackers."

"Yes, but how does that take over my life?" Jennifer asked. "It's just a way of shopping, checking on my bank account, talking to friends, and stuff."

"That it does," Debbie told her. "But it also gathers information about you. Such as what you shopped for or where you went to dinner. And if you looked at hotels or vacation spots, all of that information is stored and later sold to companies that want to get your business."

"Okay, I don't care if someone knows I had dinner at a local restaurant," Jennifer answered. "What's the harm in that?"

"Nothing, really," Debbie replied. "If that's as far as they went. But it's not just that. If you use any Wi-Fi service, they know where you are and where you've gone. If you use your phone to buy online, they know. And if you give your credit card information, they have it and can track every purchase you make. Any information passed over the internet via a Wi-Fi is out there for a smart hacker to see."

"Are you sure?" Jennifer asked starting to wonder about how much information was out there regarding her or Jim.

"I'm positive," Debbie said. "For example, I did a little research on Jim when I found out he was going to be on this flight."

"And what did you find out?" Jennifer asked.

"First, I knew that he was a Marine and served two tours in Vietnam," she answered. "That was easy since his military records are open to the public, except for some redacted areas relating to some classified operations."

Jennifer looked at Jim as Debbie continued, "I know that he served two tours on the ground, and I know about all of the medals and decorations he received.

I know that he attended flight school in Florida, where he met you, and then went back to Vietnam flying F-4s."

"How do you know that we met in Florida?" Jennifer asked.

"Pretty simple," Debbie said, smiling. "Once I had Jim's service record, I had his full name and social security number. Then, I found the marriage certificate, which included your maiden name. Then I ran a check on that, which gave me several names that matched, and then I narrowed the search to matches where Jim had been stationed. That led me to you. So, a little more research and I found that your parents owned a small hamburger place in Pensacola.”

“How long did all of that take you?” Jennifer asked, surprised at how much Debbie probably knew about their life.

“Maybe 10 minutes,” Debbie answered, smiling. “I entered my requests just before making coffee yesterday morning. I had all of that before it was brewed.”

“That fast?” Jennifer asked, shocked at how much information she had gathered in such a short time.

“That fast,” Debbie said, taking a sip of her Dr. Pepper. “And there’s more if you care to hear it.”

“I’m not sure if I like that,” Jennifer said, sitting back and crossing her arms. “How can people just go snooping around about other people’s lives.”

“That’s nothing compared to how the major companies find everything about you,” Debbie told her. “All they need to know is some basic information and have the right program in their computer system and they can look at your bank account, your credit card account, everywhere you’ve lived, or any debts you have. They know every detail of your life if they choose to find it.”

“What about if I have a password on all of my stuff,” Jennifer asked.

“Everyone has a password,” Debbie explained. “And a good hacker can find it in less time than it took you to enter it.”

“How can they do that?” Jennifer asked.

“First, most people use something that’s easy to remember, like your first name and some numbers or characters,” Debbie told her. “For example, if your name was Bob, I'd search your bank account using Bob as the start of the password. The computer would then start using every possible combination of characters until it found your password. Then, I'd try it or some variation of it on your other accounts. You'd be surprised how many people use birthdays, the last four numbers of their social security, or other things that relate to their history."

"It can't be that easy," Jennifer argued. "And I don't think that there are that many people out there who would go to all that trouble."

"You'd be wrong," Debbie informed her. "It is that easy, and you'd be surprised at how many times credit card accounts are hacked and used. Even an account at FedEx or UPS can be hacked and used to ship stuff. There are thousands of ways to use your information, not just to send you advertisements about similar purchases you made online."

"I still can't believe that it's that simple," Jennifer argued.

"Think of it this way," Debbie explained. "We've had code breakers since time began. In World War II, we had thousands of people listening to every broadcast, radio transmission, or any form of communication. They would send that information to another thousand people who specialized in breaking codes.

I'm not sure if you've ever heard of the enigma machine that Germany used to encode messages during the war," Debbie said. "It was supposedly uncrackable. But it wasn't, and we could tell what each message said. And that was just using people. The new world of computers can run thousands of bits of data every second of every day of every year. Your password is about as secure as if you just use your name or 1234567. I can probably crack it in under the time it takes to brew coffee, as I did on Jim's history."

"I don't like this," Jennifer told her. "I don't like you digging through Jim's life or mine. I don't like it one little bit."

"I understand," Debbie said, trying to console her. "But I'm just telling you what's out there. It's my job to hack computers. That's why companies hire me. And I always research anyone I know I'll be running into. It wasn't meant to be personal, just precautions on my part. I'm sorry if that upsets you, but at least now you know what's out there that may be trying to take advantage of you. As I said earlier, computers are taking over our lives, and the more you know about them, the better you can safeguard your life. At least make sure you use a secure password to log into your accounts. And for god's sake, don't use the same one over and over."

"What would you suggest?" Jim asked, trying to defuse the building tension between them. "How can anyone design an unbreakable password?"

"No one can," Debbie told him. "Given enough time, any password can be hacked. But let's not make it easy. It's much easier for someone to move on from your account if it takes too much time. Now I recommend using a phrase, such as 'damn bank' for that account. Just use the arrangement of letters on your phone to get numbers. In this case, 3262265. Then toss in a letter such as the last letter of your last name."

"And use 'damn credit card' and substitute numbers the same?" Jim asked.

"I don't recommend using damn but once," Debbie answered, smiling. "Pick some other phrase. And occasionally substitute the letter's place in the alphabet. Such as an 'E' would be a 5."

"Sort of like the POWs used in Vietnam," Jim offered. "They used a grid with five letters across the top and five rows vertically. The first tap told which row, such as one tap meant the top row, or four meant the fourth row down. Then, the second tap gave the column, such as two taps meant the second column. One tap followed by one tap was an 'A.' Two taps followed by three taps was an 'H.'"

"You can certainly use that code," Debbie said, smiling. "I'm pretty sure most people wouldn't consider that since most of the hackers today don't know about it. The biggest point is to stop using personal data. That's the main thing."

"Wait a second," Jennifer said. "There are 26 letters in the alphabet. You only have 25 squares."

"They put 'C' and 'K' on the same square, one tap and three taps," Jim explained. "Since they sort of sound the same in a word, it works. The listener can decide which letter it was.

And let's not forget the Navajo Wind talkers," Jim added. "The Marines used them in the Pacific during World War II. All they had to do was have two of them with each regiment using their ancient Navajo language. And their 'code' was never broken."

Just as Jim was finishing, John came over the speaker to update them on their progress and told them that there were snacks back in the area where Jim had gotten the drinks.

Chapter 8

A couple of hours later, after landing at Quantico and taxiing to the terminal, they were met by General Barker as they came down the steps.

"How was the flight?" he asked Jim as they shook hands.

"Smooth, but it got a little chilly," Jim answered as Jennifer joined them.

"Jennifer, good to see you again," Gene told her, taking her hand. "I'm glad you could come out with Jim for the weekend."

"Thanks for inviting me," she responded. "And you know I always enjoy spending time with you guys whenever I can."

"I'll have John and Boo take your bags to the car," he said as Debbie joined them. "Why don't y'all go ahead and get in."

"I'll help with the bags," Jim offered. "I want to thank them for the great flight."

"Jennifer, you and Debbie, go ahead, and I'll help them, too," Gene said as Jim headed back to where John was sitting with their bags. "We'll head to the hotel and then head out for a quick dinner after we get everyone checked in."

"What did you mean by it getting a little chilly on the flight?" Gene asked as they picked up a couple of the bags. "Is there something wrong with the climate control system on the plane?"

Jim took a quick glance toward the Suburban and answered, "No, the temperature was fine. It was more the interaction between Jennifer and Debbie."

"What happened?" he asked, walking back to the car. "Did Debbie say something that upset Jennifer?"

"Not really," Jim answered. "She was just explaining some aspects of her job, in particular regarding passwords on the internet. As she did, she revealed how easy it was to find information, such as where I met Jennifer and other personal information. Jennifer took it as her invading her privacy. No big deal."

"Debbie can be rather blunt at times," Gene told him. "But I'll remember that in the future. I'll make sure not to schedule them on the same plane. Should we cancel dinner?"

"Definitely not," Jim said as they approached the Suburban. "I'm sort of hungry, and I'm sure they are too. Let's just see what develops before you make any policy decisions."

"Okay, folks," Gene said as he got in the Suburban. "We'll get everyone settled and meet in the lobby. Is that acceptable for all of you?"

"I'm afraid I'll have to pass," Debbie answered. "I have some work to do before we meet tomorrow. What time will we be picked up in the morning?"

"There'll be a couple of cars here about eight o'clock," Gene answered. "I've instructed the drivers to load one car to capacity and then send it on its way. The other car will bring any stragglers."

"How many people are here?" Jim asked as they headed for the hotel.

"About 40," Gene told him. "But there's only ten or so of you at the hotel where you're staying. The others will meet us at Black Water headquarters in the morning. The hotel does provide a complimentary breakfast buffet, and we'll have one set up as well when you get there."

"When will Jim get back tomorrow?" Jennifer asked as they sped to the hotel.

"I'm hoping we can break for the day by five o'clock," Gene answered. "Then, I've made dinner arrangements at the Kobe Japanese Steak and Seafood restaurant for all of the people staying at the same hotel you guys are."

"What hotel are we staying at?" Jennifer asked.

"The TownePlace Suites," Gene told them. "It's only about 20 minutes or so from Quantico, which makes it an easy commute in the mornings or evenings."

"Is there anything around to do tomorrow while you guys are doing whatever you're doing?" she then asked.

"I'm not sure," Gene answered as he turned to look at her. "But, I'm sure the desk clerk can recommend something tomorrow morning if you'll ask him. By the way, I've made arrangements for the hotel to have a car at your disposal if you need to go out."

"Maybe I'll just relax in the room for a change," she responded as she turned to look out the window.

Gene glanced in the rearview mirror at Jim, rolled his eyes slightly, and watched Jim's subtle shake of his head.

A few minutes later, as they were pulling into the hotel, Gene parked by the entrance and asked, "I've made reservations at a restaurant called Fatty's Crab House for dinner. How much time will you need to meet in the lobby?"

"I can be down in about 5 minutes," Jim answered.

"Probably 15 for me," Jennifer told him. "Do I need to put on anything more appropriate for dinner?"

"No," Gene said, opening his door. "As a matter of fact, even a sports coat is overkill for the guys here. What you're wearing is certainly appropriate."

"Well, I'd still like to change into something else," she responded as she got out of the car.

"That's fine," Jim said as he grabbed their bags. "Let's check in and get our rooms. You can decide what you want to wear when we get there."

"I'll see everyone tomorrow morning," Debbie said, grabbing her suitcase and heading for the entrance. "Have a good evening."

Jim and Gene watched Jennifer staring at her as she walked away and wondered at the attitude, she was displaying that was so unlike her normally.

"I've got to make a few calls on the rest of the folks," Gene said as they followed Debbie to the front desk. "I'll see you down in the lobby in a few minutes."

After getting their keys and getting to their room, Jennifer said, "I'm glad she's not coming to dinner with us tonight. And I hope she doesn't come tomorrow either."

"I'm not sure what your problem is with her," Jim said, setting down their suitcases. "But she hasn't done anything I know of to cause you to dislike her. And frankly, you've been rather rude to her."

"She spied on you! On us!" Jennifer exclaimed. "What business did she have doing that?"

"She didn't spy on us," Jim argued as Jennifer opened her suitcase. "She did a background check because she didn't know anything about me. That's her job with Black Water. I'm sure Gene would have told her anything she needed to know, but he's got more important things to worry about. I wish you'd just let it go."

"But why did she have to look into me?" Jennifer asked. "She doesn't need to know anything about me."

"Believe it or not, a security background check includes any members of the family. Father, brothers, wives, everybody," Jim told her. "Now, you can let it bother you, or you can dismiss it. And, I'll bet that any financial institution, such as a credit card application, does pretty much the same thing."

"Well, I still don't like it," Jennifer said as she dug into the clothes she had brought.

"The other thing to remember is that you started this by asking about passwords and other stuff," Jim told her as he took out the clothes he would need in the morning. "Personally, I found her knowledge about codes and computer security pretty interesting."

"So, you think she's pretty interesting?" Jennifer asked as she started undressing.

"Yes, I do," Jim said, knowing where this was headed. "Just as I find an expert in almost any field interesting. Except maybe for those guys who call themselves ancient alien theorists. What a bunch of malarkeys. I also think that we should pay attention to what she said about our passwords. I know that I tend to use my name or social security number a lot, and she said any hacker can break that in seconds.

Anyway, I'm going down to the lobby to meet Gene," Jim told her as she was looking at a couple of outfits for the evening. "I'll see you when you get there."

Chapter 9

Early the next morning, Jim stepped from the elevator and spotted Debbie heading out to the waiting Suburban for the drive to Quantico.

"Good morning, Debbie," he greeted her as he caught up and opened the rear door for her. "Did you get all of your work done last night?"

"Most of it," she answered as she got into the Suburban's rear seat. "How was dinner?"

"Very good," Jim said, smiling. "Jennifer and I shared a Steampot of Snow crab legs and clams. Rather messy, but certainly good."

"I ordered something from the Sake Thai Sushi Bar," she told him as a man joined them in the car. "Pretty good. I'm a big fan of Thai food, and they brought it to my room."

"Good morning," the new arrival told them, nodding. "I'm Andy. I've eaten there before, and I agree that it's very good."

"Morning," Jim replied as Andy took one of the seats just behind the driver. "I'm Jim, and this is Debbie. Where'd you come in from?"

"Los Angeles," Andy answered. "And you?"

"Dallas and Fort Worth," Debbie told him. "Are you Andy Bailey?"

"Why, yes, I am," he answered. "Do we know each other?"

"No," Debbie told him as another man approached the car. "I just prepared dossiers on everyone attending, and there's only one Andy."

"And just exactly what is your job with the company?" Andy asked, staring at her.

"Computer security, among other things," Debbie replied as another man joined Andy in the middle seats. "I'm sure the General will brief everyone on my role this morning when we're all there."

"What about you, Jim?" Andy asked. "Are you part of the computer security thing?"

"No, I'm more in the operation aspect of things," he answered as another man got into the front passenger seat. "Probably like most of us will be."

"Okay, folks," the driver said, starting the car. "If everyone will make sure their seatbelts are buckled, we'll head for Quantico."

For the next few minutes, everyone except Debbie exchanged names and where they had come from. Jim quietly watched as the others repeatedly glanced at Debbie and wondered what information she had gathered on them.

As they passed through the entrance gates to Marine Corps Base Quantico, Jim noticed the crisp salute the guard rendered their car and the nod their driver returned.

As they pulled up to the first set of gates of the double fence that surrounded the Black Water headquarters, the driver handed the guard a list of the passengers. As the gate slid open, he waved them into the space between the fences and closed the gate. Once the gate had fully closed, the second gate opened and allowed them to drive to the concrete block that was the headquarters building.

"Pretty paranoid about their security, aren't they?" Andy remarked, glancing at Debbie and then Jim.

"I'm guessing it's your first time here," Debbie responded with a slight smile.

"No, but I would have thought that just being on a Marine Base would provide enough security," Andy replied. "Who are they trying to keep out that hasn't already been denied entrance?"

"Who said they are trying to keep someone out?" she retorted. "Maybe they are trying to keep something in."

"Now, what could that possibly be?" Andy continued as they approached the building.

"Why don't you ask General Barker when you see him?" Debbie answered as the driver opened their door. "I'm sure he can answer any questions you have about the security, including computer security since you seem to have some issue with it."

"What's with the attitude?" Andy whispered as he joined Jim walking to the building.

"Don't know," Jim answered as they neared the door. "I just met her on the plane yesterday on the flight here."

"Well, whatever it is," Andy told him as they entered a small enclosed area and handed their IDs to the guard behind a thick glass panel, "I'm not too impressed. So, she's a computer geek. So, what."

"I'm sure the General thinks she's necessary for this operation," Jim answered as he took his ID back, and the door into the interior buzzed, signaling they could enter. "And, as the lady said, maybe you should direct your questions to him."

"I plan on it," Andy said as they walked down the hall to the cafeteria. "I don't see why we need to suffer that type of attitude from some backroom computer clerk. Probably wishes she could be on the operational end anyway."

As they entered the room full of long tables and a breakfast buffet set up against the back wall, Gene approached them and said, "Good morning, gentlemen. How'd the night go?"

"Just fine, sir," Andy answered. "But, if you don't mind, I have a couple of questions."

"We'll get to your, and the others, questions after the briefing," Gene told him. "Why don't you go ahead and grab something to eat while we're waiting for the rest of the teams."

Turning to Jim, he said, "Jim, I'd like to speak to you alone before the brief. So, if you'd get whatever you want from the buffet and join me at the table close to the briefing stand, we can talk."

"I'll be right there, sir," Jim said as he turned to follow Andy. "Just let me grab a coffee and some fruit."

"You might want to try the scrambled eggs with sausage, cheese, and jalapeno," Gene suggested. "There's a big bowl of Picante sauce if you care for it. Oh, yeah, grab a biscuit with some sausage gravy. It's excellent."

Chapter 10

When Jim sat his tray down, Gene looked across the room and asked, "What happened on the drive-in this morning?"

Jim cocked his head slightly and asked, "What are you referring to? "

"Your driver mentioned some rather pointed jabs between Debbie and one of the other passengers," Gene explained. "Do you think we have a problem with one of our operators?"

"I don't think so," Jim answered as he took a fork full of the scrambled eggs. "Yeah, there was some friction evident between Andy, the guy from LA, and Debbie, but I wouldn't characterize it as a problem."

Gene glanced to where Andy had taken a seat with some of the others and remarked, "He's pretty new. And more importantly, he's not running the LA operation. The guy that's heading it couldn't make this briefing and sent Andy. At Andy's constant urging."

"Not that I'm trying to support either side, but Debbie does have a way of, let's call it, minor snobbery, talking down to people," Jim told him. "And, of course, you remember what happened on the flight here. Could be she needs to tone it down slightly."

Gene smiled as he took a bite of biscuit slathered with the white gravy and chunks of sausage mixed in, saying, "Yeah, she is quite defensive, bordering on offensive, in dealing with some people. Not that it matters, but I strongly suspect it may have something to do with being coerced into working with Black Water. I think she still resents our interference in her previous occupation."

"That could be," Jim agreed, taking a sip of coffee, "But maybe just a little nudge toward civility would be in order. Again, I've seen firsthand how she can get under someone's skin. And granted, Jennifer is sort of easily irritated sometimes, and while Debbie's directness may be an asset on the job, some social graces go a long way sometimes when dealing with some highly inflated egos, which I suspect Andy has."

"You're right about that," Gene chuckled. "He's one of those guys who only care about getting the medal and not what it takes to earn it. And I'm sure you know the type."

"That I do," Jim agreed as a man in a black short-sleeved knit T-shirt stepped up to the podium. "Unfortunately, they seldom have the instincts or guts to do what's necessary, whereas the guys that actually earn the medals normally do it out of some ingrained desire to help their fellow man or fulfill the mission."

"And then there are the Andy's of the world," Gene agreed. "All show and no go. The constant bane of any organization. My biggest fear is that they'll put their fellow operatives in danger or the mission. And that I can't allow."

"So, what's your plan regarding LA?" Jim asked as the guy at the podium asked everyone to refresh their coffees or whatever they needed to do before taking their seats.

"I'm flying out to LA Monday to have a talk with Mike Knox and make sure Andy is solid before we launch the operation," Gene answered. "Seldom do we need to remove someone from our ranks, but it does happen."

"What happens to them then?" Jim asked as everyone scurried back from the buffet. "Do you worry about them talking out of school?"

"Not at all," Gene answered with a hint of a smile crossing his face. "They know only too well what happens to enemies of Black Water."

"That I can understand," Jim agreed, nodding. "Not a wise move to piss off the bear when he's not in a cage. Sort of like being the June bug when the duck's hungry."

"That's a fairly apt metaphor," Gene said, laughing. "But we certainly don't have the time or luxury of following the obvious litany of metaphors I'm sure are struggling to break free of your brain right now. But, if you so desire, write all of them down in your after-action report, and I'll be sure to give them due attention when this is over."

"Now, I'm deeply hurt," Jim replied with a hangdog expression as the speaker asked for the lights to be lowered. "To think you'd think that…"

"Later," Gene whispered, interrupting him. "Let's let this guy have our attention."

"Welcome, ladies and gentlemen," the man said, speaking into the microphone affixed to the podium. "Welcome to the first, and hopefully last, informational meeting regarding what we're calling 'The El Salvadorian Solution.' "

Nodding to someone in the back of the room, he continued, "I'm Larry Matthews, and I'm the director of combined operations for Black Water. As you know, Dark Water is restricted to operations outside of the United States and its territories. You also know that Muddy Water is restricted to operations within the United States or its territories."

Pausing while the organizational chart appeared on a huge screen behind him, he then explained, "MS13 is a domestic problem for us, the US, but its roots reside in El Salvador. Also, it has morphed into an international problem since it involves many of the countries in Central America."

As the picture changed, Larry continued, "As you can see here, they have spread across the United States into almost every major city."

The picture changed again into a map of the Western Hemisphere and Larry explained, "Here is the latest information we have regarding their operations within our hemisphere, and thus a threat to us. But since this briefing is specifically tailored to Muddy Water participation in support of the overall operation, we'll concentrate on exactly that."

"How do we coordinate with Dark Water if they're running concurrent operations?" came a question from the room.

"Me," Larry declared. "Through each sector, that's roughly five cities, you will be given specific directions regarding timing and extent of operations. As I mentioned, I'm the director of combined operations for Black Water. That is the coordination."

Pausing for a second, he continued, "Now, there is one other person in this room besides General Gene Barker, who is Black Water. However, during this operation, she was attached to Muddy Water for operational purposes. And even then, we, Black Water, can direct her efforts in supporting Dark Water if we determine we need her assistance there without endangering the domestic operations."

As the screen changed to a map of the United States with Long Island, New York, Fairfax County, Virginia, Montgomery County, Maryland, El Paso, Texas, and Los Angeles, California, highlighted, Larry explained, "These five cities, or more specifically areas, are the centers of the domestic operations. Long Island will additionally cover specific targets in New York City as well as Newark, New Jersey."

As a red circle appeared to encompass an area about 50 miles across Long Island, Larry moved on, saying, "Fairfax County will also include Washington DC, Maryland County includes about the same size area, including of course Baltimore, El Paso pretty much the same but less towns, and Los Angeles is from roughly Santa Anna up to Santa Clarita."

As everyone looked at the scope of the operation, Larry waited until most of the eyes were on him again before saying, "Now, I'm betting that you're wondering how you can possibly cover your assigned areas after reading what we gave you last week about how widespread and loosely organized MS 13 is.

Here's the answer," he said, nodding to the side. "May I present the person who developed the system that will allow us to know the exact location of every target, both here and overseas, and every one of our operatives, within mere feet within seconds of being asked. She'll only be known as Debbie to any of you. And, as you may have guessed, she's the Black Water asset I told you about earlier. Now, I suggest you pay close attention to what this lady has to tell you.

Mainly because the company has gone to extraordinary lengths to get her assistance, but just as importantly, especially to you, your safety may well depend on her being able to tell you exactly where your target is before he spots you."

Chapter 11

Debbie merely nodded at Larry as she confidently strode to the recently vacated podium and sat her laptop computer down. Adjusting the microphone slightly lower, she opened the laptop and hit a couple of keys. Immediately, a layout of the room appeared on the screen with small circles surrounding a number representing each person.

"You were given a package when you came in this morning with your name on it," she started. "If you haven't already done so, please open it and remove the contents."

Waiting until everyone had theirs open, she told them, "What you have is a radically new phone, an earpiece with a microphone, and instructions for their use. They've been turned on and we'll be using them in a moment. But, for now, please pay attention to the screen.

These black circles are you," she told them, making sure they were paying attention. "Each of you."

Pausing while everyone looked around to try and identify which circle represented them, she hit another key and said, "The circle that has turned green is you, Andy.

Would the gentleman to your left please rise and walk to the rear of the room?"

As he rose as requested, his circle turned green and was seen moving across the screen towards the back of the room.

"Now, will everyone please raise their hands if they are convinced that what you are seeing is real-time tracking?" she asked.

Pausing for a second, she continued, "If you aren't fully convinced, stand up and go join the man in the rear."

One man did stand up and head to the side of the room but returned as he watched his circle turn green and follow his movements.

As he retook his seat, Debbie looked at the man at the rear and said, "You can return to your chair, too, sir."

As he took his seat beside Andy, each circle except Andy's changed back from green to the original black. "Now, if you aren't convinced, there's nothing more I can do to prove the capabilities of my tracking program."

Nodding to the rear of the room, she continued, "Now, by itself, knowing exactly where you are has its benefits, but that's not why I developed this program."

As everyone watched the screen, a black circle with a number appeared at the rear of the room and started moving up the side. As it approached the table where Andy sat, it paused and then moved toward him.

By now, everyone was watching the man approach Andy and wondered what was coming next. Andy merely turned his head and watched until the man was standing next to him.

"Now," Debbie said, "What do you think about having someone get that close without you knowing who it is?"

The circle around the man suddenly turned red, and Debbie announced, "The enemy has just arrived at your doorstep, Andy. Wouldn't it have been nice to have seen him coming?

Maybe you could have done something instead of just sitting there and getting shot," she continued with a look of satisfaction. "And this is really why Black Water paid me to develop this program specifically for this operation.

Now, if you would look at the phones you were given," Debbie directed as she watched them reach for their phones, "You'll find a small gun figure on the screen. Touch it. As you will notice, all that is required to activate a feature of the phone is a touch. More about its capabilities later.

As you've probably figured out, these phones are at the cutting edge of the next generation of cell phones," Debbie explained. "The company, Black Water, and other agencies within the intelligence branches of our government have been sponsoring a program that developed them. In addition to this operation, we'll be running a field test of various aspects of the phone itself for the company that is developing it for commercial use in the next few years. Within a few years, everyone will have one of these for their personal use.

Now, the towers that normal cell phones use will also support these phones as well," she continued. "We have augmented them with several mobile towers in each area dedicated solely to our operation.

A quick history lesson is appropriate before we continue," she announced as the screen changed.

"The first wireless communication tower was developed by Nikola Tesla in 1893," Debbie explained as everyone followed the dates on the screen. "It was followed in 1901 by Guglielmo Marconi, who developed the first useable long-distance wireless transmission capability, 1905, Tesla again with the first cell tower, and in 1920 by AT&T's development of the frequency multiplying complex that allowed multiple telephone conversations at the same time.

Communication towers were first used by the military in World War One," she continued. "Then, as we entered World War Two, the need for communication with our submarine fleet expanded our knowledge of wireless communication over long distances.

The use of mobile towers has been around for decades to support a fast-moving army," she concluded. "And it's these towers, somewhat modified to fit our needs, that'll give us the number of towers necessary to triangulate the position of any person, more specifically his phone, to the parameters we need. With the number of towers, we'll be using, that accuracy is a mere three feet under the worst conditions."

Noticing Andy's hand up, she asked, "What is it this time, Andy? Is there something you don't understand?"

"Okay, I get it that you can put on a display of your new little gadgets here in a controlled environment," he argued. "But the guys we're after don't have these magic phones...."

Cutting him off, Debbie explained as she glanced at her laptop and typed in a quick command, "They have cell phones, don't they? Just as you have one in your jacket pocket, its number is 213-877-2121, and it's ringing.... now."

Just as the ring could be heard throughout the room, a red circle replaced the green one that had been around Andy's seat.

"Does that answer your question, sir?" Debbie asked, slightly shaking her head and looking down condescendingly at him. "Or is there anything else that you need explained before I finish my presentation of how this is going to help you find your targets and save your asses?"

Looking around the room before glancing down at Gene and Jim in the first row, she suggested, "Why don't we take a short break and get some coffee or maybe find deep within ourselves the courtesy to wait until the real question period arises?"

Chapter 12

As Debbie came down from the raised stage, Gene motioned for Jim to follow him and approached her. "Debbie, got a second?" he asked.

"Certainly, General," she answered. "What can I do for you?"

"Don't you think you're being a little harsh with Andy?" Gene asked. "Is there something between you two that I need to know?"

"Not that I know of," she told him. "But I don't appreciate his attitude, and I'm not going to just stand there and let him take over my presentation with his questions, which are nothing except subtly veiled aspects of what I think is a misogynistic attitude in general."

"I understand," Gene replied. "But questions are the reason why we're here instead of just sending out an informational package. Don't you agree?"

"Definitely," she answered, nodding. "But I think it's a waste of our time to be constantly interrupted when I haven't covered each aspect of my part of the operation. I want these people to have complete confidence in the program I've developed. I certainly plan on fielding any questions when I conclude the presentation, but if I'm repeatedly interrupted….we could be here days."

"But he only asked one question," Gene argued. "Maybe just asking everyone to hold their questions until you ask would be the appropriate method."

Debbie thought for a split second and replied, "Maybe, but now that everyone has seen how interruptions are handled, they won't be so anxious to be publicly embarrassed. Though, I honestly don't think Andy will get the message. Like I said, I think the man is a misogynist and just wants to demonstrate his dominance over any female that's threatening to his warped sense of importance."

"Okay," Gene conceded. "Tell you what I'm going to do. As soon as everyone is back in their seats, I'm going to politely request that they hold their questions until the end. At least it will give Andy an excuse to hold back and not appear to have been bested by you. Is that an acceptable compromise?"

"Of course, General," Debbie answered. "Now, if you have nothing else, I'd like to get something to drink before we restart."

Nodding at her, Gene turned to Jim and said, "Let's grab a drink ourselves."

"By the way," Jim asked as they walked toward the buffet table. "Did you say that a man named Mike Knox was running the Los Angeles operation?"

"Yes," Gene answered, reaching for a glass of unsweetened tea. "And I'm sure your next question is if he's the same guy you flew with down at NAS Pensacola."

"That was exactly my next question," Jim said, smiling. "How long has he been with us?"

"About the same as you," Gene answered, squeezing a lemon into his glass. "But he never worked with Dark Water. He stayed on active duty until he retired, and we picked him up when he got hired by Pacific Southwest Airlines, PSA. Then, when US Air acquired them, he stayed in California and joined Muddy Water."

"He was a good pilot," Jim remarked as they headed back to their table. "And a good instructor. I learned a lot from him. Maybe I'll get a chance to see him again."

"Maybe so," Gene agreed, setting his glass down. "Now, if you'll excuse me, I have to try and unruffle some feathers."

Stepping up to the podium, he paused a second and then announced, "Folks, if you'd please get back to your seats, Debbie would like to conclude her presentation. And, if you don't mind, I'd appreciate it if you'd hold your questions until she's done, at which time she'll gladly entertain them.

Oh, one other thing," he added before stepping down. "The staff will be removing the breakfast buffet items and replacing them with lunch over the next hour or so. Please allow them access to the tables by getting anything you think you may want now and quickly return to your seats."

A few minutes later, Debbie returned to the podium and announced, "The next thing we'll discuss is how we know which phones our friends in MS 13 will be using. That may alleviate some of the misgivings that have been previously brought up."

Quickly typing on her laptop, she continued, "Here are the phones currently being used by their organization."

Pausing while all of the phone numbers scrolled across the screen, she finally told them, "What you see here are about 8,000 phones. I realize that current estimates of MS 13 membership are closer to 10,000, but some of the lower-level members don't have a phone. However, that could change as we conduct the operation.

Another issue that I'm sure you're interested in is how we know when phones are tossed and new ones, basically prepaid untraceable phones, are acquired," she told them, seeing many of the heads nodding in agreement.

"Here's the dirty little secret that nobody wants to admit," she announced. "It's called Voice Recognition Technology. It's only been around to the public for four or five years. In case you aren't too familiar, it's what allows you to speak to an electronic device, and it understands what you want.

It's been around since the '50s when it could only understand numbers," she continued. "Then, in the 60's, it learned a few words. In the 70's the Department of Defense funded the DARPA Sur (Speech Understanding Research) program. About the same time, Bell Laboratories also developed a program that could differentiate between voices.

In the 80's, a doll named Julie was developed that would respond to children's voices. Finally, in the 90's, the first Voice Activated Portal was developed by Bell South," she finished.

"Now, something most of you don't fully understand: your phone has the capability to hear your voice, and with a little modification, it will constantly transmit anything it hears," she told them. "Just as it picks up background noise when you're talking, with a little technological manipulation, it can be broadcasting, even when it's turned off.

That, combined with a far more advanced speech recognition program, I will have any new phone number within minutes," she said. "That, combined with cooperation from the NSA, or National Security Agency, my staff has the capability to monitor every phone conversation in the United States. Combined with the ability to key in on certain words or terms and begin recording the conversation, we can isolate those phones we are interested in monitoring.

To put it bluntly, we have the capability to monitor any phone conversation, or just background conversations if the phone is supposedly turned off, of any phone in the world," she concluded. "For example, here's a conversation we just picked up from phone number 213-877-2121."

As Andy's voice came clearly over the speaker, Debbie said, "I can pick any phone I want to monitor and do the same. Just as you just heard, I have hundreds of people monitoring the MS 13 numbers you saw on the screen. Twenty-four hours a day, seven days a week, for as long as Black Water wants to pay me. I can hear every conversation, and that is how I can give you the information you will need to complete your portion of this operation.

I could continue about how we can also use your personal computers to find out anything we want, from your search for pornography on the internet, to your credit card numbers, your passwords, your shopping habits, or every detail of your personal life," she told them. "Trust me. I know how to do this. And so do thousands of others. As much good as the internet has provided to the majority of the people, it's a gold mine for unscrupulous computer hackers.

A good hacker can even tell what you're interested in on the internet by how long you pause on an article," she finished. "If you're using any computer on the internet, private or public, I'm listening. If you're using a cell phone, I'm listening. I can tell which keystrokes you use on your computer or the numbers you punch into your phone. I am virtually residing inside your electronic devices. Now, are there any questions?"

"Is all of that really possible?" a man at the back asked.

"All of it and more," Debbie told him. "The computer power is growing exponentially. And with that comes more power to intrude into your life. Just think, the Wright Brothers' first flight was 30 miles per hour. If they could have doubled their speed every year, they have been flying at Mach 21 by 1913. That's only ten years. What would it be today?

The advancement of computing power is doubling faster than that," she added. "You have no concept of what's going to happen in the next five years. It's impossible to know what advances we'll have."

"But can you really monitor us as you've described?" came another question.

"Let me put it this way," she answered. "If I want to target you, I'd know when you farted. Maybe I couldn't smell it, but I could damn sure tell you which room in your house you were in. If your phone is in your bedroom when you go to bed, I can listen to you and your wife or girlfriend. Or your wife's lover."

"How is that possible?" a guy in the middle of the room asked. "How can you get a phone or a computer to let you control it?"

"I call your phone, you accept the call, our phones are connected, I send a bug, or cookie if you like that word better, to your phone," she answered. "If it's your computer, it's even easier. I send you an email, you open it, I'm ensconced in your computer. This is all going on right now.

There are voice-activated electronic devices on the drawing boards that will allow you to turn on your lights, your television, change channels, anything you want. But it's listening to every word you utter. And it's talking to someone else. Me, if I chose to listen.

Privacy? A thing of the past, unless you return to the 50's lifestyle and only use cash. Even then, cameras are being installed everywhere that'll send your license plate numbers to a central location. All I have to do is do a search of your plates and I'll know where you've been," Debbie continued. "And facial recognition programs are rapidly developing. Possible? I've only touched on what I can do and have done today.

Tomorrow? Even I don't know. But I wouldn't get a cavity filled until I have a close friend watching to make sure nothing's going to be put in my mouth besides whatever material is required to fill the cavity," she concluded. "Now, if that's all, I need to get back to work on what I certainly hope will make this a successful operation, with the only fatalities being MS 13. Thank you for your attention."

As she stepped away from the podium, Gene stepped up to the microphone and said, "Thank you, Debbie. Now, if everyone will please grab something from the buffet for lunch, we'll continue with more briefings in an hour or so."

Chapter 13

As everyone was finishing their lunches, another man in a black knit T-shirt stepped up to the podium and announced, "If everyone would please return to their seats, we'll try to wrap this up."

Waiting until the last few stragglers were back in their seats, he continued, "First, we'll cover the basics of the phone, some of its capabilities, and more importantly, how we'll be using it during the El Salvadorian Solution."

"I'm Robert Wheeler," he told them. "And I'm the head of the technology department for Black Water. We monitor applications for patents, keep our eyes on new companies that seem to be working on things we're interested in, and basically prowl the world trying to keep one step in front of everyone else, including the Department of Defense."

As the screen behind him depicted an enlarged picture of the phones they had been given, he continued, "This phone, as Debbie mentioned, is truly a cosmic leap in technology. It has more computing power than NASA had back in 1969 when we put the first man on the moon. That took a room full of computers and now we can hold it in one hand. As Debbie said, the exponentially growing computer industry is practically unfathomable.

So, let's have a crash course on how to maximize this little miracle," he told them. "I can't possibly cover all of the capabilities of the phone, so we'll concentrate on the basics that we'll need for this operation. You can read the manual when you get to your rooms or back home and practice each operation until you're comfortable.

First, there's a small button on the top right side if you're holding the phone with the screen facing you," he told them. "Just pushing it in for a couple of seconds will turn it off or turn it on. The only difference is that it's still unusable when turned on until your personal password is entered into the display that fills the screen. Please don't play with it now. You can change the password when you get home. For now, it's 123456.

Now, you've been told that it operates with just a touch," Robert continued as the screen changed to a video showing various operations available. "You'll notice that you can use two fingers to expand or compress whatever is on the screen. Again, play with it when you get back to your rooms tonight.

The next thing we want to look at is the earpiece," he said as the screen changed. "Pretty simple. Just put it in your ear, and you can hear or transmit without using your hands.

Let's try it out," he said, putting his earpiece in. "Just touch the earpiece once to activate it."

Waiting a few seconds, he said, "Now, you're listening to me via the phone. These phones are all paired, so they are basically an intercom system. We'll pair them to the phones you'll be using in your different areas before you go home tomorrow.

Your voice will activate the microphone," he continued. "Now, there's a priority system built in that only allows one transmission at a time. If there's anyone talking, it blocks all of the other phones, with the exception of the phone used by the head of your area."

Pointing to a man in the first row, he said, "Say something."

"Hello," the man said. "How's this?"

"Did everyone hear that?" Robert asked. "Hold your hand up if you didn't."

Not seeing any hands, he pointed to another man and said, "Start counting from one to twenty when I give you the signal."

Robert pointed to another man and told him to say something when directed and keep talking until told to stop. Pointing to the guy to start counting, he waited until he reached five and pointed to the other man.

When the first man reached twenty, the second guy talking could be heard.

Giving the cut-off signal, Robert asked, "Do you see how this works? It's a hands-free communication system for members of your team. That, along with your phone's capability to show your location and that of your target, will allow you to safely execute your mission.

The phone will mirror what Debbie showed you on the screen as to how it tracks locations," he continued. "The expansion or compression of the screen will let you look in great detail at your immediate surroundings or out to encompass the entire United States. Play with it later.

You are expected to teach every member of your team back in your area how to operate this device," he advised them. "A phone for each of them will be given to you before you leave tomorrow. They'll be paired and ready to use. And there will be a charger included that works with the phone.

Are there any questions?" Robert asked, turning off the screen.

"Am I supposed to teach everybody on my team?" Andy asked, raising his hand. "Or will the head of the team?"

Robert looked down at Gene before answering, "I think we should go with the head of your team, Andy. Now, if that's all, I'll turn it over to Gary Kirby, who'll discuss logistics. If you want to refresh your drinks or anything, please do so quickly and return to your seats."

Robert stopped by where Gene and Jim were sitting and commented, "I'm starting to get a bad feeling about that guy, Andy. He's either the dumbest piece of shit I've had to work with here, or he's so intent on being the center of attention that he could present a problem."

"I understand," Gene replied. "I'll discuss this with Knox and let him make the decision. Andy is part of his team, and I want him to take care of it."

"Good," Robert said, turning to leave. "We've put too much time and money into this to let one egotistical moron ruin it. Especially since I firmly believe that fool could jeopardize not just the mission but lives."

Chapter 14

Gary Kirby stepped up to the podium and glanced around at the people scurrying back to their seats. As the last one left the buffet table, he began, "Good afternoon. I'm Gary Kirby, and I'm the Chief of Black Water's logistical department. I'm hoping to make this a short and sweet briefing, so if you keep your questions until the very end, I'm going to try and get you out of here in about an hour. After that, it's up to you as to how you want to stick around asking questions. Or listening to others asking questions.

First off, we have rented the top two floors of the Embassy Suites hotels under different fictitious corporations in the five cities where you'll be working," Gary said. "We've got two cars and thirty vans, all white, all with nonexistent government tags, for each of the teams.

Each of you will be given a package containing 60 phones and earpieces along with charging cables and instructions when you leave tomorrow," he continued. "All of the vehicles have a modified electrical system to ensure the phones are fully charged throughout the day or night.

You'll also be provided with two weapons for each of the six members of the ten teams assigned to each location.

Each team member will have two handguns, and there will be one shotgun per vehicle," Gary told them. "There'll be a resupply of ammo delivered to the hotel at the end of every day according to the expenditure.

Each member will have a credit card matching the company he's working for that can be used for fuel, meals, or any other incidentals," he said. "Each of the hotels has a breakfast buffet; if you can make it, however, feel free to dine out as necessary. But, as always, don't overindulge at the company's expense. Such behavior would not be to your benefit.

Now, following your shift, you'll take the cars, or vans, to a location that will provide disposition of any material that needs to be gotten rid of, and they'll clean the vehicle afterward," he continued. "If you have gathered too much baggage before your shift is over, proceed to the disposal site and wait for your vehicle to be returned to you.

Remember, there are approximately ten teams with six members each, two per vehicle, at each location," Gary explained. "So, please coordinate through your leader before all of you pull into the disposal site at the same time. That just might draw unwanted attention, and I think 30 white vans sitting there would do just that. And it would also most certainly cause you unnecessary waiting.

Should there be any accidents, such as injury to one of the team members, there is a facility we've staffed with doctors and nurses to provide any medical care you may require," he informed them. "But, if it's critical, head to the nearest hospital, and we'll worry about the fallout later. If you run afoul of the local police, don't resist or draw attention to yourselves, especially if you've already collected some of your assigned hits. And for god's sake, no speeding, use turn signals, and come to a complete stop at the appropriate times.

Black Water will be sending travel instructions to the team leaders within a day or so for each member," Gary told them. "That will include both directions and local transport to the hotel if flying in. If you haven't received yours within three days, call me. My number is on a card inside the package with the phones. Now, are there any questions?"

"What's going to happen to the baggage, as you called it, when we take it to the disposal site?" Andy asked.

"That's well beyond your level, sir," Gary answered. "All you need to know and do is to follow your assignment regarding each one and leave the rest of it to the people we've put at each location. Now, are there any questions regarding the issues I've covered? If not, General Barker would like a few minutes to brief you on the rest of the day and what to expect tomorrow. Thank you for your attention."

"Thank you, Gary," Gene said as he stepped up to the podium. "I know it's been a lot of information in a short period of time. As we used to say in the Marines, it's like trying to drink from a fire hose. I've made arrangements for each of you to be taken from your hotel as a group to a nearby restaurant, selected by a good friend of mine who dines out here all of the time. He assures me that the menu has a wide selection, and the food is excellent. The restaurants have been notified of your arrival, and the meals have been covered, as well as the tips. Drinks included. But discretion is appreciated.

If asked, you're all up here interviewing for a civil service position on base," he advised. "There'll be transportation tomorrow morning starting at 8 o'clock to bring you back here for any final issues you've thought about tonight. I plan on having each of you on your way home by noon.

One final suggestion before I cut you loose," he added. "Please take as much time as you need to learn how to use those phones we've given you. Your life, and those of your teammates, may well depend on them. This operation has been in planning for over a year and the coordination with the Dark Water folks has placed additional stress on everyone, so please learn to use those phones. You probably won't have time to screw around with it during the heat of the operation. Do it now so we can answer any questions tomorrow and keep working with them when you get home."

Looking at each of them, he concluded, "That's it for today, folks. I'll see you here tomorrow. Enjoy your meals and have a good night."

Chapter 15

The following morning at Black Water headquarters, Gene was waiting for Jim to arrive. Seeing him enter the briefing room, Gene walked over and joined him at the buffet, saying, "I figured you'd be in the first car. I was starting to get hungry but figured I'd wait for you."

"Thanks," Jim said, taking a tray from the stack. "It's always more pleasant to enjoy a meal with someone than by myself. And I spend too many meals alone when I'm flying."

"Why's that?" Gene asked, getting a glass of orange juice and a cup of coffee. "I figured you'd either meet your Captain or some of the Flight Attendants most of the time." "Actually, the Flight Attendants seldom come down, and at least half the time, the Captain has other plans," Jim replied as he heaped scrambled eggs on his plate and put a helping of gravy and Picante sauce on them.

Putting a spoonful of potatoes au gratin beside them, he continued, "So, I just either eat in the hotel or find something nearby. Most of the hotels will take me and come get me if it's not too far."

"That's good," Gene said, filling his plate. "I called Mike in LA last night after we got back from dinner."

"How'd that go?" Jim asked, taking a seat at the table closest to the podium.

"Fine," Gene answered setting his tray down. "He's aware of his problem child Andy and says he'll probably pull him. He knows how important this operation is going to be and can't take any chances with the other members of his team."

"Is that it?" Jim asked, taking a sip of his orange juice.

"For now," Gene answered. "But he wants Andy to keep thinking he's important to the team until this is over. Then, if he recommends, Andy will be released."

"Is Mike going to let him operate in the field?" Jim asked.

"No, he's going to keep him at the hotel. He's planning on telling Andy that he wants him to be available to send out if any of the teams get in trouble," Gene explained. "That way, Andy will think he's more important than the other members, and Mike can keep an eye on him."

"Good idea," Jim agreed as he took a forkful of eggs. "Hopefully, he'll be able to teach the others how to use the new phones without pissing too many of them off."

"Speaking of that, how are you coming with it?" Gene asked. "Do you understand it well enough?"

"I think so," Jim said, nodding. "I'll play with it while Jennifer's at work. Make a few calls to the others and see how it's going with them. We'll have it down by the time we get to El Paso."

"I have no doubt," Gene said as Larry walked up to the podium, and a map of the United States lit the screen behind him. "I've had the opportunity to work with Debbie and the tech guys on this for most of the development stage. Once you get the hang of it, it's damned impressive and easy to grasp."

"Speaking of Debbie, I noticed she didn't come to dinner with us last night," Jim said. "Any problem?"

"No," Gene answered. "She stayed here last night to do some last-minute updates to the target list based on the latest intelligence."

"Anything major?" Jim asked.

"Some shakeups in the Los Angeles area. Looks like someone wanted an early promotion," Gene answered. "Fortunately, he took care of a couple of our targets before he got his termination orders."

"Too bad we can't depend on them to annihilate each other like the other gangs do," Jim remarked. "But then you'd be out of a job."

"Sure, as if gangs are the only problems in the world," Gene replied, shaking his head. "Crap is really heating up over in the Middle East again. I guess we can't expect centuries-old rivalries to disappear overnight."

Larry tapped the microphone and announced, "Ladies and gentlemen, please take your seats as quickly as possible. We're going to try to wrap this up in the next couple of hours so you can get back home."

"If you have any questions from yesterday or with the operation of the phones, now's the time," he continued as everyone hurried to find their seats. "Robert and the other members of Black Water are here to make sure you leave here as well-prepared as possible."

Not seeing any hands go up, he introduced Debbie again before leaving the podium. Nodding to Gene as he left, he motioned for him to join him. Excusing himself, Gene slid his chair back and headed to the door where Larry had left.

"Good morning," Debbie said as the screen changed to show several sets of numbers beside each of the cities. "Here's the latest number of targets each of you will be assigned."

Waiting until she was sure she had their attention, she continued, "As you can see in red, these are the targets that must be removed with extreme prejudice. To refresh your understanding of this group, it contains any member of MS 13 who has directly participated in the murder, rape, beating, or dismemberment of anyone. That includes other members of MS 13 or members of any other gangs.

As you can see, there are approximately 600 in Long Island, 500 in Montgomery County, 1,000 in El Paso, 700 in Fairfax County, and last but certainly not least, 1,800 in Los Angeles," she pointed out. "That's about 4,600 hits out of the approximately 10,000 known or suspected members.

That's a lot of blood, ladies and gentlemen," she continued after a short pause. "But we've gamed this every way in the world, and this is the solution we came to. There's almost as many scattered across Central America and a few in other countries around the world.

Now, what about the other four or five thousand?" she asked as numbers in black were added. "These are the ones that have committed a crime, but generally non-violent. These will be collected and delivered to the same location we discussed yesterday.

And, before anyone asks, we would prefer that they be in the same van as those less fortunate," Debbie explained. "The behavioral folks think that we can give them a chance at life after we either incarcerate them here or return them to their country of origin.

Concurrent with planning this operation, the company persuaded the countries in question to accept their citizens and pass judgment," she told them. "And, the countries of origin understand that whatever judgment they elect to use, our government will be paying attention, and those much-desired foreign aid dollars or lucrative trade agreements will evaporate faster than mouse piss on a blacktop in the summer in Arizona."

As another set of numbers in green appeared, she said, "These are those who are under twelve years of age and not formal members. They are to be treated the same as the group seen in black. Also, make every attempt to have them staring at the results of MS 13's trademark being tattooed everywhere on their deceased bodies.

Speaking of the MS 13 tattoos, if you encounter any individual bearing them, treat them as you do the blacklisted individuals," she said. "We'll let their fate be decided by the behavioral folks. However, if they want to make it difficult, color them red. And the same goes for the black list. Anyone on that list that attempts to interfere resolve the situation immediately."

As everyone looked at the magnitude of the numbers in each category, Debbie reminded them, "Some of your targets may change from black or green to red during the operation. Some of them may disappear for unknown reasons. But the list will be updated as often as necessary. The people monitoring their location and actions will be making inputs minute by minute.

You may even need to make a judgment call on the spot," she said. "Let's not be overzealous, but don't take a chance and wind up dead. And we're aware that some mistakes will occur. But err on the side of your safety. We'll take care of it later.

Now, are there any questions?" she asked as Larry joined her at the podium.

Shaking her head as she saw Andy raising his hand, she said, "And what's your question this time, Andy?"

"I thought you said you could pinpoint each target. I believe you said within three feet. And now you're saying that you don't even know who our targets are?" Andy asked. "How are we supposed to have confidence in what you tell us now?"

'Well, sir, over the year we've been working on this, members of MS 13 have come and gone," Debbie explained. "Some die, some go to prison, new ones join. It's a dynamic situation.

If you'd ever had any field experience, I'm sure you'd understand. But you don't," she chided him. "And you'll probably never truly understand.

But, let me put it this way," she continued. "If an MS 13 member was on the list to be taken care of tomorrow, but he's in a car wreck and dies this afternoon, do you think we should go ahead and kill him again tomorrow? Only a complete moron would think that. Now, if you folks have nothing else for me, I'll turn you over to Larry. Good luck out there and stay safe."

As Debbie walked off shaking her head, Larry announced, "Well, that about wraps it up. Any further updates will be provided once you get back to your base. Again, I want to stress the importance of the little phone we gave you. Work with it. Call your teammates. There's a shit load of information in the manual. Learn it. If there's one single item that is the key to this operation, it's this. Now, I'll let you folks go and head home. Thanks for your attention."

Chapter 16

Jim was picking up everything he needed to take with him when Gene came back to the table. "Ready to head to the hotel?" Gene asked.

"Yeah," Jim answered. "What time do Jennifer and I need to be at the airport to go home?"

"We'll discuss that on the ride to the hotel," Gene answered. "There's something we need to discuss without anyone else around."

"Okay," Jim told him. "I'm ready whenever you are. Just let me hit the john first."

"No problem," Gene said, gathering his notes from the table. "I'll meet you out front."

The first thing that Jim noticed when he reached the Lincoln Town car was that Gene was driving. Opening the passenger door and getting in, he said, "I see you've opted to go it alone instead of having a driver."

"What we're going to discuss is better with just the two of us," Gene told him as he headed for the double gates that would allow them back into the Marine portion of the base.

Finally clear of the base, Gene said, "You remember when I went out to meet with Larry during the brief?"

"Sure," Jim answered. "I suppose it had something to do with the operation, probably involving the Dark Water side since I know you wouldn't discuss that aspect with the domestic side that this briefing was for."

"Partially correct," Gene confirmed as they headed toward Stafford. "What Larry told me worried me about one aspect of our domestic operation."

"What was that?" Jim asked, taking a glance at Gene.

"Andy," Gene said, taking his eyes off the road for a second to see Jim's reaction.

"I thought you were going to let Mike resolve that issue," Jim replied. "And I thought the solution was to keep him out of the field and in the hotel with Mike."

"That was the plan," Gene confirmed. "Until Debbie did a little more digging. What she found, and we confirmed, led us to believe that Andy would most likely jeopardize the operation if he remained involved in any aspect."

"And what did Debbie find that led to this conclusion?" Jim asked.

"Remember the little jab she delivered about field experience after Andy asked if we could trust her regarding the MS 13 members' location?" Gene asked.

"Sure," Jim answered, nodding. "I just thought it was more of the ongoing tit-for-tat crap between the two."

"Oh, no," Gene explained. "As you know, Debbie is rather blunt, even brutal, when someone questions her professionalism or denigrates her work. Well, she started looking into Andy's time with Black Water and discovered some rather unpleasant issues."

"Wait a second," Jim quickly remarked. "I thought he was Muddy Water."

"Yes, he is now. He was brought over after being with Black Water for a couple of years," Gene explained. "He was one of the staffers at our Los Angeles office. We, Black Water, hired him based on his experience in the Air Force personnel area. He applied for an opening, and one of our guys who had served with him in Korea recommended him."

"So, he was just a shoe clerk shuffling papers in the Air Force and had no operational experience of any sort," Jim remarked critically. "I guess I'm sort of surprised that the company would hire someone like that."

"We have numerous people in the support offices," Gene explained. "These are the folks that arrange transportation, make reservations, submit expense reports, all of the stuff that goes on behind the scenes. The thing different in this instance is that he wormed his way into an operation because Mike decided to give him a chance."

"How did Mike even know about this little weenie?" Jim asked incredulously.

"Well, Andy knew some information about Mike's involvement with Muddy Water," Gene explained. "And he more or less approached him about a year ago when Mike was trying to resolve some routine paperwork issues.

Then, he sort of found out where Mike went for a beer or what gym he used and slowly worked his way into his trust," Gene continued.

"Let me understand this," Jim remarked. "This shithead uses privileged information about Black Water's employees and then stalks him. Does that about sum it up?"

"That's about right," Gene reluctantly admitted. "But it was more insidious than that. Mike just thought the guy was one of the team and probably lonely since he couldn't discuss his job with the usual public. Basically, he felt sorry for him and finally agreed to help him if he wanted to get into the operational end."

"Now you're going to tell me that Black Water approved moving a friggin' desk jockey into an operational slot," Jim replied, amazed. "How the hell could the company approve that?"

"It was a mistake," Gene admitted. "But appropriate measures are being enacted to ensure this never happens again."

"Okay, mistakes happen," Jim agreed after pausing to consider how it happened. "So, we, you hired the wrong guy. Fire him and move on."

"Not that simple," Gene told him. "Along with Debbie's digging around, she, along with Mike, discovered that Andy has a rather loose mouth."

"What do you mean, loose mouth?" Jim asked, astonished that a member of Black Water hadn't been vetted to ensure this would never happen.

"It seems that he was regaling one of the ladies from his former office about how he had been hand-selected to be a member of a very high-level operation," Gene said. "Apparently, he had a rather self-glamorizing manner around the office. Constantly making innuendos about his other work with the company."

"Let me guess," Jim said, shaking his head. "He had personalized license plates that read 007."

"Not that blatant, but he was definitely delusional," Gene confirmed. "Now, the problem is how to resolve the situation."

"You mean Mike's problem," Jim corrected him.

"No, I mean our problem," Gene said assertively with a quick glance at Jim. "And by our, I mean yours."

Taking a deep breath and slowly letting it out, Jim finally asked, "And what do you suggest I do to resolve my problem?"

"Eliminate the problem," Gene answered. "We can't afford to let him just walk around with extensive knowledge of the operation he's just listened to. And we damn sure can't trust him to keep his mouth shut. I don't see any other solution. If you do, please let me know."

After a couple of minutes, Jim finally answered, "I don't know of any other way. I'm still not sure why this is my problem, but I agree with the solution."

"It's your problem because I'm asking you," Gene told him. "I need someone I trust explicitly. This is coming from the top of the organization. We don't want anyone else to know that we're willing to remove personnel this way."

"Mike's going to know," Jim argued. "Why not let him do it?"

"He's too close," Gene said. "I talked to him, and he understands that this has to be done, but I don't want him to be the one. Just as I wouldn't ask you to do it to someone you've gotten close to. No, you're my choice. However, if you don't think you can, I'll find someone else."

"No, I'll do it," Jim said quietly. "You know I'll never refuse you. You're as much family as anyone else. More than most of my real family. When do you need this done?"

"You're flying to Los Angeles and laying over Monday, aren't you?" Gene asked, already knowing the answer. "You'll be meeting him at a small bar called Harley's just down the street from the hotel."

"Why would he meet me?" Jim asked.

"Mike is going to tell him to meet you regarding some changes to the operation," Gene explained. "The laboratory here has prepared a lethal extract from the cone snail, more specifically, the geography cone snail, and it'll be at the hotel when you sign in tomorrow evening."

"How's it administered?" Jim asked.

"It's a liquid," Gene answered. "Simply pour it into his drink."

"How does it work, and how quick is it?" Jim asked.

"Basically, it's a form of insulin," Gene told him. "But extremely toxic. As a matter of fact, the nickname for the Conus Geographus, cone snail, is the cigarette snail. Supposedly, you only have time to smoke one cigarette if you're stung by one of these guys."

"I thought insulin had to be injected," Jim replied. "And what if there's an autopsy? Do we have a problem there?"

"Insulin can be taken orally, but it's very ineffective that way," Gene explained. "This shit is massively effective with over 100 different toxins, and the quantity you'll be using would put an elephant down.

The autopsy issue is nonexistent," Gene continued. "Even if we somehow lost control, Andy is diabetic, so it would be unusual for him not to have some amount of insulin in his system.

"I guess you've been busy these last few hours," Jim said as they pulled into the hotel.

"Not really," Gene explained as he parked. "The toxin has been in our labs for several years. The coordination with Mike was merely a phone call after he confirmed what Debbie had discovered. And everything else just fell into place."

"What would you have done if I hadn't been laying over in Los Angeles tomorrow night?" Jim asked as they walked into the hotel.

"I'd have thought of something," Gene answered, smiling. "Now go get Jennifer, and we'll grab a bite to eat before I stick you on the plane going back to Dallas."

"What about Debbie?" Jim asked, punching the elevator up button. "Is she going with us?"

"No, she's got some work to do here before she goes home," Gene answered. "There are a couple of glitches with our computer system in El Salvador that need her attention."

"That'll make Jennifer happy," Jim remarked as the elevator doors opened. "And I really didn't want to sit listening to her not talking for four hours either."

Chapter 17

Monday morning, after Jennifer had left for work, Jim finished packing his suitcase for the three-day trip and was almost out of the door to head to the Dallas Fort Worth Airport (DFW) when the phone rang.

"Hello," he answered, glancing at his watch.

"Good morning," came the response. "This is Don Jackson with crew scheduling, and I need to take the first two legs of your trip today to finish a new Captain's checkout. So, your sign-in will be this afternoon at three o'clock for the remainder of the trip. Will that be a problem?"

"No," Jim answered. "I'm assuming that my Captain is also being taken off the Chicago turn and will be with me on the LA portion."

"That is correct, sir," the scheduler answered. "His trip and yours will both complete the remainder of the original trip, and you'll both be paid for the entire sequence."

"Sounds good," Jim replied. "Thanks for the call."

"No problem, sir," Jerry said. "Have a good trip this afternoon."

After hanging up, Jim called the Black Water headquarters and waited to be transferred to General Barker. "Good morning, sir," Jim said as he answered. "Just thought I'd give you a quick call to update you on my schedule today."

"Any problems?" Gene asked.

"No, the company needed my first two legs for some training issue, but I'll still fly the leg to LA just as originally scheduled," Jim answered. "I wanted to make sure you were aware that I wouldn't be on the Chicago turn if you were monitoring the flight crews."

"I would have checked on it later today to make sure it was on schedule just in case I needed to make some alternative arrangements regarding the scheduled meeting tonight," Gene told him. "But I appreciate your call. Saved me some time and effort trying to find out if you were going to make the meeting."

"Good," Jim replied. "I'll let you get back to work, and if anything else comes up, I'll give you a call."

"Thanks," Gene said. "Let me know if there are any problems later this evening. Everything has been arranged at the hotel and where you'll be meeting the other party."

"Yes, sir," Jim said. "I'll give you a call afterward from the hotel. Good day."

Taking this opportunity to look at some of the unique characteristics of the new phone, he took it out of his suitcase and turned it on. As it powered up, he looked at the manual and reviewed how to make a simple phone call.

As the screen came to life, he touched the phone symbol and saw a directory of contacts and their numbers. Scrolling down the list, he stopped when he spotted Mike Knox.

Tapping on it, he saw the name pop up and heard it dialing. "Good morning, Mike," he said when it was answered. "This is Jim Lashley."

"Hey, Jim," Mike replied. "It's been a while. How have you been?"

"Good," Jim answered. "I was just playing with this new-fangled phone and saw your number. I hope I'm not disturbing you."

"Not at all," he told him. "I saw your name on the list General Barker gave me regarding the upcoming operation and I had thought about contacting you."

"I guess Gene told you that I was going to be out there this evening," Jim said. "I'm sorry about the situation, but I'm sure you understand."

"I do," Mike answered. "Completely. I'm just embarrassed that I was taken in. Guess I'm getting soft in my old age."

"Well, we can't always see everything," Jim sympathized. "I'm just glad we figured it out before it caused a major problem."

"Me too," Mike agreed. "Is there anything I can do to help you?"

"Not really," Jim answered. "Everything is supposed to be in place, but I appreciate the offer. If something comes up, I'll give you a call."

"I know Gene didn't want me involved because I'm close to the issue," Mike told him. "But I feel as if I'm passing my problem off to you. If you need or want my help, please let me know. If nothing else, maybe we can get together afterward. I'm not scheduled to fly until Wednesday, and it would be good to catch up."

"Sure would," Jim said. "Tell you what, give me your usual number, and I'll call when I finish this evening. Maybe we can meet somewhere and grab a beer."

"Sounds good," Mike answered. "I'll call your layover hotel and leave it with them. And I'm serious about helping you if you want. Matter of fact, I'm going to call Gene and let him know that I'm available and more than willing to take care of it since it's my fault to start with."

"That's up to you," Jim replied. "But I'm glad we had a chance to talk. Letting Gene know you're willing to help will give him an alternative in case something goes wrong with my trip. Anyway, I look forward to seeing you this evening, and I'll give you a call from the hotel when my meeting is over."

"Good," Mike responded. "And I'll leave you a message at the hotel if anything has changed. See you this evening."

Hanging up, Jim used his house phone and called Jennifer at work to let her know he was still home and asked if she wanted to go have lunch. Hearing that she did, he replaced the phone and was changing from his uniform into a pair of starched Wranglers when the phone rang again.

"Hello," he answered, buttoning his shirt.

"Jim, slight change of plans," Gene told him. "I just talked to Mike in LA, and he told me you and he had spoken about this evening. I agreed with his involvement, and he will meet you at the hotel. Everything else remains as planned. Do you have any questions?"

"No, sir," Jim replied. "I think that's a great idea. It would be good to have another man in case I have to move the problem afterward. It could be a lot easier if there were two of us."

"Agreed," Gene said. "Let me know if you guys need anything else. Have a safe flight."

"Yes, sir," Jim said before hanging up. "I'll call from the hotel when I get in."

After having lunch with Jennifer, Jim changed back into his uniform and headed to the DFW airport for the remainder of his trip. Arriving early, he looked around the flight operations area for his Captain. Spotting him at one of the computers, he walked over and said hello.

"Good afternoon, Jim," Terry said, shaking his hand. "What a nice way to start the day. Told to stay home and get paid. That's always good."

"I agree," Jim answered. "Gave me a chance to have lunch with my wife, which is a rare opportunity."

"I just hung around the house and caught up on some honey-do's," Terry said, nodding. "Do you have any plans for tonight in LA?"

"Yeah," Jim answered. "I'm meeting an old Marine buddy for a glass of iced tea. He was my first Flight Instructor when I was a Cadet."

"Sounds like fun," Terry said, handing Jim the paperwork for their flight. "Take a look at this and let me know if you have any questions. I'll hit the head and meet you at the gate."

"Yes, sir," Jim said, glancing at the assigned route and weather for their flight. "I'll head on down and see if the Flight Attendants are there already."

Chapter 18

After landing at the Los Angeles International Airport (LAX), Jim rode with the crew to their layover hotel. As he signed in and got his key, the desk clerk handed him a large envelope and a note with Mike's phone number.

Telling everyone he would see them in the morning, he headed for the elevator and exited on the third floor for his room. Changing quickly, he called Mike and told him he would meet him in Harley's bar down the street.

As he got off the elevator to leave, he saw Terry with one of the Flight Attendants going into the hotel restaurant. Remembering how the Flight Attendant had called the cockpit several times during the flight from DFW, Jim wondered if there was some romantic interest between the two.

As he walked into the bar, he spotted Mike sitting at a corner table near the rear. As he approached, Mike rose and smiled, saying, "Damn, it's been a long time."

"Sure has," Jim replied, shaking his outstretched hand. "But you look the same as the day I met you."

"Bullshit," Mike said, laughing. "And the Pope doesn't like little altar boys. How the hell have you been?"

"Good," Jim answered. "The airlines are a far cry from the old days. No sweaty flight suits, plenty of days off, and coffee in the cockpit."

"True enough," Mike agreed as they took their seats. "I'm not sure how things are at American Airlines, but US Air takes pretty good care of us."

"American is good," Jim responded as he took a small Ziplock baggie from his pocket. "Boring most of the time. Sort of like being a bus driver with disgruntled people riding in the back."

"But coffee in the cockpit," Mike offered again, smiling. "And nobody is shooting at you."

"That's a plus," Jim agreed. "Not to change the subject, but when is Andy supposed to be here?"

"Supposed to be here in about 30 minutes, but it wouldn't surprise me if he's early. He has a tendency to get somewhere early so he can survey the situation," Mike answered, nodding at the baggie. "Just how strong is that stuff in the baggie anyway?"

"Supposed to be enough to put an elephant's nose in the dirt," Jim told him. "What did you tell Andy about why we're meeting?"

"I told him that you were coming out to get his opinion of some minor changes to the operation," Mike answered. "I let him believe that the company valued his input and was thinking about letting him take charge of one of the sectors."

"What a douche," Jim said, looking around the bar. "What would you like to drink? More importantly, what does numb nuts drink?"

"Just get me a Heineken," Mike said. "Andy likes Old Grand Dad. I'm pretty sure that's because James Bond drank it in Live and Let Die. Ever since the General and Debbie told me about this little twerp, I've remembered all the little things he did that should have been a clue as to his fantasy of being a secret agent. Like you said, a real douche."

"I'll go get the drinks, and we'll mix his last cocktail," Jim said, getting up. "If he shows up before I get back, you'll need to distract him while I do it."

Jim had just reached the bar when he saw Andy walking in, looking around. "Hey Andy," he called, waving at him. "Just getting a couple of beers for Mike and me. He says you like Old Grand Dad, is that right?"

"Perfect," Andy answered, shaking Jim's hand. "No ice."

"No problem," Jim told him. "Mike's over there at that corner table. Why don't you go on over, and I'll bring the drinks.

Shit," Jim thought, remembering that he had left the baggie on the table. "Hey, Andy! How about giving me a hand carrying the drinks to the table."

"No problem," Andy said, turning back. "Glad to help."

As Andy stepped up to the bar, Jim looked at Mike and saw him pat his pocket, nodding. Sure that it was safe to go to the table, Jim said, "Just grab your bourbon when the bartender pours it, and I'll take the beers to the table."

"Hi, Andy," Mike said as he sat. "Glad you could meet us on such short notice. Jim said that the General wanted to know what you think about how the operation planning went."

"It's got some holes," Andy answered, looking from Mike to Jim. "But I think most of it is workable."

"Cheers," Jim said, holding up his beer and waiting for everyone to tap it. "And what do you suggest we do to fill these holes?"

"I think most of the problem is with that computer bitch, Debbie," Andy said, taking a sip. "For someone with no field experience, she doesn't have a clue about what it's really like."

Jim cast a quick glance at Mike and asked, "Can you be a little more specific? Just give me an example of what you'd change."

"Sure," Andy said, sitting his glass on the table and holding up his hand. "First thing, I don't trust that her phone thing will give us any real information. I mean, why don't we just look at pictures of our targets and go get them?"

Jim nodded and asked, "How would you figure out where they were without her program? You saw how accurate it was during the briefing. What's your option?"

As Andy was shaking his head as he started to answer, Jim noticed Mike sit back and ease the baggie from his pocket. "I'd do it the old-fashioned way," Andy said. "Follow him until I find an opportunity. Then take him out."

"You think we could possibly trail that many people in the short amount of time we have?" Jim asked, watching Andy's eyes as Mike emptied the baggie into his glass. "I think that part of the operation will expedite it. I mean, to know where each target is at any specific time will save a shit load of time."

Just as Mike finished and was pulling his hand back, Andy turned his head and asked, "What did you just do? Did you screw with my drink?"

"Of course not," Mike answered. "There was just a fly on the rim, and I shooed it away."

"I don't believe you," Andy said, pushing his glass away. "I'll tell you what I do think. You two are here because that bitch knows I have a better idea, and she's afraid that she'll lose her big important job when I show her up. That's what I think.

I saw how cozy you were with her at Quantico," Andy said, looking at Jim. "You and that General were always agreeing with her when she couldn't stand that I was exposing her for the fraud she is. And you're here to shut me up. That's what I think."

As Andy started to stand up, Jim reached out and put his hand on Andy's shoulder, saying, "You've got it all wrong. The General and I talked about what you had asked, and we wanted to know if you had a better idea. That's all."

"You guys must think I'm a fool," Andy said, brushing Jim's hand away. "You both think you're so much smarter than I am because you were Marines. Hey, I've done my research too. Big airline pilots. Big fighter pilots. Well, you don't know shit as far as I'm concerned. And you can tell that smartass bitch and the General that I'm not sitting by and let you idiots ruin this operation."

As Andy pushed his chair back, Mike quietly said, "Hey, Andy. We aren't going to ruin this operation. And we're going to make sure that you don't."

Slipping his hand from beneath the table, Mike put the barrel of the silenced Walther P22 22 caliber pistol against Andy's forehead and pulled the trigger.

Jim grabbed Andy's shirt as his head snapped back and pulled him forward onto the table, whispering, "We better get the hell out of here as quietly as we can. Where did you park?"

"Right outside," Mike answered, looking around the bar. "You grab his left side, and I'll take the right. If anyone says anything, we're just taking our drunk friend home."

Wiping the table where Andy's head had come to rest with his napkin, Jim put twenty dollars under his unfinished beer and said, "Okay, whenever you're ready."

Mike stood and told him, "Now. Just stand up and put his arm around your shoulders. I'll do the same when you get him up."

As they maneuvered their way toward the door to the bar, the bartender asked, "Little too much to drink? You guys need a hand?"

"No," Jim answered. "We got it, but thanks. I left enough to cover our drinks on the table. Sorry for the inconvenience."

As they exited the bar, Mike nodded in the direction of the car and said, "Little worthless prick. I hated to do it this way, but I didn't see any option."

"No," Jim agreed as they approached the car. "I'm just glad you came armed. Now, all we need to do is dispose of the body."

"I've already taken care of that," Mike told him as they placed Andy's body in the rear seat. "I've got a place we've used several times, and that's where I was going to take him anyway. Do you need a ride back to the hotel before I drop off our little buddy?"

"No, it's not far, and I'll just walk," Jim answered. "I'll give Gene a call and explain what happened."

"Okay. I'll call you when it's done. And I'll call Gene and let him know it's taken care of," Mike said as he got into the car.

"All right," Jim said, glancing back at the bar. "I probably wouldn't go back to Harley's for a while if I were you. I don't think anyone was paying attention except the bartender, but I'd play it safe and stay away."

"That's not a problem," Mike said, starting the car. "I live way the hell across town, and this is the first time, and now last time, I've been here. Take care of yourself, and we'll talk later."

Jim glanced at the door to the bar one final time as he headed back to the hotel. Not seeing anyone, he shook his head at the incredible luck that nobody had noticed. "I guess good luck is just as important as good planning," he thought as he headed down the street. "Maybe even better."

Chapter 19

As soon as Jim was back in his room, he made a quick call to Gene to explain how things had gone wrong. When he heard Gene's voice, he began, "Things didn't quite go according to plan, sir."

"I know," came the reply.

"Has Mike already called you?" Jim asked, surprised that he already knew.

"The bartender," Gene answered.

"The bartender was part of the plan?" Jim asked, again surprised.

"What, did you think I'd send you out there without at least having someone covering your back?" Gene explained. "This was all arranged before Mike wanted to get involved."

"Why didn't you say something?" Jim asked. "It would have been nice to know there was someone else there in case we ran into a problem."

"I wasn't worried about it," Gene replied, chuckling softly. "I've known you and Mike long enough to know that either of you could handle it. The bartender was just additional insurance, as were the other two guys in the bar."

Shaking his head, Jim just said, "I still think it would have been nice to have known. But, as I said, things didn't quite work out according to the plan."

"I disagree," Gene told him. "You went there to execute the man, and you were successful."

"What do you mean successful?" Jim asked.

"Sort of like that line in The Green Mile," Gene answered. "You know, where the guy intentionally didn't wet the sponge?"

"I remember," Jim replied. "The guy they were executing sort of caught on fire."

"And the warden asked what the hell happened," Gene continued. That's when Hanks said it was an execution and a successful one."

"I remember," Jim added. "And then when the warden asked how that was a success, he said the man was dead, wasn't he."

"Exactly," Gene told him. "Andy is dead, isn't he?"

"I understand," Jim finally said. "But I still think it would have been nice to know we had backup."

"Nice is for birthday cake, or as Willie Nelson said, good and firm feeling women," Gene replied. "As you well know, there are always things going on behind the scenes that most of you guys in the field don't know about.

And some of the people out there supporting you are just that, support," he continued. "In this case, the bartender was originally there to take care of the body after you spike Andy's drink. But, when Mike joined you, it wasn't necessary.

And finally, some of them don't want to be involved with the actual operation, just a last resort," Gene concluded. "And we, the company, try to protect their identity whenever possible."

"Understand," Jim agreed. "Anyway, it was a good thing that Mike brought that little pistol. I must say that I'm a little surprised that he didn't have at least a 9 millimeter or a 40 caliber."

"That's more or less Mike's trademark," Gene told him. "He favors the close-up headshot, and the 22 caliber hollow point is the ammo of choice since it will penetrate the skull on entry but won't exit, thus ensuring any non-target isn't harmed."

"Well, it certainly worked in this case," Jim said, nodding. "I was beginning to worry when Andy decided that something was wrong. It could have been disastrous if he hadn't been armed."

"That's part of the reason for the other guys in the bar," Gene told him. "They were armed also, but as I said, didn't want to be part of the operation unless absolutely necessary."

"Okay, I'll leave it alone," Jim reluctantly agreed. "I'm just glad we got rid of Andy. I agree with you and Debbie. He was a loose cannon and couldn't be trusted. It's good that we found out when we did."

"Certainly was," Gene agreed. "I'm getting more impressed with Debbie's computer skills every day. But I'm also getting more concerned about where all of this technology is heading."

"Yeah, she sort of gave Jennifer and me an insight into what's out there right now," Jim replied. "Pretty scary when someone sitting in his mother's basement eating sugar-coated doughnuts can find out everything about your personal life. In that, I agree with Jennifer. It's too easy to pry into our everyday lives."

"It's only going to get worse, my friend," Gene told him. "I've seen some of the stuff on the drawing board. If you think Big Brother is watching you now, just wait a few years. Computer chips in your phone, your car, your credit card, or anything else that uses electronic technology. And it's coming at an exponentially expanding rate."

"Maybe they'll be able to replace us with machines like the Terminator," Jim offered. "Then I can sit around getting fat and lazy."

"I don't see that happening," Gene said, laughing. "You're too much of an adrenalin junkie. No, you won't sit around watching Little House on the Prairie. Now, hit the sack, and I'll talk to you in a couple of days when you get back home."

"Yes, sir," Jim replied. "And thank you for having our backs. Even if I was a little miffed about not knowing it was there, I'm damn glad to know that you'll always be there for us."

"That's my job. Now, get some sleep. You've got a couple of long days ahead of you," Gene told him before hanging up.

"Good night."

Chapter 20

Three days later, when Jim was sitting at home trying to figure out how to accomplish everything Jennifer had asked him to do before he left for his first El Paso flight and the start of the MS 13 operation, the phone rang as he was getting up to refresh his coffee.

"Hello," he said as he refilled the almost empty cup.

"Good morning, Jim," Gene replied. "Anything new down in Texas?"

"Not really," Jim answered, smiling at Gene's attempt at small talk. "Anything new up in Virginia?"

"Well, now that you ask, yes, there is," Gene answered. "Do you have a few minutes to spare?"

"Of course," Jim replied. "Are you just down the street, as usual, or sitting in your office in Quantico?"

"I don't have time to fly down every time I need to talk to you, you know," Gene complained. "And since I'm having to do some follow up regarding the upcoming operation, I certainly can't personally visit all of the players involved. So, you'll just have to do with a phone call."

"That's certainly my loss, sir," Jim replied. "Although you always provide me with an excuse to go out for lunch. But I'm interrupting."

"Yes, you are," Gene remarked, chuckling. "And, as always, a smart ass. But, since I'm sure you're up to your neck in chores, I'll try to make this quick. The first night has been changed from a field operation to a briefing."

"Okay," Jim said. "Who's briefing, and what's changed that delays the operation?"

"In your case, a lady named Melinda will be doing the briefing," Gene answered. "The change is that the toads in the basement have run a simulation that shows a wide dispersal of the players within two days after implementation of the op. Bearing that in mind, we've brought in new teams that will concentrate on those who were to be collected for removal. They'll arrive the second day and will operate autonomously."

"How will that affect our planning?" Jim asked. "Seems to me that it'll make it easier for my group to concentrate on the real purpose of the operation."

"I believe it does," Gene agreed. "Now, instead of collecting the trash, your people will be free to move about more rapidly. That should help resolve the disposal problem."

"So, how much will that shorten the entire operation?" Jim asked, wondering how many bodies were going to be left in place as they moved through the city.

"It's likely that it will actually extend it," Gene told him. "That's because once the plan is executed, the word is going to spread, and those at the upper levels will have the knowledge and means to disappear."

"It seems to me that the entire focus of the operation is now at a much lower level than previously described," Jim countered. "If we don't get the head of the snake, the problem will return. Maybe at a different location, but the problem remains."

"That's correct," Gene admitted. "But, if the spooks are wrong in their assessment, we'll get the majority of what we're after. If they're correct, we're working on a plan to track and remove everything that escapes."

"What about interaction between our two groups?" Jim asked. "I'm sure the planners took that into account because things could get out of hand very quickly if we have two autonomous teams working in the same area, possibly within feet of each other."

"That's part of the reason for the briefing," Gene answered. "As you probably noticed, Debbie is not briefing you. She'll be remaining at Quantico, and her team up here will be sending updates to the folks in each of the cities. In your case, Melinda, as I mentioned."

"Is that going to dilute my intelligence?" Jim asked. "I was under the assumption that I would have an onsite computer specialist to give minute-to-minute updates for our field operations."

"You'll still get that," Gene assured him. "But, since we're planning on an unknown number of assignments, possibly as much as half, no longer being in the area, we increased Debbie's staff here to monitor that activity."

"Will she be providing Melinda with the information on movement, or will it be available locally?" Jim asked.

"Melinda will have the local information," Gene answered. "Each city will be seeing everything they need for their circumstances. The removal teams will also have a dedicated computer analyst. Debbie will be overseeing all of them, including those operating under Dark Water's banner."

"Let's get back to the length," Jim said. "You said it would extend the operation. By that, I'm assuming you mean the time required to remove all of the opposition.

But, from my standpoint, it looks like my portion will be substantially shortened," he continued. "There are now twice as many operators on our side working on up to half as many opposition forces. Mathematically, that should shorten my time frame by about 75 percent."

"That's correct," Gene acknowledged. "But, because of the time involved in determining the new location of those that leave town, we are left with an extended operation."

"That I understand," Jim replied. "But, as far as my people, it should be over within a week versus a month."

"Possibly," Gene confirmed. "However, if we determine that the majority of the escapees are still in the local area, or even just a few of the more important ones, your teams will be tasked to take care of them as initially planned."

"Which means what regarding our timeline?" Jim asked. "Will we still be meeting as previously planned but with no specific targets?"

"More or less," Gene told him. "If one of our assignments leaves the area but is reasonably close, we'll have one of the teams sent to resolve the situation. Or, if we get intelligence that he is returning, the same result.

But to be more accurate, some of the evenings you may not have anything to do except watch reruns of the Andy Griffith show," Gene finished. "Or it may be a single assignment at three o'clock in the morning."

"I guess you're going to rehash the old adage about how air power works," Jim countered. "You know, flexibility is the key to air power, and lack of information is the key to flexibility; therefore, the less you know, the better you are."

"Close," Gene said, laughing. "But, following that formula, I'd just give you a weapon and point you in the right direction. Then, you'd provide the best possible outcome. Is that what you're saying?"

"Sort of," Jim countered. "But, if you gave me the means and the goal, I'm pretty sure the result would be the same. Sort of like Occam's razor."

"I'm not going to follow you down that rabbit hole," Gene said. "But the principle is true. Less is sometimes more. Now, are there any other worthy questions before I call the other team leaders?"

"One," Jim answered. "Maybe more of a suggestion than a question. Are you going to provide both my teams and the recovery teams with identifying apparel? Something that wouldn't be too noticeable to the casual observer but readily identifiable to us?"

"We haven't discussed that, but what would you suggest?" Gene asked.

"I think a baseball cap would be appropriate," Jim answered. "Maybe white for the removal teams and red for the others. Possibly a logo on the front to ensure it's not just a plain cap that could be confused with an innocent bystander."

"I'll look into that," Gene said. "That's a good idea. I'll get with the folks at the front office and see what they can come up with. Anything else?"

"One other thing," Jim answered. "Security cameras. We need someone to get any security camera and video from any location after the removal teams are out.

Oh, before I forget it, I got the El Paso bid for next month," Jim informed him. "But I'll get back to you if I think of something."

"I heard you got the bid from one of our guys down there in scheduling," Gene told him. "I'll try to have everything ready for you when you get to the hotel in El Paso. Until then, take care of yourself. Goodbye."

Chapter 21

Two weeks later after Jennifer had left for work, Jim tossed his suitcase and flight bag in the truck and headed for the airport. Once in operations, he checked for any updates to his flight manuals and printed the list of the crew for the trip to El Paso. Noticing that one of the Flight Attendants was one he had flown with several times before, he smiled and headed for the gate, hoping she would already be there.

As he walked up to the gate, he noticed her sitting with three other Flight Attendants in the chairs closest to the windows, looking out over the ramp. "Good morning, ladies," he said, stopping by the seats. "I'm Jim, and I'll be assisting Captain Kirby for the next few days."

"I know you," Mary said as she stood up to give Jim a hug. "We've flown together a few times before. How did you get so lucky to get this horrible trip?"

"Yeah, I remember flying with you," Jim replied, returning her hug. "And it's not that bad of a trip."

"What do you mean, not bad?" Mary asked. "Dallas to El Paso to Dallas to El Paso, spend the night. Then El Paso to Dallas to El Paso, spend the night. Then El Paso to Dallas. I figured you were too senior for something like this."

"It fits the days I needed off," Jim explained. "And I have a couple of friends in El Paso that I'll get to see. How about you? Still riding your bicycle up and down the Trinity River?"

"When I get a chance," she answered, taking her seat. "Do you know our Captain?"

"No," Jim told her. "I saw his name when I signed in, but I don't think I've ever met him."

"We haven't heard of him either," Mary said, looking at the other Flight Attendants. "And that's usually a good sign."

"I understand," Jim replied, smiling. "I've heard about you guys 'A' list. I'm just hoping I'm never on it."

"Trust me, you'll never be on the Ass list," Mary said, laughing. "Not that you're really memorable, but you just sort of fall into the 'I remember him as a nice guy' category if you're remembered at all."

"Wow!" Jim exclaimed, shaking his head. "What a compliment!"

"You know what I mean," Mary said. "By the way, this is Susan, Lorinda, and Paula. Ladies, I give you the remarkably unremarkable Jim Lashley."

"Ladies, nice to meet you," Jim told them as he tipped his hat. "I'm hoping that none of you ever remember me either."

"Stop it," Mary said as the others nodded their acknowledgment. "I told you I remembered you. What more do you want than to be somewhat remembered and not be on the 'A' list?"

"I guess that's about as good as I can ever hope for," Jim answered as a man in a Captain's uniform walked up.

"I'm guessing that you guys are on the El Paso trip," he said, sitting his roll-aboard down. "I'm Ray."

"Hi, Captain," Jim said, extending his hand. "I'm Jim. Nice to meet you."

"Just call me Ray," he said, shaking Jim's hand. "And that goes for the rest of you. I like to keep things informal and friendly whenever possible."

"I'm Mary, the number one," Mary said, standing. "And these ladies are Susan, Lorinda, and Paula."

"Good to meet all of you," Ray said. "Now, if it's all right with you, I'll give you my quick one and only brief for the month or however long we're flying together."

Pausing to make sure they were listening, he then continued, "You guys are professionals; just do your jobs. Jim and I will do ours. If you have any problems, call me, and I'll try my best to take care of it.

As far as the passengers go," he told them, "We don't put up with any crap. If you're concerned about someone before we takeoff, let me know. I'd rather solve it on the ground here at DFW than at 30 thousand feet over Midland.

Once in the air, take care of it if you can. If not, call the cockpit, and one of us will come help you," he finished. "As I said, we're not here to take crap off the passengers. I won't tolerate rude behavior or vulgar language. Are there any questions?"

Seeing everyone nod their head, Ray finished his brief by saying, "Good. Now, let's make these miserable three days of flying in circles as pleasant as possible. And always remember, I'm up in front to take care of you as well as the passengers."

Seeing their plane pulling into the gate, Jim said, "I'll go on down and get the preflight out of the way unless you have anything else for me."

"Nope," Ray said. "And, if you don't mind, I'll do the walk around on the legs I'm flying. Unless it's too cold or too hot, that is. Or too windy."

"Your choice," Jim answered, smiling and shaking his head. "Just let me know when it's not too cold, too hot, or too windy, and I'll sit in the cockpit drinking a cold Dr Pepper while you suffer the moderate weather."

Chapter 22

After landing back at El Paso on the third and last flight of the day, Jim and the crew took the courtesy van to their hotel. As Jim checked in, the receptionist handed him an envelope saying, "Mr. Lashley, this was left for you earlier this afternoon."

"Thanks," Jim said as he put the envelope in his jacket pocket and took the electronic key card.

Seeing Ray holding the elevator, he hurried to join him and the Flight Attendants. "Anything important?" Ray asked as the elevator began to rise.

"Probably not," Jim answered, looking at the floors as they passed them. "Most likely something from my friend I'm supposed to meet this evening."

"Well, if it falls through, let me know, and we'll have a debrief tea and dinner here," Ray said as the elevator came to a stop on their floor. "And the same goes for you ladies if you're so inclined."

"Thanks, but we've made plans for the evening," Mary said as they got out. "We'll see both of you in the morning."

"I'll give you a call in a few minutes if I'll be available this evening," Jim told Ray as he stopped in front of his room.

As soon as he shut the door, Jim pulled his jacket off and tossed it on the bed. Opening the envelope, he saw a number and instructions to call using the phone he had gotten from Blackwater.

After two rings, he heard a voice saying, "Mr. Lashley, this is Melinda, and a car will be at your hotel in 10 minutes to take you to the Vista Del Sol Conference Center, where the other members of the team will be meeting. Will that give you sufficient time?"

"That'll be fine," Jim said, opening his suitcase. "I'll be ready when the car gets here. What hotel are we using for the operation?"

"It's the Motel 6 just down the street from the conference center. But you won't be staying there tonight. However, a room has been reserved for you along with the rest of the members of the teams," she answered. "Matter of fact, the entire hotel has been reserved for our operation for the entire month. As has been the conference room, we'll be using this evening. Both were contracted for through the Army out at Biggs for a special operation."

"Great. I'll see you in a few minutes," Jim told her as he started changing into his jeans and a T-shirt.

Five minutes later, he was in the elevator, heading down to the lobby. As he stepped off, he saw a black Suburban pulling up to the door in front of the hotel.

As he walked out, the driver came around the back of the car and opened the rear door on the passenger side saying, "Good afternoon, Mr. Lashley. I'm Nolan, and I'll be your driver for the month. How was your flight in?"

"Uneventful," Jim said, opening the passenger door to the front seat. "And, if it's all right with you, I'd prefer to sit up here."

"That'll be fine," Nolan said, shutting the rear door and returning around the back of the car.

"Are you from El Paso?" Jim asked, noticing the pistol on the driver's belt as he was getting in the car.

"No, sir," he answered. "I'm from Virginia."

"Quantico?" Jim asked as they pulled away from the hotel.

"Boswell's Corner," he answered, accelerating down the road. "It's a little town about five miles from the Marine base at Quantico."

"Then I guess you're part of the group here for the briefing," Jim remarked as they pulled onto I-10 heading east.

"Yes, sir," Nolan said. "I've been here for a couple of days helping Melinda set everything up. And, as I said, I'll be your driver, or maybe I should say assistant, for the time you're here."

"Blackwater?" Jim asked as Nolan maneuvered around the cars starting to clog the freeway.

"Yes, sir," Nolan answered, passing several cars before crossing back to the right lane. "About ten years now."

"No need to call me sir, just Jim will do," Jim told him as he admired how Nolan was handling the increasing traffic. "What do you do at Quantico when you're not assigned to babysit somebody like me?"

"I teach advanced driving, small arms marksmanship, and hand-to-hand combat techniques," Nolan answered as they took the exit for Gateway Blvd. "And I get loaned out to help any operation where they think I can be useful."

"Sounds like they keep you busy," Jim offered as they came to Lomaland Drive and made a left turn.

"Pretty much," Nolan answered, heading north. "The motel we're using is just a block or so on the right. It's not bad. The rooms are clean, and the folks back at Quantico have made some arrangements for catering for the guys staying here. I've been assigned worse."

"Military?" Jim asked as they turned right on Rojas Drive.

"Navy," Nolan answered as they pulled into the parking lot for the conference center. "Six years active and still in the reserves."

"Well, I'm glad to have you around," Jim told him as they parked. "I'm not sure if you'll need to do more than ferry me from the layover hotel to here and back, but it's good to know that you aren't just some shoe clerk from the admin area if things get out of hand. Which they seem to do with regularity."

"I understand," Nolan acknowledged as they both exited the car. "And I had a chance to read your resume before I came here. I like to know what to expect if you know what I mean."

"I understand," Jim said as they entered the Conference Center. "We occasionally misjudge some of the people who get into the organization. Thank goodness it's a rarity."

"I heard about the little issue out in Los Angeles," Nolan told him as he led the way to the room they'd been assigned. "As the old saying goes, shit happens."

"Yes, it does," Jim agreed as they walked into the room.

Chapter 23

"Good afternoon, Mr. Lashley," a young lady said as they walked into the conference room filled with rows of tables and chairs facing the front of the room. "I'm Melinda Carrillo, and Debbie assigned me to help you with the communications and tracking for this operation."

"Hi Melinda, please just call me Jim," he answered, looking around at the crowd that filled the room. "Looks like most of the people are already here. Sorry if I delayed the start of the briefing."

"That's not a problem, sir," she answered. "I have just a few things to go over with you before we start if you don't mind."

"Please, go ahead," Jim replied as they walked toward the podium set in front of the tables and several screens covering most of the wall behind it.

"First, everyone is here, and I've given them an additional piece of equipment that'll make this operation a lot smoother," Melinda said as she pulled a small packet from a box sitting on the table at the front of the room.

"This is a Bluetooth headset," she explained as she opened the cellophane-wrapped object. "It's something new and will fit into your ear, requiring no cords or hands to use the phone we provided."

"How does it work?" Jim asked as he examined the tiny object.

"Just hand me your phone, and I'll set it up for you," she said, holding out her hand. "I just need to do a quick update that enables your phone to connect directly with the earpiece and microphone. I've already done it with the rest of the phones we're using, and it only takes a few minutes."

Handing her his phone, Jim glanced around the room to see if he recognized anyone there. A couple of the faces looked familiar, but he couldn't place their names or why they did.

After a couple of minutes, Melinda handed him back his phone and explained, "Right here, under the settings icon, is the Bluetooth section."

Touching it, she continued, "Here you can see the letters MS Op. That's the earpiece, and you can tell it's connected to your phone because it says 'connected' beside it."

Taking the earpiece, she turned it on and handed it back, saying, "I've turned it on for you, and I'll give you an informational packet on how to use it when we're done. Just put it in your right ear for now, and I'll give you a demonstration."

As Jim followed her instructions, she put her earpiece in and pulled out her phone, placing a call to his phone. "All you have to do is touch the back of the earpiece to answer. Then, just talk normally."

"Hello," he said. "Can you hear me?"

"Yes," she answered. "Can you hear me?"

"Amazing," Jim replied, looking at her standing there without the phone in her hand. "Truly amazing."

"Now, just touch the earpiece for a couple of seconds to hang up," she directed as she touched hers.

"Now, everyone's hands will be free, yet they're able to hear and talk with their phones," she informed him.

"Will the protocol for the priority of the phones still remain the same?" Jim asked, seeing most of the people with their earpieces in.

"Yes," she answered. "All this does is allow the guys to communicate without having to hold the phone or have it connected with a wire. Much simpler and definitely more efficient. Any questions about it for now?"

"No, not yet," Jim answered. "Is there anything else before we start?"

"Not unless you have something for me," she told him. "I reserved a seat for you at the table just in front of the podium, and if you're ready, I'll start."

"Go ahead," Jim said, pulling out one of the chairs and looking at the papers on the table.

Melinda stepped up to the podium and announced that they were ready to start as soon as everyone took their seats.

"Good afternoon, again, everyone," she said, looking around and turning on the screens behind her. "Mr. Lashley has been briefed on the Bluetooth system, and I'll just give you a quick update on the latest information we've received from Quantico.

As you can see, there are 30 separate screens behind me," she continued. "Twenty-five of them are dedicated to the teams and their targets. The others are backup screens and for communication with Quantico.

As everyone knows by now, we've accelerated the operation from the aspect of removing the bodies," she said as the screens showed groups of dots representing each of them. "I can switch from your location to the exact location of your assigned target if necessary by zooming in or out, or I can keep track of both of you, within reason.

With Bluetooth, I, or Jim, can communicate with any of you, and you can communicate with your teammates," she told them as she manipulated one of the screens to zoom out and show both the team members and their designated targets.

"I can also add the pickup operations, when necessary," she explained as additional information came onto the screen. "However, your mission is to neutralize the target and be prepared for the next one as soon as possible. We'll handle the pickup and disposal from here.

Most of the initial targets are still in reasonable proximity to their original locations," she said as the screens changed to depict just the targets as black dots. "However, we now expect many of them, especially those at the upper echelon, to rabbit as soon as they figure out what's happening. That's why we've restructured the target assignments to prioritize them.

Because the pickup teams have a more or less secondary role, they'll be briefed as their assignments come in," she explained. "Since we can't assign specific targets until you complete your part, they'll be dispatched once we determine the location and what sort of recovery operation they'll be performing. Either alive or not, and where to deposit the subject.

This is explained more thoroughly in the papers in front of each of you, as well as the newest targets and assignments by teams," she finished. "I'll give you a couple of minutes to find the information relating to your team, and then I'll ask Mr. Lashley to finish the briefing and answer any questions.

By the way," she added before stepping down. "Those papers are not to leave this room. Everything will be destroyed after the meeting. We can't afford for any evidence concerning this operation to leave this room. I hope you fully understand how serious the folks at Quantico are about the security of this operation. We've already had a leak, as I'm sure you're aware, and it didn't end well for that individual."

Chapter 24

A few minutes later, Jim stepped up to the podium and announced, "I guess you know by now who I am. Please, just call me Jim. I'm sorry that I won't be able to meet each of you personally, but as you're aware, time is in rather short supply. Especially since Quantico thinks a lot of our targets will probably disappear after the first or second night of the purge.

I'm not here to tell you how to manage your team or which tactics you employ in accomplishing your mission," he continued. "I'm here only to make last-minute decisions as to the overall operation. You have your targets, and you'll be directed to them. You should know what you plan to do with each particular individual before you actually confront him.

If he is on the kill list, I expect you to expedite it and move on to the next target," Jim said, looking from face to face. "If you get a valid face shot, call in the kill. If it's not readily apparent that the target is terminated, fire a second shot and call in a maybe. We'll direct the retrieval folks to complete the task if necessary. But make sure the target is immobile. We don't want him crawling away.

Above all, if you need assistance for any reason, call me," Jim said. "The company has spent thousands of hours and millions of dollars on this operation over the last year, and just a few days ago, things changed. It's inevitable. I'm more concerned about one of you getting ambushed or an unknown player showing up. Do your best to beat a hasty retreat and call me.

If you have an equipment problem, get your asses back here and get it resolved," he directed. "I don't want you out there blind. We can relocate your target. Melinda and the other folks have given us one hell of an advantage over our targets by being able to know where they are at any moment. That's useless if you can't get the information. And, back to the ambush, we can't tell you what your threat is if we can't talk to you. A 30-minute delay in completing the assignment is irrelevant compared to losing an agent or an entire team.

Speaking of the team," Jim stressed, "You are a team. With multiple assets. Such as your phones. If one is operational, you can usually speak to each other and complete the mission. But, when in a position to get back here, do it. Or if verbal communication between you is impossible, get back here.

I'll be working closely with Melinda and any other people she'll have to assist her, as well as the folks back at Quantico," Jim continued. "If some information comes in that affects the entire operation, I'll make the decision to either give everyone the information or direct a withdrawal. If it's target specific, I'll make sure the team involved gets it.

Regarding weapons and ammunition," he told them. "Take this evening to make sure everything is in working order. There should be a 12 gauge assigned to each team. Make sure there's sufficient ammunition for it as well as your other weapons.

Try to get a good feel for each target on the list for your team tomorrow," Jim advised. "Study the pictures, the probable location, choice of weapons, habits. Anything you can learn about the target may be the key to success. The old adage is true: know your enemy better than he knows himself.

I won't be available here until shortly after noon tomorrow, but the company has ways of getting in touch with me if absolutely necessary," he told them. "And I honestly don't think tomorrow will be much of a problem. If we hit them quickly, the word of our operation won't have a chance to spread. The next day may be different. We may need to revise our strategy, but until then, stick to the basics. Learn your target, develop your strategy, and execute the mission. Now, if there are any questions, please ask them.'

A hand went up in the back, and a man asked, "What's going to happen if we enter a store armed and the cashier or someone triggers an alarm or calls the police?"

Jim looked at Melinda and motioned her to come up as he said, "I really don't know. But, if Melinda doesn't have the answer, I'll have it for you before we leave tonight."

Jim stepped to the side as Melinda lowered the microphone slightly, saying, "We are monitoring all police or other law enforcement officials, such as the border patrol or ICE. If we hear a dispatch to your location, we'll advise you on what's happening.

We'll probably get a good read on the time for the response," she continued. "Then you'll have to make the decision whether to continue the mission or leave."

Jim stepped back up and asked, "Does that answer your question?"

"As well as I guess it can be answered," came the man's answer. "Isn't there some way of letting them know it's us?"

"Absolutely not," Jim said vigorously, shaking his head. "We can't afford to have anyone outside this room knowing what we're doing. That could crater the entire operation across the country.

If you see any law enforcement arrive or hear sirens, get the hell out of there any way you can," Jim told them. "If you can't, lay your weapons down away from you, get down on your knees, and lace your fingers behind your head. Say nothing. Let them do their job, and we'll take care of you as soon as we can.

Guys, you've most likely heard about the leak we had in Los Angeles. Now, imagine that possibility a thousand times over," Jim said. "Besides that, you guys know the rules of the game. This isn't your first Black Water assignment. We operate outside of the law. That's why we're called. To resolve problems that the government can't because of either some restriction or just political blowback.

Mission accomplishment is the paramount issue," Jim reminded them. "But we, and I specifically, don't want any of you to get injured. Do as I ask. If confronted by any law enforcement officer, even if it's Barney Fife, lay down your weapon and present no threat to the officer.

We can get you out of the situation at a later date," he continued. "It's easier to get you out of jail or the hospital than out of the morgue. We'll still complete the mission. Maybe another team. Maybe you the next day or next week.

Now one other thing before I resume the question and answer part," Jim said with a slight smile. "This is a rare opportunity."

He paused a moment to let them wonder what the opportunity was before he continued, "Most, if not all, of the previous operations you and I have been assigned were more or less extremely clandestine. We always tried to execute the mission in ways that couldn't be detected. Or at least presented doubt as to who it could have been or if it had been natural causes.

This time, we don't give a shit," Jim emphasized. "This time, we want MS 13 to know that they are no longer welcome in the United States of America. If there's ever been a small desire to wreak havoc on some of the most low-life worthless assholes on the face of the earth, this is where you get to exercise it.

And I don't mean just eliminating someone," he continued. "I mean eliminating them with a vengeance. Hell, if I was in your position of getting the privilege of removing one of these monsters, I'd put the 12 gauge three inches from his nose and pull the trigger.

Now, having said that," Jim told them as he looked from face to face, "If you want to requisition another shotgun, I'll sign off on it tonight, and we'll have it for you by tomorrow when you come back here to begin the operation.

But the tactics are up to each individual team," Jim reminded them. "And the tactics I just espoused aren't necessarily those of the company, but they are mine. And, since the company put me here to run this operation, I'm making the decision that you can be as ruthless as you want when confronting the target.

The only caveat is, make damn sure it's your target," he said. "Make sure it's a wet target, not one of the possibly salvageable kids that are just trying to survive with no family other than MS 13. But, if there's any doubt and there are tattoos denoting gang affiliation, then you have carte blanche."

Seeing no other hands go up, Jim finished by saying, "All right, I have to get back to my hotel. I'll be leaving in the morning, and I'll be back around noon tomorrow. In the meantime, if you have questions, ask Melinda.

I fully expect to get back here tomorrow and learn that most of the targets for the day have been taken care of, and we're starting on the next list. I truly hope so," he said. "Thank you for your attention this afternoon, and please, do what you've proven you can do repeatedly since you've been with Black Water or one of its subsidiaries. Complete the assignment. And keep yourself and your teammates safe. Good evening."

Chapter 25

The next day, after Jim had flown to DFW and back to El Paso, he quickly hurried to his room at the layover hotel after telling everyone he would see them in the morning and then called Melinda to let her know that he was back and would be ready to go when Nolan got there with the car.

Hearing that Nolan was already on his way, he hung his uniform in the closet and changed into his standard layover clothes, jeans, T-shirt, and boots. Closing his suitcase, he took a final look around the room and left, taking his suitcase since he would be staying at Motel 6 with the rest of the teams for the night.

Nolan was waiting just outside of the hotel when he stepped off the elevator, so he waved his recognition and went directly to the exit.

As Nolan got out of the car to greet him, Jim said, "I hope you have some good news for me."

"Pretty good," Nolan said, opening the front passenger door for Jim. "I'll try to get you up to speed as we go."

"Great," Jim replied, tossing his suitcase in the back seat before getting into the front seat.

As Nolan got behind the wheel, he said, "Things have been going pretty much according to plan…..so far."

"That's what I thought would happen," Jim replied as they headed east on I-10. "But I sense a little hesitation. I'm guessing there have been a few hiccups."

"A couple," Nolan admitted as they passed every car on the highway. "But, like the first day of any operation, we're learning and sort of refining how we coordinate the teams."

"Any problems with locating the targets?" Jim asked, watching the arid desert scenery pass.

"Not at first," Nolan replied. "Melinda did a hell of a job getting the teams to the exact location. Those little ear things made it so easy. She, or one of the other ladies working with her, would basically walk the teams right up to where the targets were standing. They'd take their shots and be gone as she was directing the pickup teams to where the bodies were laying."

"Technology," Jim mused. "It's going to change our world. A lot of good, but I'm betting that there's a bucket of crap that goes with it. What you could call unintended consequences."

"That may happen," Nolan remarked as the conference center came into view. "But, right now, they are handier than a pocket on a shirt."

As they pulled into the parking lot, Jim said, "Once we get inside, I want you to get me a pistol, preferably a Colt model 1911 45 caliber. And a 12 gauge. Get one for yourself if you'd like."

"Are you expecting trouble?" Nolan asked, parking the car.

"Not necessarily," Jim answered, getting out. "But I want to be ready if we need to take over for one of the teams. Or anything else that's unexpected."

"Do you want me to bring them to you in the conference room?" Nolan asked, following Jim to the building.

"Bring me the pistol and a holster, and put the shotguns in the car," Jim directed. "And make sure we have a couple of boxes of shells for each gun."

"I'll take care of it," Nolan replied, nodding. "Anything else?"

"Not that I know of for now," Jim answered as they headed down the hall to the room they were using. "Did Melinda give you a Bluetooth ear thing?"

"No, sir," Nolan told him. "Do you think I need one?"

"I hope not, but I'd prefer that you do in case I need to contact you if you're not in the room," Jim said as they acknowledged the rather large man who was sitting just outside of the door to their room.

"Okay, I'll head out and get the artillery while Melinda brings you up to speed on the operation," Nolan said, holding the door open for Jim. "I'll see you in about 30 minutes."

"Good afternoon, Jim," Melinda said as he walked up to the table where she was watching the screens. "How's your day been so far?"

"Pretty routine," he answered, watching the moving dots on the screens. "Nolan says there've been a few problems. Anything that I need to know about?"

"Not really," she told him as she typed on her keyboard, changing one of the screens. "Guys not turning on their earpieces before they headed out. Or touching it and turning it off unintentionally. Little things like that."

"Learning curve," Jim acknowledged, watching the screen zoom in on what appeared to be two red dots moving toward a black dot inside a small store. "Speaking of the earpieces, I want Nolan to have one. Will that be a problem?"

"Not at all," she answered as the red dots merged with the black dot. "I'll get him one as soon as I make sure this is complete."

A few seconds later, the two red dots started moving away from the stationary black dot. Melinda expanded the screen and made a call to the recovery team assigned to the target.

Within minutes, two white dots were seen moving toward the building where the black dot remained motionless. "That's the recovery team," Melinda said as the red dots were rapidly leaving the area.

Jim looked around at several other people typing on keyboards and staring at the changing screens. "How many teams are each of these people monitoring?"

"Five," she answered. "It's not too difficult since there are very few times that multiple teams are actively engaged. Just think of it as one of those FAA controllers watching a lot of planes on their screens. How many planes do they control at once?"

"Sometimes quite a few," Jim acknowledged. "Sometimes none. Depends on the time of day, the airport, the weather, size of the area they're controlling, lots of factors."

"That's as good an analogy as I can think of," Melinda said, sitting back and watching the white dots arrive at the black dot's location. "And I'm here to take over any team if there's too little time span between different teams' activities. Such as now."

"What's next?" Jim asked as he remembered to take his earpiece out of his pocket."

"Just waiting to see the removal of the target, and then I'll get the closest security system guys into the operation," she answered. "And I was just about to mention your earpiece. That's sort of the type of learning curve thing I alluded to earlier regarding minor problems."

"I get your point," Jim said, accepting the chastisement gracefully. "Habit patterns. Good or bad, we all have them."

"And sometimes we need to modify them," Melinda told him, smiling. "I'd say something about old dogs learning new tricks, but I won't."

"I believe you just did," Jim said laughing as he watched the black and white dots moving together.

"Did I say that out loud?" Melinda looking up at him with a twinkle in her eye. "I certainly didn't mean to."

"Right," Jim said. "Why can't I hear any of the conversations out there?"

"You're not paired with the communication system," she answered as she typed a command on her keyboard. "I'll take care of that as soon as I get the security team rolling."

Shortly, Jim saw two green dots from several blocks away superimposed on a map of El Paso start moving in the direction of where the white dots were leaving. "Amazing," he thought, looking at the other screens that were constantly changing. "Controlling an operation this size with a few keystrokes. Amazing."

Chapter 26

"Here ya go, Jim," Nolan said, handing him a pistol as he approached him and Melinda. "Colt model 1911 45 caliber, as you requested."

"Thanks," Jim replied, taking the pistol out of the holster and ejecting the clip. "What's the load?"

"G2 RIP 162 grain," Nolan answered. "And I've also loaded the shotguns with the G2 RIP 303 grain slugs."

"That should take care of any problem children," Jim said as he slammed the full clip back into the pistol. "Melinda will get you a Bluetooth system as soon as she finishes getting the security team at one of the latest assignments that's completed."

"Just finished," Melinda said, turning in her chair. "I'll be right back."

"Learning anything?" Nolan asked Jim as they watched the screens with moving red, white, green, and black dots.

"Unfortunately, yes," Jim said, watching Melinda walk toward the back of the room. "I've learned that I'm way behind in the technology department. I thought I had this communication thing figured out, but I was clueless about Bluetooth, pairing, sharing, touch to activate or something. A whole new world of shit to learn."

"Here you are," Melinda said, returning and handing Nolan an earpiece. "I'll get you fixed up as soon as I get Jim's paired to his phone and tied into the communication net."

"What did I tell you?" Jim asked as she took his phone and earpiece. "I haven't a clue as to what she's talking about. And all of this computer stuff? Not a clue. Oh, I can muddle through some of it. But it's not coming easy."

"You can fly a plane with computers that help you navigate and let you sit back and enjoy your steak and mashed potatoes, but you don't understand computers?" Melinda asked sarcastically as she handed him his phone and earpiece. "Maybe you just need to take a basic computer class. Sort of like the classes you obviously took to learn about the airplane."

"Maybe so," Jim replied as she worked on Nolan's phone. "And I'm still thinking about that old dog thing you didn't mean to let slip."

"Here you are," she said, smiling at Jim as she handed Nolan his phone and earpiece. "Now, the basics. Touch the earpiece to turn it on. Hold your finger against it for a few seconds to turn it off. Tap it twice to connect to your partner's earpiece, which makes it an intercom between the two of you.

If you want to answer a phone call, tap it once," she continued as she watched them follow her instructions. "Hold your finger against it for a couple of seconds to hang up. I'll give you a quick startup sheet that'll explain these simple functions so you can read them later."

Jim tapped his twice and said, "Can you hear me?"

"Yes, and me?" Nolan answered, looking at him.

"Fine," he replied, nodding.

"How far apart will these things work?" Jim asked Melinda as she handed him and Nolan a single sheet of paper each.

"Probably a hundred feet or so if you can see each other," she answered. "If there are walls or something between you, maybe half of that."

"What about the phone? How close do I need to be to it?" he asked.

"I really don't know," she told him. "Why would you be separated from your phone using Bluetooth? Just keep your phone with you, and you'll be fine."

Just as he was taking his phone out of his pocket, he heard someone yelling in his earpiece, "We need an ambulance! We need it immediately!"

"Who's that?" he asked, looking toward the screens. "Who needs medical help?"

"It's team six," one of the people typing on her keyboard answered. "I've called 911 for them and also sent the recovery guys in their direction."

"This is Jim," he quickly said into the microphone that was now connected to the phone. "Who's this?"

"I'm Tim. My partner's been shot, and our target's making a run for it," came the reply. "Marty's bleeding like shit. You need to get someone here now!"

"Help's on its way," Jim told him as Melinda pointed to the screen where team six was shown as two red dots. "Try to put pressure on the wound until they get there.

Who was their target?" Jim asked, looking at the screen.

"Sanchez," the lady monitoring the team answered. "He's the team's top priority, but we had trouble locating him this morning. The team executed three other assignments before we found him."

"Where's Sanchez now?" Jim asked, looking for a black dot on the screen.

"He's moving east," the lady answered using a laser pointer. "That's him right there."

"Hell, he's heading this way," Jim exclaimed. "Go get the car, Nolan. We may be able to catch him and prevent him from disappearing again."

As Nolan ran from the room, Jim turned to Melinda and said, "Keep me informed about the medical assistance and take care of Tim and Marty. They're your top priority for now."

Turning to the lady working with team six, he said, "Stay on Sanchez. Don't lose sight of him. Once the medical guys are on the scene with Tim and Marty, your job is to direct Nolan and me to Mr. Sanchez."

"Yes, sir," she replied, expanding her screen to ensure the black dot stayed in view.

"Do you want me to take over for her on Sanchez and let her handle the medical issue?" Melinda asked.

"No," Jim said, shaking his head. "Marty is your priority. Losing Sanchez would be unfortunate, but taking care of our people is more important. Just let me know when the ambulance gets there and what his condition is."

"What's your name?" Jim asked the lady following Sanchez's movement.

"Vicki Jean," she answered. "Or just Vicki. Either way."

"All right, Vicki Jean. You just get me behind Mr. Sanchez as quickly as possible," Jim told her. "You've done great. Now, let Melinda handle team six. Just keep your eye on me and the target. Are you okay, or do you need to let someone else handle this?"

"No, sir," she answered emphatically. "I'm fine. And I won't let you down. I want the man who shot my team caught. I won't let him get away."

"Good," Jim told her, putting his hand on her shoulder. "Now, just make sure you're tied to my phone so I can hear you."

She glanced at a sheet of phone numbers and quickly entered Jim's, saying, "Can you hear me now?"

"Perfect," Jim answered, heading for the exit. "How far away is he now?"

"About five miles, still heading east," she replied. "I've also got Nolan on my screen along with you. He's just pulling up in front of the building."

Chapter 27

Running from the building to the car, Jim jumped into the front passenger seat and asked, "Vicki Jean, which way should we go?"

"Turn right on Rojas and then left on Lomaland Drive," she answered. "Then head west on I-10. He's on Piasano Drive coming east. He's almost to I-110. If he takes it north, he'll be at I-10 about four miles in front of you."

Nolan floored the accelerator and sped out of the parking lot as he listened to the directions. "You might want to buckle up, sir," he said as he skidded onto Rojas. "This is going to be one hell of a ride."

"Where are the shotguns?" Jim asked as he pulled the seatbelt across his chest and lap.

"On the floor of the rear seat," Nolan answered, slowing slightly as they approached Lomaland Drive.

Jim ripped the seatbelt back from his chest and leaned over to grab one of the shotguns from the floorboard behind his seat.

Putting the butt of the shotgun on the floor in front of him, he reattached his seatbelt, picked up the gun, and pulled the slide back to make sure a shell was in the chamber.

"Got a second, Jim?" he heard Melinda say in his earpiece.

"Go ahead," he answered, laying the shotgun across his lap with the muzzle pointed toward his door.

"The ambulance just arrived to get Marty," she answered. "Tim called right before they got there and advised me that he had shot someone who was with Sanchez. That was the man who shot Marty."

"Do we know who he was?" Jim asked as Nolan slid into a right turn to join the service road that would lead them to I-10.

"Not yet," Melinda answered. "But I've got the removal team on their way to get the body. Maybe he'll have some sort of identification on him."

"Okay," Jim told her as they sped past two cars on their left and cut in front of them to enter the ramp to I-10. "Get someone with a list of the targets and photos or any other information on the targets to meet the recovery team at the drop-off. We need to know who this guy is and why we weren't aware of him."

"I'm on it," she replied. "I've also got the security folks on their way."

"Anything else?" Jim asked as Nolan narrowly missed the front of an 18-wheeler as he accelerated west on I-10.

"Tim's asking what you want him to do now," she answered.

"Bring him in," Jim told her. "I'll figure out what to do when I get back."

"Sanchez just passed I-110," he heard Vicki Jean say as Nolan zipped from lane to lane around the traffic. "It looks like he's slowing, maybe to take 54."

"How far away?" Jim asked.

"Still maybe four miles in front of you," she answered. "Keep heading west on 10. Sanchez could go either north or south on 54. I'll know in a minute or so."

"What's to the north?" Jim asked.

"A lot of residential areas," she answered. "Biggs Army Airfield, and finally New Mexico."

"What about south?" Jim asked, seeing the speedometer passing 100 miles per hour.

"Pretty much the Rio Grande and Mexico," she said.

"Where's the nearest crossing?" Jim asked, seeing a sign saying they were approaching the exit for Yarbrough Drive.

"Well, if he goes south and then west, he's only about a mile from the nearest one," she answered. "But I think he would have taken I-110 south if he had planned on going there."

"Okay, besides that one," Jim asked as Nolan slammed on the brakes to avoid a slow-moving car that was trying to get into the left lane in front of them.

"Then he'll have to go left on 375, Cesar Chavez Border Highway," she told him. "Then he'll be six or seven miles from the crossing."

"What's our best route to head there?" Jim asked.

"Probably Hawkins Blvd," she told him. "It's a mile or so in front of you."

"Take the exit for Hawkins," Jim told Nolan. "I'm betting he wants to find a way across the border."

"Okay, he just turned right, south and east, on 54," Vicki told them. "Looks like he's going to head to the crossing we were discussing."

"Anything unique about that crossing?" Jim asked as Nolan cut off a car full of nuns to make the exit onto Hawkins.

"There's actually two bridges down there," she answered. "There's one for trucks and another one that cars normally use."

"What's our best route there?" Jim asked as they maneuvered between a couple of cars on the service road before they could turn left on Hawkins.

"Left on Hawkins, follow it for about a mile or so, then left on 76," she directed. "The crossing is about six or seven miles southeast once you get on 76."

"Tim's on his way in," Melinda said as Nolan narrowly missed a pickup as he ran the light at the intersection with Hawkins and slid left onto the road. "The body's on its way, and the security team will be there in a minute or so."

"Is that it?" Jim asked as Nolan accelerated south on Hawkins.

"No," Melinda answered. "The removal team said that the manager of the store had seen what happened and had called the police. They'd barely gotten out of the building when they heard the sirens headed their way."

"How far away is the security team?" Jim asked.

"Probably four or five minutes," she answered.

"Contact them and tell them not to enter if the police are there," Jim directed.

"What about the security cameras?" she asked.

"We'll have to worry about that later," Jim told her. "I don't want the police at the scene of a shooting and see us removing evidence. It's bad enough that the body and everyone else involved have fled the scene."

"Sanchez is on 375 heading south," Vicki Jean told them. "If both of you maintain the speed you're both going, you should get to the crossing about the same time."

"Looks like you made a good guess," Nolan said, slowing for several slow-moving cars in both lanes. "But I'm a little surprised that he'd run for the border like this."

"Why's that?" Jim asked.

"It's probably going to be packed with cars," Nolan answered. "If it was me, I'd find a place to ditch the car and try to get there on foot."

"That's a good point," Jim agreed. "Guess we'll just have to wait and see. In the meantime, the crossing is our best bet for now. If he's planning on crossing on foot, he'll get a lot closer before he abandons his car."

"Melinda," Jim called out. "Can you find out if we can get the crossing Vicki's talking about closing? Call Quantico and see if they can give us a hand."

"I'll get back to you as soon as I can," she answered. "By the way, Tim just walked in. Anything you want to ask him?"

"Ask him if he thinks the guy they shot was an MS 13 member," Jim told her. "Anything from the security team?"

"They called in that they went past the store, and there were at least five police cars there and a SWAT van," she answered.

"Let Quantico know that we may have a problem if they get the tapes from the camera there," Jim directed. "This is turning into a real shit storm."

Chapter 28

Minutes later, as they followed Vicki's directions toward the border crossing, they suspected Sanchez was heading for, Tim called, saying, "Jim, this is Tim. Do you have a second?"

"Make it quick, Tim," Jim answered as Nolan wove through the traffic, narrowly missing the front or rear of each car he was maneuvering around. "We're just a tad bit busy right now."

"I understand," Tim replied. "I just wanted to say first, we didn't know the other guy was there. We had Sanchez in sight and were just trying to get a couple of steps closer to make sure we didn't miss or hit some innocent bystander.

I was backing up Marty. He was just raising his gun when all of a sudden, a shot was fired from behind me," Tim explained.

"I saw Marty start to fall as I whirled around and saw this guy with a gun in his hand," he continued. "He was swinging it toward me, so I took the shot."

"No one's blaming you," Jim told him as Nolan cut across the right lane of traffic to run through the red light as he slid into a left turn onto 76.

"I asked if the guy was MS 13 to see if he was on our list, not to see if you had made a bad shot," Jim explained as they accelerated east. "You made a good shot. Regardless of who the asshole was that shot Marty. It was a valid shoot."

"The guy was MS 13," Tim assured Jim. "He was tatted up, and I'm pretty sure I'd seen his photo in our packet. I'm going through it now to see if I recognize him."

"Got it," Jim told him as Nolan clipped the rear of a car, making an abrupt lane change. "Just let Melinda know when you figure it out. Anything else?"

"Yes," Tim replied. "I want to join you in taking down Sanchez. He was my target, and he shot my partner. I want back in the hunt."

"Melinda, anything on closing down the border crossing here?" Jim asked as he saw a sign saying the border crossing was only a few miles ahead.

"Nothing yet," she answered. "I called Quantico, and they're working on it."

"Call them back," Jim ordered. "We've only got a few minutes until he gets there. If he crosses into Mexico, we're screwed.

Tim, leave the photos for now," Jim told him. "Have Vicki direct you to the border crossing we're heading for. I want you to take the truck crossing and watch for Sanchez if we can't get the damn thing closed."

"I'm on my way," Tim answered. "Do we know what kind of car he's driving?"

"No," Jim told him. "But we know it's not a truck. Just get your ass down there pronto and see if you can spot him."

"Quantico just called, and the crossing will be closed in about a minute," Melinda told them. "And they've got a team heading to get the camera video from the store or from the police if they have it."

"Jim, he's slowing," Vicki yelled. "It looks like he's getting ready to turn."

"Where is he?" Nolan asked as he slowed. "Behind me or in front?"

"Slightly behind," she answered. "He's taking the exit for Midway Drive. You need to get to Yarbrough Drive and make a right."

"Send Tim that direction too," Jim told her. "Melinda, make sure Quantico knows that both bridges at the crossing need to be shut down. I'll let you know if we can reopen them when Sanchez changes directions."

"I'm heading out," Tim called.

"Right turn on Rojas, left turn on Loma land Drive," Vicki directed him. "Stay on Loma land and cross under I-10. You'll come to 76 in a couple of miles after that, and you'll turn right."

"Jim, you guys need to make a right turn in about a half mile on Alameda Avenue," she said, watching the three cars. "When you make the turn, Midway will be about a mile west."

"Where can he go if he takes Midway?" Jim asked, seeing the sign for Alameda coming up.

"He'll hit Alameda in front of you if he doesn't go into the neighborhood in that area," she answered. "Okay, he's on Midway."

"Who's the closest to Midway, us or Tim?" Jim asked as Nolan used the turn lane to get onto Alameda.

"You are," she answered.

"How far is he behind us?" Jim asked.

"Maybe a minute," she answered.

"Okay, send Tim down to the other end of Midway, where Sanchez entered," Jim directed. "I want to shut the back door if he goes into that neighborhood or turns around.

Melinda, do we have any information regarding that area and other MS 13 members?" Jim asked, wondering why he would go into the area instead of heading for the border.

"I'll check," she answered. "By the way, Marty is in surgery. Looks like the bullet tore through his left lung but missed his heart by millimeters. I'll keep you posted."

"Tim, cross Alameda on Yarborough and then turn right on 375," Vicki told him. "Then Midway will be on your right in about a mile and a half."

"Sanchez just made a right turn on Knights Drive," Vicki told them. "He's in the neighborhood."

"Any other way out?" Jim asked.

"If he stays on Knights, he'll come to Yarborough," she answered.

"How far is Tim from Yarborough?" he asked.

"About a mile," she replied.

"Tim, exit onto Knights when you see it," Jim said. "Let's see if we can contain him in that neighborhood.

"I see the sign ahead," Tim answered. "What do you want me to do when I get there?"

"Just hold your position there until we figure out if Sanchez is going to stay in the neighborhood," Jim explained. "But, if he exits, he'll have to pass right by you."

As they made the left turn from Alameda onto Midway, Jim asked, "Where's Sanchez now?"

"Still on Knights," Vicki said.

"And Tim?" he asked.

"I'm pulling onto Knights right now," Tim answered. "Do you want me to block the road?"

"That's a good idea," Jim agreed. "We should have him trapped when we get to Knights, and we'll turn in behind him."

"A car just stopped in front of me," Tim said excitedly. "It's about a hundred feet from me. I think it's him. No, I'm damned sure it's him.

Shit, he's backing up," Tim added. "What do you want me to do?"

"How far are we from Sanchez?" Jim asked as Nolan sped down the narrow street.

"Less than a mile," Vicki answered. "Looks like he's going to turn left on Riverside."

"Follow him, Tim," Jim said. "Is there any way for us to get in front of him now?"

"Not really," she informed him. "He'll end up back on Alameda if he keeps going. And even if he turns left when he gets there, I don't think you can get there fast enough."

"It's up to you for now, Tim," Jim said. "Just stay on his ass and don't lose sight."

"No problem," Tim answered, sliding onto Riverside just a couple of hundred feet behind Sanchez. "This asshole just got a new hemorrhoid."

Chapter 29

"Okay, we're going to turn around and go back to Midway and up to Alameda," Jim said as Nolan whipped the car around. "Let me know what direction Sanchez goes when he gets to Alameda."

"By the way," Vicki said. "I just heard that there was a hit and run at 76 and Hawkins. There are at least six police cars, and the eastbound side is completely at a standstill."

"Maybe we can funnel him up there," Tim suggested as he narrowed the gap on Sanchez. "Let him get caught up in the traffic."

"I don't think so," Vicki told him. "You're south and east of that intersection, and there aren't many ways to cross the canal north of Alameda."

"He's going right on Alameda!" Tim yelled as he watched the car sliding around the turn.

"I see him," Vicki said. "Jim, when you guys get to Alameda, make a right turn, and they'll be about three miles in front of you."

"Does Alameda run into the border crossing?" Jim asked as Nolan skidded onto Midway, heading north.

"Yes, if he keeps heading east, he'll come to 375 in about five miles," she answered. "Then, if he turns right, the crossing is about a mile and a half in front of him."

"Since the crossing is closed, what's his next option if he does head that way?" Jim asked as they saw Alameda just ahead.

"If he does make the right turn, he'll probably see the traffic backed up before he gets to the crossing," Vicki answered. "Then I think he'll just continue following 375 to the north along the Rio Grande."

"He's slowing approaching Yarbrough," Tim reported. "I think he's going to turn."

"Jim, I just found out that Sanchez has some friends in the neighborhood you guys just left," Melinda told them. "He was probably trying to get there when he saw Tim."

"Are they MS 13?" Jim asked.

"Yes," Melinda answered. "And they're on the list."

"Which team had them targeted?" Jim asked as they turned right on Alameda.

"My team," a voice joined them. "I'm Renee, and my guys were scheduled to get them tomorrow."

"Where's your team now?" Jim asked as they accelerated down Alameda.

"They just finished up an assignment about eight miles north of you," she answered.

"Are the targets in this neighborhood at home?" Jim asked, watching their speed increase past 100.

"He turned right on Yarbrough," Tim announced. "What do you want me to do?"

"Just keep him in sight," Jim told him. "We think he's trying to get to some friends in the neighborhood."

"Yes," Renee told him. "There are three of them there."

"Debbie just called from Quantico and said Sanchez has been on his phone telling those guys that he's on his way and to have their guns ready," Melinda told them. "She's monitoring all of their phones now and thinks Sanchez is trying to lead Tim into a trap."

"Renee, can you get your team headed down here now?" Jim asked.

"They'll be on their way in about 30 seconds," she answered. "Where do you want them to go?"

"What's the closest intersection to the target house?" Jim asked.

"It's at the northwest corner of Fresno Drive and Starr Avenue," Vicki answered. "Fresno dead ends at Starr."

"So, if he goes there, there are only three streets at the intersection," Jim said. "What's he doing now?"

"He isn't speeding up," Tim said. "I'm less than a block behind him. Where's the turn to his friend's place?"

"Fresno's about a half mile in front of you," Vicki told him. "But he may turn left on Cinecue Way; that's only a quarter mile or so."

"Back off a little, Tim," Jim said. "Give him some room since we think we know where he's going."

"Okay, he just passed Cinecue," Vicki told them. "Fresno is just ahead on his left."

"What about the targets at the house?" Jim asked as they approached Yarbrough. "Are they still inside?"

"No, two just left," Renee announced. "Looks like they're going around the sides of the house. The other one is still inside."

"I see him turning," Tim said. "Do you want me to follow him down that street?"

"Any streets between Tim and Starr?" Jim asked as they turned right on Yarbrough.

"There's a cross street, Lowd Avenue," Renee said.

"Make the turn behind him," Jim told Tim. "Then, if he doesn't turn on Lowd, cross that intersection and wait."

"Where's your team now, Renee?" Jim asked.

"They're about three minutes out," she answered. "What do you want them to do?"

"Melinda, if Tim blocks Fresno at Lowd, Renee's team is coming from the north on the west side; where do I need to be to block any exit from the house?" Jim asked.

"I'd say take the next street on your left, Cinecue," Vicki answered. "Then go down to Starr and turn right. The house will be about a thousand feet in front of you."

"Where's Sanchez now?" Jim asked.

"He's sitting at the house," Vicki answered. "I've got the four targets on my screen, and they are all stationary."

"Renee, can your team block the other end of Starr?" Jim asked as they turned on Cinecue.

"Yes, they are almost to Yarbrough," she said. "They can turn left there and then right on Starr."

"Are there any cross streets between Yarbrough and the house on Starr?" Jim asked as Nolan slowed and turned on Cinecue.

"Chapel Place and Schwabe Street," she said. "Chapel is a block from the house on the north, and Schwabe is slightly closer on the south."

"Have them turn left on Chapel, turn around, and hold their position," Jim said as they stopped short of Starr. "Let me know when they're there."

"They're two minutes out," Renee said. "Anything else to tell them?"

"Yes, let's get everyone on the same frequency," Jim told her as he saw Fresno just ahead. "And everyone, hold your positions until I get back to you. I don't want to rush this and screw it up. And I damn sure don't want Sanchez on the streets again. And I really don't want any more of our people shot."

Chapter 30

"Okay, Tim, can you see Sanchez from your location?" Jim asked.

"No, he turned right on Starr, and the house faces it," Tim answered. "I'm guessing the driveway is on Starr. Or he parked on the street."

"He pulled into the driveway," Vicki told them.

"Can you see the house?" Jim asked as a plan began to take form.

"No, there are several houses between us," Tim answered.

"Renee, is there any movement of the targets?" Jim asked.

"None," she answered. "There's one on the west side of the house, one on the east, one inside, and Sanchez seems to be just sitting in his car."

"Okay, Tim, I want you to back up to Lowd and come east to Cinecue Way," Jim directed. "Then come down Cinecue to where I'm parked just short of Starr. "You'll be guarding this exit until everyone else gets here."

"What about you?" Vicki asked. "I can see you on Cinecue."

"Nolan and I are going to replace Tim on Fresno," he answered. "Is the other team on frequency yet?"

"We are," he heard someone answer. "I'm Ronnie, and my partner's name is Johnny. I understand you want us to come in on Starr and then turn north on Chapel."

"That's correct," Jim answered. "I don't want the targets on Starr to see you guys. Let me know when you're there."

"Back up and turn around," Jim told Nolan as he developed a mental picture of the area.

"We're turning on Starr," Ronnie announced. "We'll be in position in a few seconds."

"I've got you in sight," Tim said as he turned south on Cinecue. "What do you want me to do?"

"Just stop beside us," Jim told him. "Okay, guys, this is the plan. Pay attention because we don't have time to practice or fine-tune this. It's by the seat of my pants planning.

I don't want Sanchez to see anyone except Tim's car," he continued. "He's expecting it. He doesn't expect anyone else.

Vicki, I want you to take over monitoring us and the targets," he continued as Tim came to a stop next to their car. "Make sure you let any of us know if any of the targets move and how close we're getting to them."

"What do you want me to do?" Renee asked.

"Help Vicki, you two work together to make sure none of us get surprised," he told her. "Four eyes on the screens have to be better than just two. I just don't want too many voices on the radio. Just Vicki and us down here."

"Got it," Renee said.

"Now, Nolan and I are going back around to Fresno and stop in front of one of the houses before we reach Starr," Jim explained as he and Nolan headed north to come back around to Fresno. "When everyone is in position, we'll start moving behind the houses towards the one where Sanchez and his boys are waiting for Tim.

Vicki, this is where it's crucial that you keep us informed of each of our progress," Jim said. "I want Ronnie and Johnny to be behind the neighboring house to the west as Nolan and I arrive in front of the house to the east."

"Do you want me to come down Starr and join you?" Tim asked.

"When we're all in position, I want you to come down Starr and stop just before you get to Fresno," Jim told him. "The plan is for Sanchez to see you down there right before we come around the neighboring houses to take out the two guys on the sides and the guy in the house."

"We're ready," Ronnie called. "Do you want us to start walking toward the targets?"

"Yes," Jim answered. "Just don't come past the house next to Sanchez until Nolan and I are ready. You and Johnny figure out who's going to enter the house and let me know. Nolan will be going in the back door with him."

"I'm going in," Ronnie said. "Johnny will take out the outside guy."

"Okay, everybody, check your weapons," Jim said as they stopped in front of the last house before Starr. "Vicki, do you have all of us? And the targets?"

"I've got you," she answered. "And the targets."

"Okay, start talking," Jim said as he and Nolan got out of their car with their shotguns. "Tim, start easing down the road and stop out of pistol range."

"Ronnie and Johnny are two houses away," Vicki announced. "The targets haven't moved.

I see you and Nolan beside the house next to Sanchez," she continued. "And Tim is about 300 feet from the house."

Jim took a look around the house toward where he thought one of the targets would be and whispered, "Where's the east target?"

"He's beside the house about 40 feet from you, slightly left of your position," she answered.

"Ronnie and Johnny are behind the next house," Vicki said. "The west target is about 50 feet to their right beside the house."

"Sanchez and inside targets?" Jim asked as he motioned Nolan to come beside him.

"No changes," Vicki said. "The inside guy is close to the front door. No more than three feet from it."

"Johnny, are you ready?" Jim asked, trying to make sure everyone moved at the same time.

"Ready, sir," came the response.

"Okay, Vicki, give us a countdown from ten," Jim said. "If anything changes, stop the count. On one, Ronnie, take the outside target. Johnny hit the back door with Nolan. I'll take out my guy.

Tim, when you hear the shooting start, haul ass down and block Sanchez's car in the driveway," Jim directed. "Stay in the car unless he starts to get out. Then, blow his ass away."

"What if he stays in his car?" Tim asked.

"Ronnie and I will have him surrounded on each side," Jim said. "Nolan and Johnny will be in his face. Vicki, start your count."

Chapter 31

"Ten…nine…eight…seven…six…five…four…three …two…one," Vicki counted. As she said one, the four members sprinted toward their objectives.

Jim spotted his as soon as he stepped from behind the corner of the house with his shotgun pointed in the direction where he'd assumed his target would be. As the man saw him and stood trying to bring a pistol to bear on him, Jim looked down the barrel at his face and pulled the trigger.

Not even pausing as he continued toward the front of the house, he fired another shot at the falling man's chest. As he got to where the bloody mass lay, he stuck his head around the corner to look for Sanchez.

As he did, he heard the distinct sound of a shotgun blast coming from inside the house. Added to that were the sounds of several pistol shots from the opposite side of the house as well as inside.

Seeing Tim roaring down the street, Jim stepped around the house and leveled the shotgun at the startled man sitting in the car. No sooner had he taken his first steps toward Sanchez, Ronnie came around to the other side with a pistol pointed through the driver's side window.

As Tim slid to a stop inches from the rear of the car, Nolan stepped out of the front door with his shotgun leveled at the windshield as Johnny moved to join Ronnie.

"Hands on the wheel!" Jim ordered as he put the barrel of his shotgun through the open passenger window. "Now! You move even a hair except to do as I say, I'll turn your face into chorizo. Comprender?"

As Sanchez realized he had no other options, he glared at Jim as he slowly gripped the top of the steering wheel. Ronnie kept his pistol pointed at his head as he opened the door and stepped back.

Tim had walked up almost to the door and stuck his pistol against the back of Sanchez's head, saying, "Your friend shot my friend, mother fucker. Now, I'm going to blow your burrito-eating brains across the inside of your car."

"Hold it!" Jim said, glancing at Tim's face. "I want this piece of shit for questioning. "Vicki, call for the removal folks and tell them to get their asses here pronto. Someone in this neighborhood is going to start wondering what all of the gunfire was about."

"Got it," she answered.

"Border crossing?" Melinda asked.

"Tell them to open it," Jim answered as Sanchez turned his head toward Tim. "This asshole isn't going to make it across today. Or any other day."

No sooner had Jim said that, Sanchez dropped both hands from the steering wheel and grabbed a pistol with his right hand that had been between his legs.

As he twisted to the left, he tried to swing the barrel up toward Tim's face. Tim pulled the trigger almost simultaneously with Sanchez's movement. Then he pulled it again as the front of Sanchez's face exploded across the inside of the windshield.

For a second, nobody moved except Sanchez as his body slowly fell forward against the steering wheel.

"Asshole," Tim muttered as he kept his pistol trained on what was left of Sanchez's head.

"Well, shit," Jim said, pulling his shotgun from the window. "Guess he won't have much to say now, will he."

"Probably not," Ronnie said as he lowered his gun. "Wonder what the hell was he thinking."

"That I don't know," Tim replied. "But I do know what the last thing to go through his mind was."

"What's that?" Nolan asked, holding his shotgun in his right hand and pointing it at the ground.

"A couple of 45 caliber bullets," Tim answered with a slight smile on his lips.

"Okay, guys," Jim said, looking around at everyone. "We need to get the hell out of here before the El Paso police arrive, and I don't think it'll be too long now.

Ronnie, you and Johnny get back to what you were doing before this little cluster fuck began," he said, looking at them. "Get with Renee and head for your next target. Leave the same way you came in. I don't want all of us on the same road if the cops get here too soon.

Tim, head back to the center, and we'll find you another partner if one's available," he continued. "Same for you. Take Fresno. Nolan and I will take Cinecue.

Nolan, go get the car, please; we'll head back there, too," he added as the sound of distant sirens filled the air.

"Vicki, how far away is the recovery team?" he asked as Nolan left, and Tim got in his car.

"Probably ten minutes," she answered.

"Okay, have them come in on Yarbrough to Starr," he told her. "They can tell if there's a chance to clean up our mess unless the cops are already here before they turn on Starr.

Melinda, any word on Marty?" Jim asked.

"Still in surgery, and the police are waiting to question him," she answered.

"Call Quantico and see if they can scrounge up a local surgeon to take over," Jim told her as Nolan pulled up to the curb. "Then, we can manage the situation and get him out of there as soon as we can move him."

"Anything else?" she asked.

"Not for now," he answered as the sounds got closer, and he got in the car with Nolan. "But I don't think the removal team will get here soon enough. In the meantime, Noland and I will stop off for something to eat before we get back. I'm sort of in the mood for a medium rare hamburger with some greasy fries."

"What are you having to drink with that?" Nolan asked as they sped away. "A bloody Mary?"

"Yeah, with a sprinkle of a little Texas Gunpowder," he answered.

Chapter 32

Tim was in the conference room talking to Vicki Jean when Jim walked in with Nolan. Walking over, Jim offered his hand and said, "You did good, Tim. You probably saved Marty's life and maybe those of us with you when you dispatched Sanchez."

Shaking Jim's hand, Tim said, "Thanks. That asshole may not have shot Marty, but he's the reason for it. And you guys were ready to take the shot on Sanchez."

"That's true," Jim acknowledged. "But I would've been shooting toward Ronnie and Nolan, and Johnny would've been shooting through the windshield. You had the best shot without possibly hitting anyone else. You did good."

"I wish we could have taken him in as you wanted," Tim said, shaking his head. "Maybe we could have learned something."

"Probably not," Jim told him. "He was willing to get shot instead of being captured. I doubt if he would've given us jack shit."

As Melinda joined them, Jim asked, "How's it coming with Marty?"

"A Dr. Robbins joined the surgery team and will be accompanying Marty as they move him to a more advanced facility to repair the damaged lung," she answered. "He'll be flown to Quantico as soon as he's stable."

"What did the locals have to say about that?" Jim asked.

"Not much," she told him. "We sent one of our guys to volunteer what he saw as an innocent bystander who was merely shopping at the store."

"What about the security camera?" Jim asked.

"It wasn't working," she answered, smiling. "Once we talked to the store manager and discovered that, we developed a story about Marty just being in the store and someone, who looked a lot like Sanchez, and the dead guy just happened to get into a gunfight."

"Shades of a Marty Robbins song," Jim remarked, almost laughing. "All that's missing is a girl named Felina and being in Rosa's Cantina instead of a piss poor 7-11."

"What the hell are you talking about?" Tim asked with a quizzical look.

"Your partner, Marty, gets shot. A Dr. Robbins is called in. Marty Robbins?" Jim said. "We're out in the West Texas town of El Paso? Come on, guys. Don't tell me you've never heard the Marty Robbins song El Paso?"

Not seeing any recognition on their faces, Jim said, "What a total lack of education in the classics. I suppose all of you know Beethoven's Fifth. And every song Bach or Mozart ever composed."

"And don't forget Van Gogh," Noland added.

"Van Gogh was a painter, numb nuts," Jim said, shaking his head. "We're talking about music, not art. Neanderthals."

Finally, he looked at Melinda and said, "Okay, you're not versed in the Texas classics. I forgive you. All of you. Now, who can tell me why Marty and Tim weren't aware of the shooter in the store?"

"I can," Melinda answered. "It's simple. He didn't have his phone on him. It was back in his house." "How did you figure that out?" Jim asked, seeing an obvious flaw in their program to monitor all the targets.

"Once we identified the body, we looked for his phone and saw that it hadn't moved from his house," she admitted.

"Did you notice Sanchez at his house before they went to the store?" Jim asked.

"Yes," she admitted. "But it wasn't abnormal for these guys to stop at each other's house, or a car, or some other location, and leave alone."

"That's going to be a problem," Jim said. "Especially if these guys figure out that we're tracking them through their phones. They could intentionally leave one, or several, phones somewhere as they accompany someone to ambush our guys."

"Isn't that somewhat like the folks at Quantico predicted?" Melinda asked.

"They predicted they would abandon their phones as they ran," Jim corrected her. "This is them using our plan to track each of them individually and turning it against us."

"What can we do about that?" she asked.

"I don't know yet," he told her. "But I'll see if I can't get the answer from the spooks at Quantico.

For now, I want any target that comes in contact with another target to be flagged and monitored to see if this reoccurs," he told her. "Make sure every team knows if there's a potential for an unknown assistant with any target they're tracking. Don't just assume that their target is alone. Be extra vigilant about another MS 13 member being there."

Jim walked to the back of the room and pulled out his phone, dialing Debbie's number. As she answered, he said, "I, or more likely we, have a problem."

"And what would that be?" she asked.

"First, have you, or any of the other controllers, noticed an unknown accomplice at any of the target takedowns?" he asked.

"Hang on a second," Debbie told him. "I don't know of any, but I'll check."

A few seconds later, she returned and answered, "Not that we know of. Every target was either solo, or we knew who was with him. Why is this a problem?"

"I just had a man shot by an unknown, who was, coincidentally, a target himself," Jim explained. "His phone wasn't with him. Therefore, nobody knew he was at the location."

"That's probably just a coincidence, as you termed it," Debbie said. "What makes you think this is going to be a problem?"

"I don't know if it is or not," Jim argued. "But these guys aren't stupid. If they figure out we're tracking them via their phones, as Quantico thinks they will, they could very well start staging ambushes instead of just dropping their phones and running."

"You have a valid point," she agreed after a second. "What do you suggest?"

"First, tell every city operation that we had a team surprised by someone who was supposed to be at home," Jim answered. "Tell them to start monitoring the targets for interaction just prior to executing their missions. If the target just left another known MS 13 member, assume that they have paired up and be extra vigilant.

We've gotten somewhat complacent about our ability to know where everyone is because we trusted the technology," he continued. "That complacency is going to get people killed. Our people. And that's unacceptable."

"What else do you suggest?" Debbie asked as she tried to think of any other solution.

"You said that you had the capability to monitor these guys' phones, didn't you?" Jim asked.

"Yes, we do," she answered. "How will that help?"

"Have your people start listening to what's not being heard," Jim said. "What I mean is, if there's a normal conversation or something that ceases right after a meeting of two or more MS 13 members, flag it for potentially a phone left behind as a decoy."

"I can handle that," Debbie said. "I'll just work out a program that will highlight the activity of any phone that's within a specified distance of another one. That'll give my people something that'll pop up as abnormal."

"That sounds good," Jim agreed. "But in the meantime, make sure everyone at each city location is aware of the potential and have your people aware of the problem until you can get your program installed."

"I'll take care of it," Debbie said. "I should have thought about this before. So simple."

"Sometimes it's the simple that gets missed when you're dazzled by the shiny new," Jim told her. "But I have to admit that I didn't think of it earlier either."

Chapter 33

"Okay, where are we?" Jim asked Melinda when he returned to the front of the room and looked at the screens.

"We're basically ahead of schedule," she answered. "Sanchez was the only target initially, so that was scheduled. The guy with him was a plus, as were the three at the house."

"Do you have another guy to partner with, Tim?" Jim asked, glancing at him talking with Vicki.

"On his way," Melinda answered. "Should be here within the hour."

Glancing at his watch, he noted the time was almost five o'clock and asked, "Have you seen anything that resembles the incident with Tim and Marty again?"

"No," she answered. "And all of the people here have been told what to look for. I'll brief the folks that come in later so that we don't miss it."

"What time will you be leaving today?" Jim asked wondering how long each group was on duty.

"Midnight," she answered, glancing across the screens. "My assistant will be coming in then until I come back at eight in the morning."

"Does everyone here follow that schedule?" he asked, wondering how hard it would be to remain sharply focused for a sixteen-hour shift.

"No, these guys are here for eight-hour shifts," she explained. "Three groups, Midnight to eight, eight to four, four to midnight.

The reason I split it with my assistant the way I did was because most of the targets are pretty much stationary after midnight," Melinda continued. "And I normally get back here around six to get up to speed or see if there are any issues before I send her to the motel."

"Hey, Melinda, can you come here for a minute?" Jim heard Vicki call out.

"What's happening?" Melinda asked as she stepped over and looked at Vicki's screen.

"Look at the number of targets moving," she said. "Nearly all my target list is suddenly moving. That's unusual."

Melinda stepped to the lady next to Vicki and asked, "Are you seeing any unusual activity from your targets?"

"No, ma'am," came the answer.

"Okay, everybody, listen up," Melinda announced. "Pay attention to your targets that you aren't actively working. See if there's anything out of line with what you've been watching for the last few hours."

Not hearing of anything unusual, Melinda went back to look at the group of targets that were moving and said, "These targets were all for team six, Tim and Marty, weren't they?"

"Yes," Vicki answered. "Along with Sanchez, they were all scheduled for this evening and tomorrow morning."

"All right, we know that Sanchez made a couple of phone calls to the people at the house where we shot him,"

Melinda said. "I'll call Debbie and see if we have a transcript of those conversations."

"Have her also look at the phones of the other three guys," Jim suggested. "They may have called those guys that appear to be rabbiting on us."

"I'll know in a minute," Melinda said as she pulled out her phone.

"How many targets are moving?" Jim asked Vicki as he looked at the screen.

"Looks like thirteen," she answered. "Some of them may just be going for a beer or something. I can't tell if they are running or not yet."

"Are they going singularly or in a group?" Jim asked as Vicki pointed out the targets she was watching.

"There are a couple that are solo, and the others are now in four cars," she answered, watching the dots move.

"Keep watching," Jim said, motioning for Nolan to join him. "I'm hoping that they'll sooner or later head in the same direction, and we can surprise them."

"Go make sure we have enough ammo for a minor standoff," Jim told Nolan. "And check out a couple more shotguns loaded with double-aught buckshot. Toss in a box of 303-grain slugs like we're using. And get a couple extra boxes for us. We may be heading out again."

"They made several calls after Sanchez called them," Melinda reported. "Debbie is making a transcript of any calls they made from the time Marty was shot until now. She'll also make live recordings from now on."

"Where's Tim's new partner coming from?" Jim asked, asking Tim to join him.

"He should've been at the motel," Melinda answered.

"Call him and tell him we need him right now," Jim told her. "And be ready to go to work when he walks in."

"What do you need, Jim?" Tim asked, joining him and Melinda.

"It looks like Sanchez blew the whistle on us before you cleaned his slate," Jim said. "It looks like he told his guys, your targets, that something was up and to run for the hills."

"What are you planning?" he asked, thinking about how difficult it would be to chase a large number of targets at once.

"As soon as Vicki figures out where they're going, Nolan and I, along with you and your new partner, are going hunting," Jim said.

"When will I get my partner?" Tim asked, anxious to get back on the job.

"He should be here shortly," Jim answered. "I've also taken the liberty of getting both of you a 12 gauge with double-aught buck and some special slugs for this little adventure."

"Jim, Tim, this is Brett," Melinda told them. "He'll be your partner, Tim."

"Glad to meet you, Brett," Jim said, shaking his hand. "Are you ready to get to work?"

"Always ready," Brett said. "These low-life bastards raped my brother's little girl last year, and I've been waiting for a chance to fuck them up ever since."

"I'm Tim," he said, introducing himself to Brett. "I'll be your partner, and I understand your feelings. They just shot my partner this afternoon, and I'm not done with them yet."

"I just told Tim I've ordered a couple of 12 gauges for you guys," Jim said as he saw Nolan coming in carrying a duffle bag. "With a little luck, we'll be on our way in a few minutes."

As Nolan handed them the bag, Jim stepped over to Vicki and asked, "Anything definite yet?"

"Not sure, but they seem to be headed northeast," she told him. "At least two cars are. There are three targets in each car. One car is going southeast but doesn't seem to be in a rush, and there are three targets in it. Another one, a solo, is going west. Another solo is following a car with two targets headed north."

"Melinda," Jim said, looking at her. "I'm going after the guys that are running, and I want Vicki assigned to get us together with at least the two cars going northeast. And get all of us on the same frequency. "If we're not done by the end of her shift, keep her here anyway. I don't want to have someone new trying to figure out what's going on."

Looking at Vicki, he continued, "I hope you don't mind me extending your hours, but I want someone I trust on this. It's liable to be a running gun battle if these guys don't settle in the same location.

And one other thing, Melinda," he said, turning to her. "Get Debbie to assign someone to monitor these guys' phones and be on the same frequency as Vicki and us."

Seeing her nod, he said, "Okay, Vicki, you've got us. Now, get us to the closest targets."

"What team number do you want to be assigned?" she asked.

Jim looked at her for a second and said with a smile, "Team America, World Police."

"Team America?" Vicki asked quizzically.

"No, we'll be team 6 in honor of Marty," Jim said as he headed out to join Nolan. "And have Melinda ask Debbie if she can silence the targets' phones. Maybe give them a constant busy signal or something. We don't need them calling anyone else."

Chapter 34

"Status, Vicki Jean," Jim requested as Nolan pulled out of the parking lot with Tim and Brett right behind them.

"The two cars that were together still are but heading more easterly now," she answered.

"What's in that direction?" Jim asked as he pointed to the west and nodded at Nolan to head that way.

"Not much," Vicki answered. "If they keep going east, they'll run into 76 or I-10.

"If it's I-10, how far from us?" he asked, signaling for Nolan to pull over.

"Probably five miles or so," Vicki answered. "But he'll hit 76 before he gets to I-10."

"How long until he gets to 76?" Jim asked.

"Maybe two minutes," she answered.

"What about the other cars?" he asked, holding up his hand to make sure Nolan understood they were waiting for the targets to commit.

"The solo that left alone is pulling into a neighborhood just north of where you shot Sanchez," she told him. "The other solo is following the car with two targets, and they are going south on 375. The car with three targets is heading south on 76."

"Looks like everyone is headed somewhere south," Jim said, trying to picture the city in his head. "What's south besides Mexico?"

"There's a lot of Texas south," Vicki informed him. "Looks like our two cars decided to take 76 also. Now you have three cars heading south on 76."

"That'll lead them to the border crossing we closed and then reopened, won't it?" Jim asked.

"Possibly," Vicki answered. "It'll hit 375, and then it's a right turn and three miles to the border."

"And there are two cars heading south on 375 right now, aren't there?" he asked.

"That's correct," Vicki told him. "They're about five miles from the crossing.

Now the solo car that pulled into the neighborhood is heading east toward 76, and he's got another target with him," she continued.

"All right, we're heading southeast on I-10," Jim said, motioning for Nolan to cross under I-10. "Let us know if any of the cars head for the border.

Get on I-10 and head east to where it meets 375," Jim told Nolan as he checked both shotguns and reloaded them with the slugs. "That'll take us to the border if they try that.

Tim, you are paying attention back there?" Jim asked checking his pistol.

"Certainly, looks like you're betting on a border run again," he answered.

"That's one option," Jim agreed, storing the shotguns in the rear seat. "We'll know in a couple of minutes."

"The two cars on 76 are making a left turn," Vicki told them excitedly. "They're now headed toward I-10 and away from the border.

They'll probably hit I-10 about two miles in front of you if you get on as soon as you pass Trevino, which is just in front of you," she said.

Nolan ran through the lights at Trevino as horns blared and cars slammed on their brakes to avoid hitting him. With Tim less than a car length behind, they accelerated up the ramp to join I-10.

"Where are they now?" Jim asked as they flew past an eighteen-wheeler with a load of two-by-fours.

"They're just now getting on 10," Vicki said. "Just a little over two miles in front."

"Are the two cars sticking together?" Jim asked as Nolan pushed the speed up over a hundred.

"Yes, they're only a couple of car lengths apart," she answered. "You're closing on them. Now under two miles."

"Okay, folks, here's the plan," Jim said, reaching behind the seat to get one of the shotguns. "We'll run right up beside them, and I'll take the lead car. Tim, you guys take the trailing car.

As you get beside them, start pumping rounds into the car," he directed. "Take the rear seat first, and we don't want the car to go out of control before we're finished. Two shots into the widow and then do the same to the driver.

As soon as I've shot the driver of my target, we'll speed away and hope both cars run off the road without hitting anyone else."

"We've got a problem," Nolan said, looking in his rearview mirror.

"What now?" Jim asked, looking behind them.

"We just passed a Texas State Trooper heading west on I-10," Nolan answered. "He flipped his lights on just before he went by."

"Vicki, what's the closest turnaround for the Trooper?" Jim asked, seeing the red and blue lights heading in the opposite direction.

"That'll be 375," she answered. "About half a mile behind you now."

"Okay, that gives us about a mile and a half head start by the time he gets turned around," Jim said. "By then, we should be almost to our targets."

"What are you thinking?" Nolan asked. "He'll definitely be able to see us shoot."

"Possibly," Jim agreed. "But I'm hoping that our targets will see the Trooper's lights coming and think he's after us, which he is, and they'll not pay attention to us passing them.

While they're watching the Trooper, we'll blow their faces off," Jim continued. "Then the Trooper has to make a quick decision. Stay with the out-of-control cars swerving around on the road or chase a couple of speeders.

I'm betting on him staying with two cars with no visible drivers and obvious holes in the sides," Jim finished as Vicki told them they were less than half a mile behind the targets.

"That's got to be them there," Nolan said, looking at the two cars in the right lane close together with three heads showing in each.

"Looks like they've spotted the Trooper," he added, seeing them turn their heads. "I think you're right. They probably think the Trooper is after us."

"Good," Jim said, rolling down his window. "Now, just slide up beside them, and I'll bring hell down to visit.

Call when you're ready, Tim," Jim said. "I'll be in position in thirty seconds."

"I'll have Brett beside them at the same time," he answered, slowing slightly so as not to pass the car.

Seconds later, Jim swiveled in his seat and put the barrel of the 12 gauge out of the window. Firing two quick shots into the rear window, he fired two more into the front window and saw the driver's head disappear in a red mist as Nolan accelerated away.

"Haul ass," he said as he looked back to see the car swerve to the left and clip Tim's car as he passed it. "I think Mr. State Trooper will have his hands full with the mess we just left."

"How far until we can get off I-10?" Jim asked, looking back to make sure Tim was still with them.

"About a mile," she said. "Take the exit for FM 793 and turn right. That'll take you to Alameda. Then a right turn will bring you back up this way."

"Are you still watching the other targets?" Jim asked as Nolan slowed to take the upcoming exit.

"Yes," she answered. "All of them are heading south on 76. Three of them are close together, and the car that went into the neighborhood and picked up a target is about a mile in trail."

"Put us on an intercept," Jim said.

"You already are," she told him. "As soon as you take 793, you'll see Fabens Airport on your right. Shortly, a quarter mile or so down the road, you'll come to 76. The cars are all about three to four miles up the road from you at that point."

"Let us know when we're close," Jim said as he tried to figure out what was coming next.

Chapter 35

"Looks like we're coming into a neighborhood," Jim said as they passed the airport. "Where is 76?"

"It crosses 793 about a half mile in front of you," Vicki said. "If you make a right turn there, you'll meet them head-on in a couple of miles."

"Are there cross streets between where we get on 76 and the targets?" Jim asked as a plan began to form.

"Several," Vicki said. "Once you make the turn onto 76, there are two that actually cross 76 and a couple that dead end at 76."

"How far apart are the closest ones?" Jim asked.

"When you make the turn, there's a small unnamed road, could be an alley, about a hundred feet on the left," she explained. "Then, about three hundred feet further down, 1st street crosses 76 but dead ends on the west side. The next one, 3rd street, is about a thousand feet further and dead ends into 76."

"What's the fastest way to get us to the little road, or alley, on the left, and the one you said was about three hundred feet down," Jim asked. "I think you said it was 1st Street."

"It is," Vicki answered. "If you want to box them in at that point, one of you should take Davis Street to your right in about half a mile. Go north on Davis for about five hundred feet and turn left on 1st Street. That comes to 76 in about three hundred feet.

The other one should continue on 793 to 76, turn right, and look for the alley I mentioned on your left in about two hundred feet," she continued.

"Is there enough room between those two spots to trap their cars?" Jim asked as the plan came together.

"Should be," she told him. "Right now, the three cars are about two miles north on 76, and they're pretty close together, maybe thirty feet between each of them."

"And the fourth car?" Jim asked as they approached Davis Street.

"He's still a couple of miles behind them," she answered as Jim told Nolan to pull over.

"Here's the plan," Jim announced, looking at the intersection of Davis and 793. "Nolan and I will head north on Davis and be on 1st Street waiting for the three cars to pass in front of us.

Tim, you and Brett go on down to 76 and turn right looking for the alley," he continued. "You back into it and wait. When the first of the cars passes me, I want you to come out of the alley and block the road. I'll come in behind the last car, and we'll have them trapped.

When you get in position, make sure you have the shotguns loaded with the double-aught," he continued. "As soon as the first car comes to a stop, I want both of you coming out running toward it with your guns up.

Nolan and I will be doing the same from behind them," Jim said, looking at Nolan. "You might expect some return fire, but I don't think they'll have any heavy artillery. Probably a couple of 9 millimeters or 38 calibers. They'll probably be too surprised to do anything.

Go past them, taking a shot from each side into the front and rear windows," he continued. "Stagger your approach so that both of you aren't shooting into the same window toward each other at the same time."

Pausing so everyone could envision the approach, he then said, "One shot in each window. We'll probably meet at the middle car, but I want you to take it out. Nolan and I will hurry back to our car to try to get the solo car that's back a couple of miles."

"What do you want us to do then?" Tim asked.

"I want you to come to the back car that Nolan and I shot and make sure there's no one left alive," he answered. "Then, return toward your car, making sure everyone in the other two cars is dead. I'd recommend using your pistols because you won't have time to reload the shotguns. With a little luck, I'll be right behind the final car as he comes down 76. When you get to the lead car, duck in front of it and wait.

We'll stop right behind him so he can't turn around or back up. "We'll all use the shotguns for these last two guys," Jim finished. "Nolan and I will probably get to them first, but come as fast as you can to back us up."

"How do you plan to get behind the new car?" Tim asked.

"We're going to back up and return to Davis and go north to 3rd street. Vicki said it was about a thousand feet further north," Jim explained. "We'll be waiting there at the intersection with 76 for them to pass, and we'll pull in behind them and trap them behind their friends.

We don't have any more time," Jim said, motioning for Nolan to drive to Davis. "Let's get in position and hope this works. How far away are the three cars now, Vicki?"

"Little over a mile," she answered. "And the other one is still a couple of miles behind them."

"Let's go," Jim said. "Vicki, make sure you keep a running commentary about where we are and how far the targets are from us."

"Nolan's making a right turn on Davis, and Tim is approaching 76," she broadcast. "The targets are a little over a mile away.

Nolan's approaching 1st street, and Tim's turning right on 76," she continued.

"Tim's backing into the alley, and Nolan's turning left on 1st," she said. "Targets are less than a mile away, still close together. The trailing car is still two miles behind.

Tim is stationary at the alley, and Nolan is stopping short of 76," Vicki said as her voice became more excited. "Targets are now crossing 3rd street, about a thousand feet from Nolan."

"I've got them in sight," Jim said. "Tim, can you see them?"

"Yes," Tim answered. "And I can see the nose of your car. I'll pull out as soon as I see you move."

"Okay, guys," Jim said. "This is it. Get out fast and move before they can react.

Now!" Jim ordered as the last of the three cars passed, and Nolan peeled out behind them.

Chapter 36

Nolan accelerated until his car was almost on top of the last of the three cars. Slamming on the brakes at the last second, he had barely put the car in park when Jim jumped out of the open door and ran to the rear passenger window with his shotgun at shoulder height.

He fired a quick blast into the window and then stepped quickly to the front window. As he pulled the trigger, he heard a shot from across the car as Nolan fired into the rear of the car.

As he ran toward the next car, he saw Brett coming from the lead car on the run toward him. Nodding, Jim whirled around and yelled at Nolan, "Get back to the car! Let Tim and Nolan finish this."

As he reached the car, he called, "Vicki, you're on. Talk to us."

Nolan left a heavy streak of black rubber as he slammed the car into reverse and accelerated backward. Stomping on the brakes as he came to 1st Street, he spun the steering wheel to the left and hit the accelerator.

As they headed east on 1ˢᵗ Street, Vicki told them, "The last car is about a half mile away. Tim and Brett are just now getting in front of the first target's car."

Skidding around the left turn onto Davis, they headed north as Vicki yelled, "They're almost to 3ʳᵈ street!"

Nolan floored the gas pedal, and they flew down the last two hundred feet of Davis. Sliding into a left turn on 3ʳᵈ, Vicki said, "They're passing 3ʳᵈ and slowing."

"I just saw them go by in front of us," Jim replied as Nolan whipped around behind them.

"Hold on," Nolan said as he prepared to hit the back of the stopping car. "I'm going to push them into the back of the last car ahead."

As the two cars made contact, Jim was pitched forward slightly but could see the two heads in the car in front snapping backward. Nolan kept the pedal on the floor as smoke from his spinning rear tires filled the air, and Jim saw Tim and Brett coming from where they'd been waiting.

As the targets' car hit the rear of the last car in front of them, Brett reached the passenger side and fired his shotgun into the closed window. As glass flew across the inside of the car, the head of the target sitting in the passenger seat exploded, covering the driver in blood and brain. Firing a second shot, it hit the driver in the side, knocking him against the door.

As Jim was running toward them, Tim fired his shotgun into the driver's window and sent a spray of blood toward the passenger side from the driver's head.

Shotgun in hand, he reached the front seat passenger side in time to see splatters of blood and brain from the driver pass through the blown-out window and plaster Brett's shirt.

Looking across the top of the car, he saw Nolan stop beside the rear window and raise his shotgun. As the noise from the blast subsided, Jim looked inside at the rear seat and said, "Shit, where did he come from."

"I never saw that guy in the back," Tim said, staring at the small piece of the driver's head still attached to his body.

"Me neither," Brett said, wiping small pieces of flesh from his chest.

"Hey guys," Melinda broke in. "I just heard over the police band that there are at least half a dozen cops headed your way. You need to get out of there, muy pronto."

"Guess we'll have to figure out who he is later," Jim said, looking at the line of cars with all of the windows splattered in red and flakes of grey. "Vicki, what's the fastest way back to the center? And avoiding I-10."

"Alameda is the next road to the west," she answered. "Take it north to Lomaland and turn right. That'll put you back where you know the area. I'm sure you can find the center from there.

"You guys head out," Jim told Tim and Brett. "You probably better stop somewhere soon and get a clean shirt or two before you get back to the center."

As they headed toward their car, Jim asked, "Do you think our car will get us back without drawing too much attention?"

"We'll see," Nolan answered, smiling as he headed to the car. "It doesn't look that bad compared to most of the cars I've seen driving around here."

"Still, let's not do anything more to get ourselves noticed," Jim said as he got into the passenger seat.

"But let's not dilly dally either," he mentioned as they heard sirens approaching. "I don't want to have to explain why you couldn't stop before you rear-ended that car with three dead bodies inside."

"Not to mention the other cars," Nolan said as he backed toward 3rd Street. "You want to head over to Alameda and follow Tim?"

"No," Jim answered. "Let's just turn around and go north on 76. I'd rather not have both of our cars seen together from here on. If the Troopers have any brains at all, and sometimes they do, they'll put two and two together with the cars on I-10, and everybody will be looking for us."

"You mean to put two and four together," Nolan said as he headed north on 76. "Two on I-10 and four here."

"You're getting to be a rather wise-ass, you know," Jim said as they saw approaching red and blue lights. "I'm not sure that's good.

Melinda, are you listening?" Jim asked as they passed the two southbound speeding El Paso police cars.

"I'm here," she answered. "What do you need?"

"Find us a place to ditch these cars," he told her. "It doesn't have to be a final resting place, just somewhere they won't be noticed for a couple of hours until we can make better arrangements to make sure they disappear."

"There's a Walmart on Yarbrough just a couple of blocks from here," she answered. "I'll have a car sent there to pick you guys up."

"That sounds good," Jim replied. "Tim, did you copy that?"

"Yeah. Where's that from here?" he asked as two more cars with their red and blue lights flashing passed him, heading south.

"Just keep going north," Vicki told him. "You'll come to Yarbrough about two miles after you cross 375. Take a right and go beneath I-10. You'll see Walmart on your right, but you'll have to go a block or so past it to make the right turn into their parking lot."

"Got it," Tim said. "I'll let Brett run in and change shirts while we wait."

"Why don't we let the guy that's coming to get us run in and grab him a shirt?" Jim asked. "What size do you need?"

"A large T-shirt will be fine," Brett answered. "I'm going to toss this one as soon as I can. It's pretty damn nasty."

"Put it under the seat," Jim said. "And you both need to look at your shoes and make sure there's nothing on them that can show up on a DNA scan."

"I'd suggest that for all of you," Melinda said. "Maybe stop by your rooms and clean up. We'll take care of the laundry later this evening.

By the way, Jim," she added. There's a certain General that wants you to call him as soon as you get back. He said you'll know who he is. Should you be worried?"

"To quote the immortal Alfred E. Neuman, "What? Me worry?" Jim said as he wondered what Gene wanted to talk about.

Chapter 37

After dropping everyone off at the motel, Jim went with the driver to the conference center since his clean clothes were at the layover hotel. After checking himself over carefully, he'd decided that he'd wait until he got back there to clean up.

"Anything new?" Jim asked as he walked to the front of the room, where the constantly changing screens showed a flurry of activity as the controllers directed the teams toward their designated targets.

"Not really," Melinda answered. "So far, there hasn't been the mass exodus that Quantico expected. Other than the Sanchez cell."

"That's good," Jim replied, nodding. "Makes it a lot easier than trying to chase them down on the highways."

"Have you called the General yet?" she asked, changing the subject.

"Not yet," Jim admitted. "I wanted to be up to speed on the entire operation before I did. Where are we regarding eliminating the scheduled targets?"

"Actually, we're ahead," she answered, smiling. "Thanks to you guys. It was never expected to get so many in such a short time."

"I certainly didn't expect to get involved at that level," Jim told her. "But shit happens."

"Speaking of shit happening," Melinda said, leading Jim away from the front of the room. "The media is having a fit. The local police can't tell them anything. Neither can the local czar of the Texas Highway Patrol. They're raising holy hell."

"How much do they know?" Jim asked, wondering if this was why Gene wanted a call.

"Nada," she answered. "Other than there were two cars on I-10 filled with bloody bodies, and a couple of fender benders there that shut down the eastbound side for almost an hour.

Then there's that little hit-and-run incident at 76 and Hawkins," she added. "Another traffic jam while the police tried to sort out what had happened. Weren't you somewhere in the vicinity when that happened?"

"Possibly," Jim answered, shaking his head. "Could have been after we went through that area."

"I'm not even going to get into that little thing down in Fabens," she continued. "Then toss in Marty getting shot, dead bodies scattered across El Paso like rice on the floor of a Chinese restaurant, and you sort of get the idea of why the local news is having a field day."

"How's Marty?" Jim asked, thinking about how close they'd come to possibly having more men shot. Potentially killed.

"He's doing well," she answered. "We flew him to Biggs as soon as he was stable. Dr. Robbins told the staff at the hospital that initially treated him he needed the expertise at the trauma center at Biggs."

"What did the folks at Biggs say?" Jim asked. "Sort of unusual for them to take a civilian, isn't it?"

"Quantico sent us documentation showing that Marty was a member of a special forces reserve unit that had been conducting a training exercise north of Biggs and had accidentally been shot," she explained.

"Well," Jim said, "If that's all, I guess I better call the General and see what he wants."

"Oh, one other thing," Melinda said, smiling. "You might get asked why the Mayor of El Paso is spending more time on television interviews along with the Chief of Police, the County Sheriff, the head of the drug and gang task force, the Commander of the State Troopers, and a few other local officials than Louis Farrakhan, Jesse Jackson, and Al Sharpton did after Malcolm X was shot in San Francisco."

"Well, I guess I better make the call and face the music," Jim replied, shaking his head as he took out his phone and walked to the rear of the room.

As Gene answered, Jim said, "General, I heard you wanted to talk to me."

"I did," Gene replied. "First, Marty's doing fine. He should be out of the hospital within a week, and we'll send him home to recuperate.

I know that's been bothering you," Gene continued after a pause. "And that leads to how this happened. I've been with Debbie over the last couple of hours to see if there's a solution."

"You probably haven't heard yet," Jim interrupted, "But there was another MS 13 member who showed up unexpectedly today."

"When was this?" Gene asked.

"An hour or so ago," Jim answered. "He was in the last car we targeted after Sanchez was taken care of. One of the initial targets made a stop before heading south, presumably to join the rest of Sanchez's cell.

Once was bad enough, but two?" Jim continued. "From the same cell? We need to get this resolved before more of our people potentially walk into a trap."

"I understand, and Debbie thinks she has the solution," Gene told him. "She's programming all of the known phones to send a signal if it hasn't been moved in any thirty-minute period.

Also, it'll activate the microphone, and the folks at NSA will monitor it until it moves," Gene continued. "If there's no conversations or background noise that's normally there, they'll notify her at Quantico."

"What'll that give us other than knowing someone forgot their phone or is sleeping in another room?" Jim asked. "We still won't know if the guy is home or with one of the other targets."

"We're working on a program to notify the local police by calling in a wellness check where the phone is," Gene explained. "We'll give them the target's name and address. "Once they get to the house, we'll find out if they're at home."

"I guess that's better than nothing, but it still leaves a gap in our ability to know who's going to be with any specific target," Jim replied. "I don't know if this was a problem unique to the cell Sanchez ran or if it's occurring at the other locations."

"So far, just there," Gene told him. "But Debbie said she'll keep working on it to see if there's a better way. That's it for now, though."

"I guess we'll still have to be a little more vigilant," Jim admitted. "Anyway, I guess you want to know what's going on down here in El Paso with all of the public outcries."

"Not necessarily," Gene said. "We expected pretty much that. You can't slaughter that many people in a day without someone noticing, even if they're identified as MS-13. As the old saying goes, you have to break a few eggs to make an omelet.

My only concern with your specific situation is that you were sent there to oversee the operation, not to go chasing around town like Billy the Kid," Gene continued. "That's why we have the teams there, to take care of the targets."

"I understand, General," Jim replied. "But I'm not going to stand by while my people are being shot. If I have to get a little blood on my hands, that's part of being in charge. If you wanted an armchair leader, you wouldn't have sent me."

"No, I wouldn't have," Gene said. "And I wouldn't expect any less from you, Jim. I just want to emphasize that sometimes a little less aggressive approach might be considered. Think about it. Now, I've got other problems to deal with. Take care of yourself. I don't want to have to tell Jennifer why you won't be coming home from a routine three-day trip with American Airlines."

As the phone went dead, Jim wondered what would happen if MS 13 figured out how they were being targeted. If they knew it was their phones, they could have two or three members without their phones accompanying anyone going out. That would jeopardize the entire operation. And get his people killed.

Chapter 38

Jim was walking back toward the front of the room when Nolan came in. Catching up to Jim, he said, "That was some shit, wasn't it."

"Yeah," Jim agreed. "An action-packed hour, all right. By the way, good job on that guy in the back of the car."

"Hell, it wasn't a big deal," Nolan replied. "I don't think he even had a gun. And he looked sort of young. I almost didn't shoot."

"Doesn't matter," Jim told him. "At that point, age made no difference. You know they have twelve-year-olds chopping people's arms off."

"Still, it's a little different than with a hardcore guy," Nolan argued.

"Yes, but people have been using children to hide behind for years," Jim reminded him. "Either as active participants or unwitting accomplishes. Doesn't matter. You're just as dead regardless of the kid's age they're using if it works."

"Have you seen Tim or Brett?" Nolan asked as they got to the front of the room.

"Not yet," Jim answered. "Brett would have taken a little more time to be presentable."

"Melinda," Jim asked, stopping by where she was monitoring one of the teams. "Anything much going on?"

"Not really," she answered. "We're slowly marching down the target list. I'd guess that we'll finish today's within the next couple of hours."

"Then what? Let everybody off?" Jim asked, looking at all of the colored dots.

"No," she answered. "We'll start on tomorrow's list and see how far we can get before everyone goes beddie bye.

Well, look who's here," Melinda said as Tim and Brett walked up. "And not a trace of your misadventures."

"Amazing what a couple of hundred gallons of hot water will do," Brett told her, grinning. "Not to mention a clean set of clothes."

"Not to get back to business, but have you made arrangements for the cars we left at Walmart?" Jim asked. "I'm not too comfortable with them sitting there with all of the potential witnesses there on I-10. And possibly the dash camera of the State Trooper."

"There's a wrecker on his way," Melinda told him. "The guy runs a little wrecking yard down in Agua Dulce, about twenty miles south. By sundown, there won't be any identifiable car, just a bunch of used car parts."

"Good," Jim said. "Now, I know we can't do much about the guys we left for the cops, but I'd like to find out who the unknown in the last car was. Especially if he was a member."

"We've identified everyone else by their phones," she explained. "I'll have to wait until the Sheriff's office figures it out. I've got a friend over there that can get me the information."

"Unless he's one of the illegals that came across the border," Jim added. "There's a shit load of them in this country, and MS 13 takes advantage of them having no family over here."

"That could be," Melinda agreed. "But we'll still know something even if it's another 'John Doe'."

"What do you want us to do now?" Tim asked. "Brett and I can get back on the street and pick up where we left off with Sanchez."

"Go see Vicki and see where she wants you," Melinda told them. "There are still a couple of hours of daylight. And I'm sure you two gunslingers can make good use of it."

As they headed over to talk to Vicki, Jim said, "If there's nothing abnormal going on, I'm going to have Nolan get another car and take me back to my hotel. I'd like to get a little sleep before I have to fly tomorrow."

"There should be one ready," Melinda said, looking at Nolan. "Go ask the guy outside the door if it's been delivered and what kind of car it is."

"If you need anything after I get back to the hotel, give me a call," Jim said, taking a last look at the screens before leaving.

"And don't forget to remind everyone about what happened to Marty," he added. "My biggest concern right now is having an unknown shooter out there while our guys are concentrating on the targets."

"Do you think it would help to add another guy to the teams?" Melinda asked. "Sort of a third eye to watch their back. Maybe staying some distance from them."

"It's not a bad thought, but if they've figured out we're following their phones, they'll just send in someone to scout the place before anyone with a phone comes in," Jim replied.

"Or, as Debbie said before this all started, they'll all just toss their phones and get new ones."

"Melinda, can you come here?" a lady called out. "I think I have a system problem."

"If you'll excuse me, I better see what's up," Melinda said, turning to walk away. "I'll let you know if I need you again. Have a good night and a safe flight tomorrow."

"I'll give you a call in the morning," Jim said over his shoulder, heading for the door. "Have a good evening."

Jim was almost to the door when Melinda called out, "I think you better look at this before you leave, Jim."

Walking back to where Melinda stood bent over typing on the keypad, he asked, "Something wrong? I know don't shit about computers. You need to call Debbie at Quantico."

"I don't think this is a computer issue," she said, straightening up. "Look at the screen."

"Okay, what am I looking for?" Jim asked.

"See all of the red dots?" she said, using a laser pointer.

"Yes, our people," Jim answered, nodding. "Looks like twenty or so."

"Now, how many black dots, our targets, do you see?" she asked.

"Five, no, four," Jim said, looking all over the screen. "Wait, now there're only three. What happened to the other one?"

"The same thing that's been happening for the last few minutes," she explained as another black dot disappeared. "They're destroying their phones. They know."

"Melinda," two more people called out. "I'm having a problem here, too."

"Get our people back here right now!" Jim ordered. "Everybody! Call them in; however, you can do it the fastest. Just get them off the streets. Now!"

As a flurry of activity and phone calls were happening, Jim called Gene to tell him what was going on. As he answered, Jim said, "Sir, we have a problem."

"Let me guess, your targets are disappearing," Gene said. "It's happening in Los Angeles, too. And I expect it'll reach our other operations before the day is over."

"I've called all of my teams back," Jim told him. "I don't want them out there blind. We're going to stand down until this gets cleared up."

"I'm calling the other locations to do the same," Gene told him. "I'll get back to you when we figure something out. You're going back to Dallas tomorrow anyway. Just wait at home for me to call you."

Jim stared at his phone for a second as it went dead and then went to where Melinda was watching the teams moving. "How's it going?" he asked as he joined her.

"So far, so good," she replied. "We've made contact with every team and told them to cease all contact with their targets. Is there anything else we can do?"

"No, I can't think of anything," Jim answered. "But I'll stay here until they're all accounted for back here."

"I can call you when they're here," she offered as more of the teams appeared to be heading to the center.

"Thanks, but I'll stay," Jim said as Nolan walked in.

"What's happening?" he asked, looking at the serious faces around him.

"The assholes figured it out," Jim said. "It took them a little longer than Quantico planned, but they finally figured it out."

"So, what do we do?" he asked, mesmerized by the screens.

"We wait," Jim answered. "It's in Quantico's hands now."

Chapter 39

The following morning, Jim was sitting in the hotel lobby when Ray came off the elevator with his roll-aboard and kit bag atop. "Good morning, Jim," he said as he parked his suitcase beside Jim's. "Where'd you get the coffee?"

Lifting his cup and motioning to the right, he said, "There's a pot just to the right of the desk. Still tastes semi-fresh."

"Sounds good; I'll be right back," he said, walking off.

"So, what do you think about what went on around here yesterday afternoon?" Ray asked when he got back and took a seat beside Jim.

"What do you mean?" Jim asked as they saw Mary getting off the elevator.

"You didn't hear about the shootings?" Ray asked as Mary came up.

"I guess not," Jim answered as she parked her roll-aboard beside theirs.

"Good morning, Captain, Jim," she said. "Are you guys talking about that thing out on I-10?"

“I was,” Ray said. “Jim doesn’t seem to know about it.”

“How can you not have heard about it?” Mary asked, taking a seat beside them. “That’s about all the news stations were running all afternoon yesterday.”

“I didn’t watch it,” Jim replied. “I was with some friends until they dropped me off here last night. What happened?”

“There was a drive-by shooting out on I-10,” Ray told him. “It seems that someone drove by a couple of cars and blew the hell out of them.”

“Not only that,” Mary added. “There were several cars shot up in some little town just a few miles south of here.”

“Wow,” Jim said. “Any clue who it was?”

“Not so far, I guess,” Ray answered. “At least they haven’t released any information on it.”

“Probably gangs,” Jim replied. “I’ve heard that there are a lot of them around here. Or the cartel. I think that there’s a lot of drug trafficking coming out of Mexico around here.”

“I’m just amazed that you didn’t at least hear about it,” Mary observed. “They had the Mayor, a bunch of police guys, and I think even the Governor on different stations all afternoon.”

“They had a news helicopter flying over I-10,” Ray added. “I-10 was backed up for several miles for a couple of hours.”

“Must have pissed a lot of people off,” Jim replied. “I really hate getting tied up in traffic. Just sitting there wondering why.”

“They were showing a video of the cars that were shot,” Ray told them. “You couldn’t see anything except them on the road and several Highway Patrol cars with their lights on."

"There were a couple of others back behind them that looked like they had gotten into a wreck, too," Mary added.

"Sounds like a real mess," Jim said as the other Flight Attendants got off the elevator. "Glad I wasn't around there."

"Good morning, everybody," Susan said as they walked up. "Did you guys see the news?"

"It seems that everybody except Jim did," Mary answered.

"Hey, I was out with friends having fun instead of sitting around my room watching TV," Jim argued. "But I guess now I'll hear all about it from you guys."

"What else do we have to talk about? Anyway, if ya'll are ready, I guess we can head out to the airport," Ray said standing.

"Lorinda's not with us?" Jim asked, getting up.

"No, just the three of us," Mary said, standing and getting her bags. "I think she's on a later flight."

"I'm going to grab another cup of coffee," Ray told them as they headed for the exit. "Do you ladies want one?"

"No thanks," Paula answered as she and Susan joined Mary, heading for the waiting van. I'll make some fresh when we get to the airplane."

As Ray headed for the coffee pot, Jim followed the Flight Attendants out to the van and stood by his luggage at the rear of the van as the driver was loading everyone's.

"Good morning, sir," the driver said as he set another bag in the luggage area. "Did you enjoy your stay at our La Quinta?"

"Just fine," Jim answered as Ray came out.

Once everyone was in the van, the driver got in and asked, "Is this all of you?"

"Yes, sir," Ray answered. "By the way, are we taking I-10 to the airport?"

"Yes, sir," he said, looking at him in the mirror. "But don't worry, they got that mess cleaned up. Besides, it was on the other side of the highway. I'll have you at the airport in about ten minutes."

As they passed beneath I-10, Jim glanced to his right where the Walmart was and quietly asked, "Do you know what 'La Quinta' means in Spanish?"

"If you say, 'next to Denny's,' I swear I'll put you on our 'A' list," Mary told him.

"I guess you've heard that before," Jim said, shaking his head.

"Only about a gazillion times," she replied. "Everybody's heard that sad old line."

"Okay, folks, we're here," the driver said as they pulled into the terminal area and stopped in front of the terminal. "I'll have your bags off in a jiffy."

After tipping the driver, everyone headed inside, and Jim said, "I'll head on down and do the walk around."

"It's my leg to fly, so I'll do it while you pull the paperwork," Ray told him as they got to the gate.

"Sounds good," Jim replied. "I'll be down as soon as I can."

As Ray and the Flight Attendants headed down the jet bridge, Jim walked to where the gate agent was and asked, "Do you mind if I use your computer to pull our paperwork?"

"Not at all," she replied. "Pretty light load this morning. I'll have you off the gate a little early if everyone checks in on time."

"Great," Jim said as he started looking at the flight plan. "It's our go-home leg, so we'll appreciate it."

Just as he was getting the last of the paperwork off the printer, he saw four Hispanic men walk up to the gate. As one of them stepped up to talk to the gate agent, he noticed a familiar tattoo on the side of his neck.

Taking a quick look at the other three, he saw one of them had MS 13 on one of his hands. Thanking the agent, he pulled his bags onto the jet bridge and took his phone out of his pocket.

Making sure no one was coming up the jet bridge, he quickly called Gene. As the phone was answered, he said, "General, I'm just getting on the plane to go back to DFW, and I saw four men with MS 13 tattoos waiting to get on the flight."

"Are you sure?" Gene asked.

"I definitely saw it on two of them," Jim answered. "I didn't want to stare at them to see if the other two had them or not."

"I'll get a copy of the passenger manifest," Gene told him. "I'll get back to you after you land. Maybe it's just a coincidence, but I wouldn't bet on it. Thanks for the call."

Chapter 40

After pulling to the gate at DFW, Jim sat turned to the left and watched the passengers leave as Ray stood at the cockpit door, thanking them. As the last few were making their way up the aisle, he saw the four men coming.

As the final straggler walked off, Ray stepped back into the cockpit and said, "Well, I guess that's it. Do you have any big plans for your days off?"

"Not really," Jim replied as Ray finished getting his kit bag filled with the things he'd taken out for the flight. "How about you?"

"I'm hoping to finish painting one of the bedrooms I started on before we left," he answered as he stood and picked up his bag. "Guess I'll see you in a few days for the next exciting trip."

"I suppose so," Jim said, following him out of the airplane. "Unless I win the lottery."

Trying not to appear in a hurry, Jim followed Ray up the jet bridge into the terminal, hoping to see the four men before they left the area.

As he passed the gate agent, he saw two men standing against the opposite wall looking at him. When one of them nodded his head, Jim figured that Gene had sent them to watch the passengers deplane.

Telling Ray goodbye, he headed down the aisle toward the luggage pickup area. As he watched Ray leaving in the opposite direction, he turned into an adjacent gate area and pulled out his phone. Just as he started to dial, the two guys walked up and asked, "Jim Lashley?"

"Yes," he answered. "Can I help you?"

"General Barker sent us," one said. "I'm Gifford, and this is Frank Jackson. "The General said to let you know that the four guys you told him about have been identified and for you to give him a call when you can. Another guy with us is following them and will meet us outside."

"Good to meet you," Jim said, shaking their hands. "Did the General say what he wanted you to do?"

"Just follow the guys for now," Max answered. "He thinks they may be meeting someone here, but that's all he asked us to do."

"I was getting ready to call him before you walked up," Jim said. "Where are you guys staying?"

"We all live around here," Max answered, handing him a card. "I'm from Ft. Worth. Frank and the other guy are both from Plano. The General said to give you my number, and he'll let you know if he wants us to help you with anything."

Taking his card, Jim said, "Okay, I'll be sure to give you a call after I touch base with him to see if he wants me to get involved."

"I'll be waiting to hear from you if he does," Max told him. "But, right now, Frank and I need to go see if our other guy needs any help."

"Good luck," Jim said as he held up his phone. "I hope you don't have any trouble following them."

"General," Jim said, watching them go through the luggage pickup exit. "Max said you wanted me to give you a call."

"Good, you met him," Gene replied. "You were right. All four of them are on our target list. They were actually on yesterday's list."

"That doesn't surprise me," Jim told him. "Although I'm a little surprised they'd be flying. I'd have thought they'd be driving."

"Maybe your little I-10 incident and the one in Fabens gave them second thoughts about driving," Gene said. "Probably lucky for us. I'm not sure we'd have found them so fast if we had to wait for Debbie to use the voice recognition program to get the new phones we think they'll get."

"So, what's next?" Jim asked as he headed for the employee train to take him to the parking lot.

"Obviously, we need to figure out where they're going," Gene answered. "Then, we'll take whatever steps are necessary to remove them."

"Any guesses as to where they may go?" Jim asked as he waited with several other airline employees for the little two-car train.

"We think they may be trying to join up with some MS 13 members in the Dallas/Fort Worth area," Gene answered. "If they do, I may need for you to get involved."

"I don't have a problem with that," Jim told him. "But I'll probably need a little help. Especially if they team up with a member here."

"I'll get you whatever you think you'll need if it comes to that," Gene assured him. "I have a couple of assets in the area."

"I'd prefer to have Nolan," Jim suggested. "Along with Tim and Brett. I'd be much more comfortable with guys I know and trust."

"That can be arranged," Gene agreed. "Give me a day to determine where these guys are going and what you'll be up against."

"I've got another flight in three days," Jim reminded him. "That's not a lot of time if these guys spread out. And as you know, it needs to be during the time Jennifer's at work."

"I do know that" Gene said. "In the meantime, we'll just have to wait for Max to give me a call when they have more information.

I'll give you a callback, Jim," Gene suddenly said. "I've got a call from him now."

As the train pulled into the employee parking lot, Jim was approaching his pickup when the phone rang. "Hello," he answered, taking out his keys.

"The guys got picked up by someone they obviously know," Gene told him. "We're running the plates right now to determine the owner. Max and his guys are taking separate cars to follow, so we should have a location within the hour.

If they're staying in the local area, I'll have your team headed your way this afternoon," he continued. "I'll give you a call as soon as I get things arranged. If they aren't staying around the area, I'll let you know that I probably won't need you."

"Yes, sir," Jim said, getting in his pickup. "I'll be waiting to hear."

Chapter 41

Jim had barely walked in the front door at home when his phone rang again. "Hello," he said as he carried his suitcase back into the bedroom.

"I've got some new information for you," Gene told him. "One of the targets has a cousin living in Northwest Dallas. He's the guy that picked them up at DFW."

"I'm guessing that you want me to do something about them," Jim said, taking off his uniform jacket and hanging it in the closet. "Where does this cousin live?"

"Are you familiar with the Forest Lane area?" Gene asked.

"Somewhat," Jim answered, tossing his pants on the bed. "Not exactly an upscale area. I think it's just north of Love Field by the 635 Loop."

"That's where Max and his team followed them," Gene explained. "They're apparently going to stay with him in his apartment."

"Did they bring any luggage with them when they came?" Jim asked. "And, more importantly, have they gotten any new phones we can track?"

"That's negative on the phones for now," Gene answered. "At least the voice recognition program hasn't given us one. However, the cousin does have one. And it's negative on the luggage also."

"Has Debbie managed to hack his phone so we can track it?" Jim asked. "Or at least be able to monitor it?"

"She's working on it," Gene replied. "She thinks she can have it by later this afternoon. But, in the meantime, she can track it through the cell towers with reasonable proximity."

"What the hell is reasonable proximity?" Jim asked. "Ten feet? A hundred yards? A mile?"

"More like a quarter mile," Gene explained. "Maybe to a specific building. It depends on how many towers she has to work with. The more towers, the more accuracy."

"I guess that's the best I can expect for now," Jim admitted. "But I'd damn sure like to have a little narrower window of possible locations if we're going to take care of this little problem."

"I think you'll have that by the time Nolan and the other guys get there," Gene assured him. "Debbie's gotten pretty good at infecting their phones."

"Speaking of Nolan and the guys, when are they coming in?" Jim asked. "And where are they going to be staying?"

"Our plane is on the way to El Paso right now," Gene told him. "It should be on the ground in about four more hours. Then about two or so more back to Love Field.

Max will pick them up at Love, and they'll be staying at a Motel 6 up in the area where the cousin lives," he continued. "Max and his guys will be staying there also. They'll only be about a half mile from the apartment."

"I'm sure you're aware that monitoring the cousin's phone doesn't mean that the other guys are with him," Jim said. "Do we have eyes on them?"

"Yes," Gene assured him. "Max and the other two are taking turns watching the apartments. They'll know what the situation on the ground is until we can get more information from hacking his phone."

"I'm guessing that the targets will need to go shopping since you said they had no luggage," Jim mused. "Either that, or they don't plan on staying with the cousin for more than a day or so."

"Still an unknown," Gene admitted. "But the apartment is a one bed, one bath affair. So, I don't think they'll be there very long."

"What about weapons?" Jim asked. "Unless Nolan and the others are bringing them, I'm going to need some firepower."

"Your weapons or theirs?" Gene asked sarcastically.

"Mine, of course," Jim said equally sarcastically. "And for the guys coming from El Paso."

"On the plane when it gets to Love," Gene told him. "You'll have everything you had in El Paso. With a fresh supply of ammo, of course."

"Cars for the guys?" Jim asked, mentally checking off items he knew they'd need once the operation started.

"Two Suburbans," Gene answered. "Plus, I'm making arrangements for a recovery team and their equipment should the need arise. Anything else?"

"Not yet," Jim said. "And not to state the obvious, you know I can't be involved while Jennifer is home."

"Yes, that is obvious," Gene remarked. "Hang on a second, Max is calling in."

A minute or so later, he came back saying, "The cousin just left the apartment. We'll track him and see if anything changes."

"I'm going to hazard a guess," Jim said. "He's going out for food. He's going out to buy them some clothes. Or, and this is my favorite, he's going out to buy them a phone.

Of course, he could also be going to get them some artillery," he added. "If he's MS 13, that shouldn't be too difficult."

"As I said, we're tracking him and will have the answer soon," Gene told him. "Anything else on your mind?"

"Not regarding this specific circumstance," Jim answered. "But is someone monitoring all of the airlines for our missing targets? I still think there'll be some driving, but if these guys were worried about the risk or just needed to get somewhere that driving would take too long, we need to be looking at alternative means of travel."

"The shortest answer is yes," Gene told him. "The mushroom men in the lower depths of the building are pulling every passenger list from every airline servicing El Paso.

Additionally, we have people working as ticket agents at the local bus stations," he added.

"Trains?" Jim asked. "Foot traffic across the border?"

"You seem to think we're completely inept up here," Gene told him. "Yes, planes, trains, and automobiles."

"You forgot hitchhikers," Jim said with a smile on his face.

"Oh yeah, we have thousands of cars with moms and dads driving around all day picking up strange people," Gene remarked. "I think I've exhausted every bit of worthwhile information from you for the moment. Why don't you go clean house or something while I get back to work on resolving the problem that your little rampage on I-10 probably started."

"I'll be waiting for Debbie's results," Jim said, turning the conversation back to seriousness. "Although I know about the holes in the tracking problem, it's damn sure better than knowing nothing."

"I'll let you know the minute I do," Gene said before hanging up. "You take care down there, you hear? You're going to have a good team, but I'm not a fan of unplanned operations like this. Too many things may have been overlooked. Just be careful."

"I will, sir," Jim assured him quickly. "By the way, how's Marty?"

"Doing well," Gene said. "Now I've got work to do. Tell Jennifer I said hello, and we'll do steaks next time I'm in town."

Chapter 42

It was almost nine o'clock when Jim and Jennifer were sitting together on the couch watching a rerun of an old Bennie Hill show when the phone rang.

"I'll get it," Jim said, taking his arm from around Jennifer's shoulders.

"Hello," he said, turning down the volume on the television.

"Good evening," Gene said. "Got a second?"

"Sure, General," he answered, looking at Jennifer. "I'm just sitting here with my beautiful wife, watching Bennie Hill."

"Tell her I said hello," Gene told him. "Then I'll bring you up to speed on the day."

"Gene says hi," Jim said, looking at her.

"Tell him I said hello, too," she said. "And it's about time for him to get down here and bring those steaks he's always bragging about. What were they? Waggle?"

"Wagyu," Jim corrected her. "Did you hear that, General? Jennifer wants you to come to dinner and bring some Waggle steaks."

"Tell her I'll do just that," he answered. "Now, the cousin went to a couple of stores in the area. One was a clothing store, and the other was a 7-11 type store, Quick Trip or Quick Stop. Something like that."

"Waggle, Wagyu, something like that," Jim said, smiling at Jennifer.

"Anyway, the clothing place didn't have any interest to us; we already figured our targets would need to get some new clothes," Gene continued. "But, when he went to the Quick Trip, Max was following him at that time and decided to follow him inside. Especially since he hadn't parked at the gas pumps, he figured he was there for something else.

Max was lucky that there was an empty spot to park just outside the door, and there were several people in line to check out," Gene told him. "So there the guy stands with a twelve-pack of Heineken and a couple of prepaid phones."

"Heineken beer?" Jim said. "That stuff is too skunky for me. I don't see how people drink it."

"When the cousin leaves, Max walks up to the cashier and says, "Excuse me, but I'm with the Federal Communications Commission, and I want to see your records of all phone sales within the last twelve days," Gene says, chuckling. "Anyway, the guy, Max said he was from India or somewhere, says in an almost understandable accent, 'Sir, I don't know how to do that'.

You don't know?' Max asked with a typical low-level governmental bureaucrat attitude," Gene continued, almost laughing. "Then Max says, 'Well, I don't have time to call my boss or yours, so I'll just take any receipts of recent phone sales'.

The cashier is shaking like a dog shitting peach seeds and prints out a copy of the receipt for the phones saying 'Thank you, sir. Thank you so very much. You have made my life so much easier. Thank you very, very much," Gene told him. "I thought Max was going to pee his pants. He was laughing so hard telling me the story.

The receipt had the phone numbers and the serial numbers printed on it," he finished. "It took Debbie less than five minutes to hack into them. She hasn't gotten a tracer on them yet, but we're listening to every word they say."

"That sounds good," Jim said, glancing at Jennifer, making sure she was paying more attention to Bennie Hill than him.

"The first call was to a member named Juan de Carlos," Gene told him. "Mr. de Carlos just happens to have been the number three guy where we've removed the two guys above him. So, he's now El Jefe. He told them to stay where they were for a week and then to get back to El Paso.

All of your guys are at the Motel 6 we talked about and expect you to contact them there about mid-morning tomorrow," Gene said. "We have a little time to do more planning regarding how to take care of them, but I'm somewhat concerned that these guys will start tossing phones like used condoms. So, you guys figure out what you think would be a rational approach with minimum risk and get back to me."

"I'll make sure she knows," Jim said, nodding.

"Max's team will continue to monitor them so that there's no possibility of them recognizing you or your guys," Gene said. "Nolan asked if Max and his guys should get the Bluetooth stuff, and I said no because they don't need to hear you and your team talking. What are your thoughts?"

"I think you're right, sir," Jim said, rolling his eyes as Jennifer glanced at him.

"By noon tomorrow, Debbie will have all of their phones, including the cousin's, tagged so we can hear any conversations where the phone is located, and we'll be able to track them too," Gene continued. "Now, I'm going to use Vicki Jean back in El Paso to be your controller since she worked with all of you earlier. If that's acceptable to you, say it's good."

"Hell, that's good news, sir," Jim replied.

"Okay," Gene finally said, "you give me a call tomorrow morning after you meet with your team and you've established a good connection with Vicki and she can see everyone, including the targets and the cousin. Now, give the phone to Jennifer so I can tell her goodbye."

Jim handed her the phone, saying, "The General wants to tell you something."

"Gene, so nice to hear from you," she said, smiling. "Don't forget your promise to come down for a couple of days. I just learned how to make a Key Lime pie, and it's really delicious!"

"I plan on coming soon," he promised her. "But I have to ask you a favor."

"What's that?" she asked.

"Don't let Jim watch any more Bennie Hill," he answered. "I think his sense of humor is over the line anyway. If he starts tossing in double entendres, he'll be unbearable."

Jennifer started laughing and said, "He'll be unbearable? You should be around him twenty-four hours a day! Unbearable is a pretty mild description. If he wasn't so damn cute, I couldn't put up with the man. Maybe that's why you don't come down here as often. Let's blame it on him."

Hearing Gene saying goodbye, she said, "Come see us anyway. I'll tell Jim you said goodbye."

Chapter 43

The next morning, after Jennifer had left for work, Jim found the phone number for the only Motel 6 in the Forest Lane area and called.

"Good morning," he said as the desk clerk answered. "I'm trying to contact some friends that came in sometime yesterday. Probably checked in around six or seven o'clock. Three guys. One named Nolan."

After holding while the clerk checked his register, he finally was transferred to Nolan's room.

"Good morning, Nolan," Jim said. "How are the accommodations?"

"Sucks," he answered. "But I'm hoping for a very short stay."

"Is everybody up and moving?" Jim asked, watching one of the local news channels on the television.

"Pretty much," Nolan answered. "I just talked to Max, and one of his guys, Frank, I believe, is over at the apartments babysitting our friendly visitors from El Paso.

Tim, Brett, and I were just about to head out to find somewhere for breakfast," he continued. "Do you want to join us?"

"Sounds good," he answered. "Do you have any place in mind?"

"Not a clue," Nolan replied. "I'm really not sure if there's any place around here that I wouldn't have to fight off the roaches to get to my scrambled eggs."

"Yeah, I know a little about that part of town," Jim agreed. "But there's an IHOP that should be just down the road east of you. I can be there in about twenty minutes if you guys can be ready."

"That's plenty of time," Nolan told him. "Do you want me to invite Max and the other guy?"

"Sure," Jim said. "How much have you told him about why you're here?"

"Nothing," he answered. "I wasn't sure how he and his guys fit into the overall operation."

"Good," Jim said. "They're just here to monitor our targets until Debbie gets her tracking program installed on their phones. Gene thinks it'll be done around noon today. Then I'm pretty sure he'll send them home."

"Right," Nolan responded. "I'll round up the other guys and see you at IHOP in fifteen or twenty minutes."

Turning off the television, Jim grabbed the keys to his Corvette and was almost out of the house when his phone rang.

"Hello," he answered, closing the door behind him.

"Have you met with the team yet this morning?" Gene asked.

"I'm on my way right now," Jim answered. "I was going to give you a call after that, as you requested."

"I still want you to call," Gene said. "But I have a little good news for you that you can share with the others."

"I'm always happy to get good news," Jim said.

"Debbie got all of the phones fixed," Gene told him. "She had Vicki watching her screen as they popped up. She then called Max to verify everyone's location to make sure they matched. Within feet.

When you get together with your guys," he continued, "I want you to give Vicki a call, and we'll verify your locations as well. You can make sure the intercom function on your phone is working with hers as well. So, take your earpiece."

"I may have to wait until after breakfast," Jim told him as he returned to the house. "Nolan asked Max and one other guy to join us for breakfast. After that, we'll go back to their rooms and check in with Vicki."

"That'll work," Gene said. "I'm going to release Max and his team as soon as we get you hooked up with Vicki."

"Okay, if there's nothing else, I'll head to IHOP to meet them," Jim replied, going into his bedroom and getting the earpiece out of his suitcase.

"That's about it," Gene said. "Let me know how things look as soon as you come up with a plan."

"You bet," Jim assured him, heading back out. "Probably be a couple of hours."

"Oh, I forgot to ask," Jim added, getting into his car. "Actually, two things; how's Marty, and did the same thing happen at the other locations?"

"Marty'll be going home, probably tomorrow," Gene said. "And yes, the word spread like a case of the crabs on a US Navy submarine at Subic Bay."

Laughing, Jim said, "I know it's not funny, but that's a good way to describe the situation. What are your people's thoughts as to when we can finish the operation?"

"We're guessing in a week," Gene answered. "That's based on the conversation we heard when Mr. de Carlos told your targets to be back in El Paso in a week. Thank you, Juan, and another piece of information we got from a hooker in Los Angeles. One of her regulars told her he would be out of town for a week and how much he would miss her."

"Love, ain't it grand?" Jim said, starting the car. "I'll call as soon as I can."

Pulling into the IHOP a few minutes later, he walked in and spotted Nolan and Tim at a booth by the back wall. Walking over, he said, "Good morning, boys. I'd ask if you slept tight and the bed bugs didn't bite, but that's probably a little too close to the truth."

"I've been in worse," Tim said, setting his menu down. "Not much, but worse. There're some spots in DC that'll make this place look like the Ritz."

"I agree," Nolan said. "I've had a couple of assignments up there watching some junior Congressman's playful antics. I'll take this Roach Motel over that one any day."

As Jim was sliding into the booth, Brett walked up and said, "Max won't be coming. Seems that he's been relieved from watching over those pieces of shit."

"And now we get to," Tim said as the waitress headed their way.

Chapter 44

"Good morning, gentlemen," the waitress said as she stood ready to write down their orders. "Would you like some coffee first, or are you ready to order?"

Jim looked up, smiling, and said, "Black coffee and the double blueberry pancakes with lots of extra butter."

"I'll take the spicy poblano omelet, hash browns, and coffee," Tim said, laying his menu on top of Jim's.

"Two eggs over medium, ham, hash browns, and coffee," Nolan told her. "And a glass of water, please."

"Smokehouse combo, please," Brett said. "And coffee."

"I'll have your coffee and water right out," she said, writing the last order on her pad.

As she was walking away, Jim's phone rang. "Hello," he answered.

"Good morning, Jim," Vicki said. "How're the pancakes at IHOP?"

"Pretty damn good," he answered. "Looks like you guys have the location shit back online."

"It was never actually offline," she explained. "We just lost the targets because of the phones being destroyed. We saw no need to track you guys until we had targets again. Now we do. At least some, like there."

"How's the accuracy?" Jim asked, mouthing Vicki to the rest of the guys.

"Let's see, I've already told you I know you're at IHOP, obviously in Dallas," she answered. "You're sitting beside Nolan, Tim is across from you, and Brett is beside him. How'd I do."

"Pretty good," he said, smiling. "But can you tell what we're having for breakfast?"

"Yes, I can," she told him. "Debbie turned on the speakers of your phones just a few minutes ago. Right now, I'm going to make sure the intercom with the earpieces works. So, if all of you have yours, please put them in."

"Do you have your earpieces?" Jim asked, looking at each of them.

Seeing everyone nod, he answered, "Yes, hang on a second, and we'll check them out."

Laying his phone on the table, he took his out of his shirt pocket and stuck it in his right ear. As the others did the same, he said, "Testing. Jim."

"I have you," Vicki told him. "Now, the others, please."

"Tim," he said.

"Brett."

"Nolan."

"Okay, if you heard each other, we have a good connection," Vicki said. "Now, I'll let you guys get back to your blueberry pancakes and the cholesterol-loaded meals.

I'll call you back when I get something on the targets," she finished.

"That worked," Jim said, removing his earpiece. "Better than I expected."

"I'm not so sure I want to be carrying this damn phone anymore," Brett said, removing his earpiece. "They don't need to know when I have gas."

"Neither do we," Nolan said, laughing. "But I agree with the sentiment. This is too much invasion of my privacy."

"We'll return the phones and earpieces when this is over," Jim assured them. "In the meantime, just remember that they have the capability, even if they aren't using it."

"When does the government ever not use something they have the capability to use?" Tim asked looking at Jim. "Answer…never."

"Blackwater isn't the government," Brett argued.

"No, but they're bigger than half the governments in the world," Tim said. "And they damn sure have more assets at their disposal than probably our own government."

"Speaking of the technology," Jim said as their coffee arrived. "I think we need to get this over with as soon as we get a chance. I'm concerned that these guys' phones are going to be either tossed after one use or every day. Then we're back to eyeballing them."

"I agree," Nolan said. "What do you think of taking them at the apartment?"

"Too risky," Jim told him. "Too many unknowns in there. This area isn't the safest, and plenty of crime means plenty of guns. I'd prefer not to be walking into a crowded apartment building under those circumstances."

"I agree," Tim said. "I'd like to get them somewhere alone, maybe if they're driving somewhere. Or stopping for gas."

"Me, too," Brett added. "It would be nice if we could catch them on the road like before."

"That would be nice," Jim told them as he saw their waitress approaching with their meals. "But I think that was a once-in-a-lifetime opportunity. And I'd bet that everyone is paying a little more attention to the other cars around them now."

Once the waitress had left, Tim asked, "How do you want to pair up? Same as El Paso?"

"Yes, that worked well," Jim answered as he poured blueberry syrup across his pancakes. "I'm comfortable with that. Do either of you see any reason to change?"

"No," everyone replied in unison.

"Okay, let's finish our breakfast and head back to your rooms to wait for Vicki to let us know what's going on with our errant gang members."

"Is the cousin a member?" Nolan asked as he took a bite of a sausage.

"I don't know," Jim answered. "But, if he's in the way, it doesn't matter. I don't advocate taking him out if we can avoid it, but the fact is that he's helping out targets, and that gets him involved."

"I'd bet he's gang," Brett added. "If not now, he probably has ties to them. He's got to know that his cousin is. And the others at his place."

Jim's phone suddenly rang, and he answered, "Hello."

"They're on the move," Vicki told him. "You better choke down whatever you're chewing on and get ready to follow them."

"Sorry, guys," Jim said, reaching for his wallet. "They're on the move."

As everyone got out of the booth, Jim tossed four twenties on the table and headed for the door.

"All of them are already in the cars," Nolan said as they rushed out of the restaurant. "What do you want to do with your car?"

"We'll leave it here for now," Jim answered as they got to the Suburban. "We don't have time for anything else."

"If you haven't already done it, get your earpieces in," Jim yelled as everyone started to get in their cars. "And make sure the weapons are loaded."

"They're leaving the apartment," Vicki said as the cars started. "I'll have a direction for you in a few seconds. I'd recommend heading east on Forest since that's where they'll have to go."

"We're on our way," Jim said, reaching for one of the shotguns lying on the floorboard of the rear seat."

"Your pistol is under your seat," Nolan told him as he sped out of the IHOP parking lot onto Forest Lane with Tim close behind. "I made sure it was loaded when I put it in the car this morning."

"They're coming west on Forest," Vicki told them. "They're less than a mile in front of you. Now they're passing Webb Chapel, that's the next road in front of you."

"I see them," Nolan said. "Brown Chevy with five people about to pass us on the other side of the road." "That's them," Vicki said. "You need to turn around. Just don't go north on Webb Chapel."

Spotting a Starbucks just across Webb Chapel, Nolan whipped in and made a quick turn to head back out as Tim followed.

"They're turning into a gas station just ahead of you," Vicki told them. "It's on the left side. I'd recommend pulling over on the right and waiting to see what happens."

"Negative," Jim said. "We're following them in."

Chapter 45

As they neared the gas station, Jim saw the cousin shutting his door beside one of the gas pumps with the four targets still in the car.

"Pull up to the pump behind him," he told Nolan.

"Tim, take the pump on the other side," he said as they slowed to pull in.

"When you get parked, I want Brett to go inside with the cousin," he continued. "Tim, you just get out and stand beside your car. What load do you have in your shotgun?"

"I've got double-aught," he answered.

"What do we have, Nolan?"

"Slugs," he said as he eased in behind the targets' car. "Both of us do."

"Brett, leave your shotgun in the car, but take your pistol," Jim told him. "Head inside as soon as Tim stops the car. Be ready in case the cousin is armed."

"And if he is?" Brett asked.

"Blow his ass away if he pulls it," Jim answered.

"Nolan, take the driver's side," Jim directed. "I'll go first and take one shot into the rear seat, aiming for the guy sitting by the window on my side. Then, I'll take the one in the front passenger seat using two shots.

I want you to be a second behind me and take out the two others in the rear," Jim said. "Take a third shot at the guy on my side if you can't tell if he's dead.

We'll haul ass back to the car, so leave it running," Jim said as he made sure there was a cartridge in the chamber. "Tim, leave your car running. This is going to be fast.

Brett, as soon as you hear the shooting, decide if you need to shoot the cousin," Jim told him. "I'd prefer for you not to, especially inside the store. But do what you need to do.

Tim, your job is to be watching Nolan and my backs," Jim said as they came to a stop mere feet behind the car.

Okay, guys, let's make this quick," Jim said as Nolan put the car in park. "Then get back to the cars and then head west to the first road, Josey Lane; make a right turn, and you'll be on the access road for 635. Join it, and you're heading east. Just keep going, and Vicki will make sure we get back together."

"Ready, Tim?" Jim asked, glancing at his car. "Brett?"

Hearing both were, he opened his door and said, "Now!"

Leaving it open, he rushed to the passenger side and fired a shot at the target's head sitting the closest to the window. As the glass shattered and the target fell to his left, Jim stepped to the front seat and fired two quick shots into the target's face as he was turning to look at him.

Taking a quick look at the store where Brett was just about to enter, he heard Nolan shooting into the rear seat.

"Let's go! Let's go!" he yelled as he sprinted back to their car. "Tim, grab Brett as he comes out of the store."

Just as he was about to get in the car, he saw the cousin running toward them, a pistol in his hand, with Brett close behind.

Watching Tim raise his shotgun, he yelled, "No, Tim. Don't shoot. Let Brett handle it. That buckshot will scatter too much from that distance."

No sooner had he said that than the cousin whirled around and took a shot at Brett. As Brett tumbled to the ground and rolled to his side, he heard Nolan's gun roar as he sent a slug into the cousin's back.

Rising to his feet, Brett took one step toward the cousin whose chest had become a gaping hole where the slug had exited and fired two quick shots into his face.

Tim was already back in the car when Brett came running. Waiting the few seconds for him to get in, he hit the accelerator and spun around the front of the target's car heading back to Forest.

As Nolan tossed his shotgun into the rear and climbed behind the wheel, Jim took one look to make sure Brett was alright and then jumped into the passenger seat.

Nolan slammed the car into reverse and whipped the wheel to the left leaving a trail of rubber on the cement as he slid around the pump he'd been parked beside.

Dodging a car on Forest, Nolan accelerated the few yards to Josey and skidded into a right turn to join it with Tim only seconds behind.

"Vicki," Jim said as they entered the 635 loop across the north of Dallas. "Call Quantico and tell them what's happening if they don't already know. I need somewhere close for Nolan to drop me off so I can go get my car at the IHOP.

Of course, that means you need to have a car come get me," he continued as the two cars slowed to merge with the slower-moving traffic. "And find somewhere for Nolan and Tim to dump these cars. If that gas station has security cameras, we need to get that video before the cops do."

"You'll be at US 75 in about five miles," Vicki told them. "Take it south, and I'll have an answer for you by the time you do.

There's a Presbyterian hospital about three miles down on Walnut Hill," she continued. "Head there, and I'll get you a ride back to your car. Nolan and Tim can leave the cars in the parking lot, and I'll make arrangements for someone to come get them."

"You need to make sure we get these cars to disappear as soon as we can," Jim said.

"I'll take care of it," Vicki told them. "You're about two miles from 75. I'm calling one of the taxi companies to pick you up at the hospital entrance. I'll ask Melinda to start working on the other stuff while I do. Anything else?"

"When you get a hold of someone at Quantico, have them get word to General Barker that I'll call him when I get a chance," Jim said as they saw the exit for US 75.

Moments later, both cars pulled into the parking lot for the hospital. Stepping out of the car, Jim told Nolan, "See if you can snag a couple of tags from the cars close by and swap them with ours. It might buy us a couple of hours to get rid of these if one of the police decides to send some cars to cruise the hospitals in case someone was shot back at the gas station."

"All right, guys," Jim said as they gathered beside his car. "I've got to go get my car, and I'll meet you at your motel when Vicki gives me the word that you're on your way. I'd recommend splitting up these cars once you swap the plates. If the cops are looking for them, they're looking for two."

"Brett, are you all right?" Jim asked, looking at the tear on the knee of his jeans. "That was quite a tumble."

"A little road rash," he said, looking at the tear. "But it's a long way from my heart."

"Okay," Jim said smiling at all of them as he turned to head to the entrance to the hospital. "That was rather hastily concocted, but it worked. Hopefully, I'll see you in a few minutes. Maybe we can go somewhere quiet and actually get to eat our breakfast."

Chapter 46

Twenty minutes later, after the cab had dropped Jim off at the IHOP, he took out his phone and called Gene. Getting into his car, he said, "Good afternoon, sir. Hope I didn't keep you waiting."

"I do believe that I asked you to give me a call after you'd met with the rest of the team and come up with a plan," Gene chastised him.

"Well, to be honest, we never really came up with a plan," Jim offered in his defense. "We'd been discussing the problem while we were having breakfast, or I should say trying to have breakfast, and Vicki called saying the targets were on the move.

And I......" Jim was saying when Gene cut him off.

"So, you did another by the seat of your pants impromptu shootout in broad daylight," Gene said. "And in front of who knows how many people. And within the view of an operational security camera."

"I didn't know the camera was operational," Jim offered.

"Well, it was," Gene told him.

Waiting for a couple of seconds before saying anything, Jim finally said, "But the bottom line is that we eliminated the four targets. And another shooter, as well. That was our mission, and we accomplished it.

And I'll take full responsibility for everything," Jim added. "The others were just following my orders."

"You may not know this," Gene said quietly, "But we're recording each of all of the phone and intercom conversations."

"Ohhhh," Jim said. "I did not know that. But I'll still stick by everything that I did. A mere conversation can't possibly cover everything that goes into making a split-second decision."

"Are you through?" Gene asked. "Because if you are, I'd like to thank you for getting the job done. And I have a little piece of information that might interest you."

"Then I guess I'm through," Jim answered. "What's the interesting piece of information?"

"Debbie's voice recognition program is working better than we'd hoped," he said. "We managed to find almost half of the escaped targets scattered across the country. We believe that we locked in within fifteen minutes of their first phone call."

"That's great," Jim said. "Should make it pretty easy to locate them."

"Yes, it will," Gene agreed. "At least to the area where they were when they purchased the phones. But I sort of predicted what would happen next."

"You're referring to the used condom remark," Jim said, nodding.

"Yes, and these guys are doing exactly that," Gene continued. "They're making one call and ditching the phone.

Granted, we can get the conversation, but it's back to square one after that."

"It would be my bet that one of the reasons the targets were at that store was to get new phones," Gene said. "I was wondering why they only bought two phones the first time. Now I know."

"So, with that in mind, your impromptu shoot-out was probably the best thing that you could have done," Gene admitted. "We'd probably have lost them if you hadn't.

This is causing a lot of frustration at all of the locations," he continued. "Just as they find a target, their phone goes dormant, and we'll find them on another one a couple of hours later."

"What's the overall plan for the operation if we can't follow our targets?" Jim asked. "Go house to house?"

"No, that's an invitation to get our people killed," Gene answered. "For right now, we monitor all of their calls every time we determine who's using a new phone. One good thing is that they normally keep the phone for a day or so. It's only after they use it to call that they toss them."

"Pretty smart on their part," Jim said. "Of course, we knew these weren't stupid people. Ruthless? Very. Stupid? No."

"Right now, we're playing a waiting game," Gene said. "We're collecting a lot of information, but it takes time and coordination with different law enforcement agencies to make any usable plan, if we can at all.

Everything points to a week delay, as I've mentioned," Gene told him. "Then we'll modify our plan. The mushrooms are gaming multiple scenarios right now."

"So, we just sit back and let them roam around the country?" Jim asked, feeling the frustration of not fulfilling the mission.

"Look at it this way," Gene explained. "A week of them hiding out is a week of them not wreaking havoc on the communities where they were active before they scattered."

"What about the communities where they went?" Jim asked. "Are they seeing an uptick in violence or crime?"

"So far, no," Gene answered. "I have no doubt that some of it is happening, but it's not on the scale as before. So, we're making progress. And we'd planned on a month-long program anyway. So, we're still sort of on track to fulfill the contract."

"Is there a way we can give every team member a binder with all of the targets from all of the locations?" Jim asked. "Then when a Los Angeles target pops up here in Dallas, I'll know to be watching for him?"

"We looked at that," Gene answered. "What are the odds of you running into a target? Almost nonexistent. It was just a fluke of luck that those four got on the very airplane where we had someone who knew about the operation.

And I doubt if these guys are hanging out where you or other team members frequent," he continued. "Then we get into what would you do if you did come across one of them? Pull out your shotgun?

As we found out in El Paso, sometimes there's an unknown player," Gene added. "In this scenario, there's a very high likelihood of there being several unknowns. No. We wait."

"Are you leaving Nolan and the guys down here?" Jim asked.

"No, I'm sending everybody home for now," he answered. "Except for Debbie and her people up here. Most of the actual work is being done by the computer programs she developed, so there's very little for the guys who directed the local operations to do."

"Does this mean I've got the rest of the month off?" Jim asked.

"I believe I mentioned something about a week," Gene reminded him. "So, you can take off until I call you."

"With pay?" Jim asked.

"Goodbye, Jim," Gene said, shaking his head. "Go clean the toilets or something to stay busy until I call."

Chapter 47

Four days later, as Jim was driving home from the airport, his phone rang. "Hello," he said as he pulled onto 635 to loop around to Mesquite.

"How was your trip?" Gene asked.

"Pretty boring after the last El Paso trips," Jim answered, maneuvering around the traffic that was jockeying for position to take one of the upcoming exits.

"Maybe I can help you out then," Gene said. "How long until you reach your house, thirty minutes?"

"More like forty-five," Jim answered. "Could be as much as an hour, depending on the traffic. What's this got to do with helping me out?"

"You just said you were bored," Gene explained. "I have a target for you."

"Okay, but I thought we agreed that it was pointless to go chasing them since they always tossed their phones after making a call," Jim argued.

"We have an exception," Gene told him. "Debbie found this guy three days ago when he checked in with his cell leader. He was told to stay in place for now and to call back in a week on a new phone.

It seems that he decided to do exactly that and no more," Gene continued. "But he didn't toss the phone. He called someone back in Los Angeles yesterday, and Debbie decided to try to put the tracking program into his phone. It's still active."

"And where is this guy?" Jim asked.

"He's been staying at some house just north of Forest Lane," Gene told him. "How familiar are you with the area?"

"Not intimately, but I know generally where you're talking about," Jim told him.

"Okay, the guy is stationary for now, but he goes out a couple of times a day, sometimes more often," Gene said. "We think there's a good chance that you can take him when he does."

"What about doing it while he's in the house?" Jim asked.

"We know there are other people there, and we don't want to get into more than a one-on-one at this point," Gene answered. "We'd prefer to do it away from there. Specifically, we think you can do it at one of the stores or restaurants he goes to."

"So, you want me to walk into a restaurant and remove this guy," Jim said as he passed 75 now heading southeast.

"That's the plan if we can't do it before he walks in," Gene confirmed.

"What about all this security camera surveillance stuff you were worried about last week?" Jim asked. "Not worried now?"

"We've got that covered," Gene told him. "By the time you get to your house, someone will have left a white

Chevrolet pickup in front of it. Inside are a red hoodie, a Los Angeles Dodger baseball cap, and a Colt 45.

The pistol was used in a robbery/murder in Los Angeles last year," Gene explained. "We just happened to get it when the guy who used it was released due to some irregularities in his arrest. It sort of disappeared from the evidence room after that.

The guy was part of the Bloods, therefore the red hoodie, and we're going to tie the target to the robbery," Gene continued.

"So, what's the plan?" Jim asked as he saw his exit coming up. "I sit in front of my house in a strange pickup wearing a ball cap and a hoodie? Yeah, that shouldn't attract any attention.

Or do we just leave the pickup out there when Jennifer comes home, and I explain it to her?" he said, taking the exit into Mesquite.

"No," Gene corrected him. "The plan is for you to change into your normal sit around in your ass-at-home clothes, drive the pickup somewhere close, and wait for Vicki to contact you. I'm guessing you're what five, maybe ten minutes from home. So, you should be ready to go in fifteen, maybe twenty minutes."

"Okay, twenty minutes," Jim agreed. "Then what? Drive twenty minutes back to the Forest Lane area and wait?"

"Sort of," Gene admitted. "But he hasn't left the house yet today, and his habit seems to be going to a local restaurant, the El Molcajetazo, around one o'clock. That gives you just enough time to get home, change, and be there either before he gets there or as he's leaving."

"It seems to me that you're putting a lot of faith in a two-day habit pattern," Jim said as he turned onto his block and spotted the white pickup. "But I'll get changed and be ready for Vicki Jean to give me my instructions."

"Good," Gene said. "I'll be waiting for Vicki to let me know if our target is on the move. I know this might be a long shot, but I appreciate you for this. When Lady Luck gives you an opportunity, you should take it. Sort of like the four you got lucky with last week."

"Got it," Jim said as he pulled into his driveway and parked. "I'll be ready in five minutes, and I'll let you know what happens when it happens.

Oh, by the way," he said as he walked to his front door. "You need to tell the guys sitting in the blue Ford down the street that they're not fooling anyone. A small neighborhood like this notices strangers just sitting around. I'd be surprised if someone hasn't already called the police and reported suspicious behavior."

"I'll tell them," Gene said. "But I'm sure they didn't want to leave that pistol where just anyone could get it unless they could watch it.

"Just thought I'd mention it," Jim said, going into the house after waving at the guys in the Ford. "I'll let Vicki know that I'm on my way."

Chapter 48

Five minutes later, Jim came out with his earpiece in and said, "Vicki, I'm on my way. Where's the target?"

"He's still at his house," she answered. "Hasn't left all day, but he's been in and out of the house, so I know he didn't leave his phone at home. Right now, he's just sitting in his yard. That's unusual for him."

"Hell, let's just head there," Jim said. "Gene said it's just north of Forest Lane, so I'm going to take 635 back around."

"You'll need to take the Webb Chapel exit," she told him. "Then go under 635 to Forest, heading east."

"Got it," Jim answered, getting into the pickup truck. After making sure the clip was fully loaded and one in the chamber, he drove down the street and passed the two men who were still sitting in the blue car, waving as he went by, heading for 635.

Not hearing anything about the target, he sped northwest toward Webb Chapel, wondering what he would do if he got there, and the target was still in the house. Gene didn't want him entering it, but there might not be any other choice.

"Still nothing?" he asked as he saw his exit coming up.

"No," Vicki answered. "I just don't understand it. He's normally been out a couple of times by now."

"Get me to his house," Jim said, leaving 635. "I'll figure it out when I get there."

"Ok, Webb, south to Forest going east," she reminded him. "Then left turn on Cromwell Drive in about a quarter of a mile."

"How far am I from his house?" Jim asked as he passed beneath 635 on Webb Chapel.

"Maybe a mile," she answered.

"Cromwell dead ends into High Meadow Drive in about a thousand feet," she told him as she saw him turn north on Cromwell. "Turn right when you get there, and High Mesa Drive will be the first street on your right.

Okay, his house is about five hundred feet down High Mesa, on your left, so go slow, and I'll tell you when you're there," she continued as she watched him on her screen.

"You're there," Vicki said as Jim took a quick look and saw two guys sitting in the front yard drinking beer.

"I'm going to keep heading down High Mesa," Jim told her. "I saw two guys in the yard. I'll turn around at the first street and come back by."

"Did they see you drive by?" Vicki asked.

"I don't know," he said as he came to High Dale Drive. "I don't think so, but they could have."

"Go ahead and turn right on that street," she suggested, seeing where he was. "Then go left in about two hundred feet on High Bluff, and you'll be at the east end of High Mesa Drive in about a thousand feet. That'll take you back by the house."

"Alright," Jim said, making the right turn. "I wish I had a picture of him or something, so I'd know which one of those guys I saw was him."

"Sorry, I can't help you there unless one of them walks away from the other," she said as he approached High Bluff. "Then, I can say he's moving, and you can see which one it is."

"Maybe one of them will by the time I get back there," Jim said as he turned left.

A few seconds later, Jim turned left onto High Mesa and began to circle back toward the house and asked, "Still no movement?"

"Nope," she answered.

"That was High Meadow Drive that I was on before I got on his street, wasn't it?" Jim asked as he slowly passed the houses on his right.

"Yes," Vicki answered. "And if you keep going that direction past his house, you'll be back there."

As he approached High Dale, he could see the target's house just a couple of hundred feet down the street. Seeing the two men still sitting in the yard, he slowed down to a crawl and kept heading for their house.

"What are you doing?" Vicki asked. "Don't tell me you're going to stop at the house."

"That's exactly what I'm going to do," Jim told her. "I'll make sure one of those guys gets up and comes out to the street."

Stopping in front of a house two down from the target's house, Jim looked out the passenger window for a second and switched his earpiece to his left ear. Taking the pistol in his left hand and letting it hang down beside the seat, he eased forward to the next house. After sitting in front of it for a minute or so, staring at it, he pulled up to the target's house.

"Okay, Vicki, let me know if our guy moves," he said quietly, looking at the house.

After sitting there for a few seconds, he heard one of the men yelling, asking what he wanted.

"I'm looking for a friend of mine," he yelled back.

"He doesn't live here, Chorra," one of them yelled. "There's no friend of yours in this part of town."

"He told me he lives in a yellow house," Jim told them. "Do you know where there's a yellow house on this street?

"Look, whitey," one of the men said, standing. "There's no yellow house on this street. And there aren't any white folks on this street. You need to move along."

"My friend isn't white," Jim told them. "His name is Paul Gonzalez. He's supposed to live on this street."

"There's no Gonzalez around here," the guy said as he started walking toward Jim's pickup. "For the last time, you need to get your white ass out of here."

"One's moving, Vicki," Jim whispered as the guy got closer. "Is it our target?"

"No, he's not moving," Vicki told him.

"Are you deaf?" the guy said as he got to the pickup and put his hands on the windowsill. "Don't you understand English? I said there's no one around here named Gonzalez or Paul. Now, for the last time, get your white ass out of here!"

As Jim looked past the man to the other man who was getting up, he noticed that the guy at his pickup door had MS 13 tattooed on the fingers of both hands.

"The target is moving," Vicki said. "He's coming toward you."

"What's this asshole's problem?" the target said as he reached the pickup.

"He thinks some friend of his lives around here," the first guy said. "And I think he's lost."

"Lost his mind," the target said, laughing. "You need to move along, white boy, before someone decides they need this shiny new pickup."

"Look," Jim said as he started to raise the pistol, "I'm just looking for a friend. I don't want any trouble."

"You got trouble, jefe," the target told him. "You got more fucking trouble than a pissing his pants little white boy like you can handle. Do you understand?"

"Okay. Okay, I'll leave," Jim said as the target held a pistol up, showing Jim that he was armed.

Reaching for the gear shift with his right hand, he raised his left hand to just below the tricep on his right arm, pointing the pistol at the target's face. When the target's eyes dropped, and Jim saw the recognition register on his face, Jim squeezed the trigger twice in rapid succession.

As what was left of his head pitched back, Jim turned slightly to his right and pointed the pistol at the other guy's face, saying, "I guess you're just a bonus round."

As the guy released his hand from the door, two shots caught him, first in the throat and the next one in the forehead. As his body toppled backward, Jim pulled the gear shifter down into drive and sped away.

"Get me out of here, Vicki," Jim said as he came to High Meadow.

"Right turn on High Meadow, left turn on Marsh Lane, and a right turn on the access road for 635," she told him. "What happened back there?"

"I took care of the Los Angeles problem," Jim said, slowing for the turn onto Marsh. "I'd say call Quantico, but

I know they're recording this. Tell the boys in the blue Ford to stick around if they haven't left. Or to come get their pickup if they have. It may need a little wash job on the passenger side."

Chapter 49

An hour later, Jim had turned the pickup over to the guys who delivered it and was repacking his bag for his next trip when the phone rang.

"Hello," he said, snapping his suitcase closed.

"I guess there's going to be a new normal on this operation," Gene told him. "Maybe things will go back to like the first week, but it appears that we'll have to make some modifications."

"I'm going to hazard a guess that you've already gamed the scenario and found that tossing the phones is going to make this a very difficult operation," Jim told him, heading for the living room.

"Yes, much more difficult," Gene agreed.

"That's one of the things with technology," Jim told him. "It's great when you're the one holding all the cards. But the opponent can always negate your advantage given enough time. In this situation, it only took a couple of days."

"That's true," Gene said. "Now, we've got to regain the advantage, or we'll never achieve the goals that the company set."

"I have a suggestion if you don't mind," Jim told him.

"Please," Gene said. "I always welcome your perspective."

"I've been giving this some thought," he began. "First off, I don't think we'll ever get back to the first week, as you put it.

These guys, at least those with enough smarts to be in a leadership position, figured out the phone thing," he continued. "We were lucky they took as long as they did.

With the technological advantage, we had them," Jim said. "We knew who we wanted, where they were at a moment's notice, so we developed our list of most wanted and proceeded to work our way down that list.

Let's call that system a man-to-man offense," Jim explained. "Each team had a specific target and went after it. That worked well initially.

I'm not really sure when they put two and two together and came up with four," he continued, "But they did. Doesn't really matter how or when they figured it out.

What it does mean for us is that we can't continue with an offense that's not going to work anymore," Jim said. "What we need to do now is switch to a zone offense. This concept is normally used for the defense, but we're playing offense."

"How do you propose to enact it?" Gene asked. "Divide the entire city of El Paso into a system of grids and give each team one? That seems like a huge waste of manpower. Some are just sitting around while others are inundated with targets."

"Let's start with the layout of the city," Jim countered. "Have Debbie take every piece of data, a snapshot of every screen that had targets, and overlay the black dots on the entire city.

Then, take the areas of concentration and figure out how much area is in each," he continued. "Take those areas and divide them up according to street, traffic patterns, natural obstructions to movement such as rivers, railroad tracks, and anything that restricts direct travel from a central point within each specific area.

Now, let's assume that we have a small window of opportunity, say five minutes, for the team stationed there to get to any point where any target might pop up," Jim told him.

"We're not using just the distance in miles," he said. "We're looking at the areas more in light of time. No area should include points more than five minutes away.

I think given the fact that Debbie can only give you tracking data for a short period, maybe a day, we need what I'd call a quick reaction force," he told Gene. "Debbie says she can use voice recognition to determine the target within fifteen minutes. Let's assume that it's twenty.

Our teams are spread across the high-threat areas, needing five minutes to get to where Debbie says the target is," Jim explained. "It's possible that the target will toss the phone within that period of time to be in strict compliance with the single-use rule."

"I think I can see where you're going with this," Gene said. "Sort of like a spider that spins his web and then goes to where the fly landed."

"I guess that's as good of an analogy as I can think of," Jim agreed.

"And if we split the teams into singles, we'd have smaller areas," Gene mused. "With shorter response times."

"And probably more of our people shot," Jim countered. "Look at the Marty shooting. Look at what happened in Fabens. Look at what happened with the four guys here: with Nolan, Brett, and Tim. And now the last one with the guy I just shot."

"Marty was the only one," Gene argued.

"I'm not talking about who got shot," Jim explained. "I'm referring to the fact that there were unknowns every time.

And I think it's going to become the norm," he continued. "Reference the two phones for the four men here. I'd be surprised if the bottom tier got a phone. Too dangerous to have that many.

Not only in the sheer numbers, but the odds of someone not tossing their phone, like the Los Angeles guy here," Jim continued. "I'd bet maybe one out of four would be carrying a phone when they initially return.

When we leave, those that are left will probably slowly return to everyone having one," he theorized. "But during the time frame of this operation? One out of four. Possibly two, like it was here. But no more than that.

And that means that our teams will be facing two to four MS 13 members at every target location," Jim concluded. "We need a minimum of two guys working together in each zone."

"Okay, I understand," Gene said. "What about weapons? Any changes there?"

"I want every team to have at least one shotgun," Jim answered. "Preferably a twelve gauge. And, considering that they may have little time to aim, load them with double-aught buckshot. That's equivalent to nine thirty caliber bullets, which will spread out when fired. Even with shooting from the hip, at least one of the pellets is going to take down the target."

"A guy walking into a store or restaurant with a shotgun is pretty obvious, isn't it?" Gene argued. "There goes any element of surprise."

"There are a couple of solutions for that," Jim told him. "First, there's a pistol called 'The Judge'. But it's only in a 410 gauge. Maybe have the shotgun guy carry it on his hip for a backup.

My preference is the Mossberg 500 shorty with a pistol grip," Jim told him. "It can be carried in one hand with it down by your leg and be practically unseen unless someone looks down.

You raise it like a pistol, grab the slide, and shoot," he explained. "Then all you have to do is pump in another round with the slide, and you're ready for the next shot."

"Anything else?" Gene asked.

"Look into vests," Jim answered. "We're about to enter a whole new concept, and with the potential of six guys shooting within a confined space, I think it has merit. Preferably something light that can be pretty much invisible beneath loose clothing."

"All right," Gene said. "I'll attack the zone suggestion first with Debbie and the other people who were tracking the targets. We should come up with an answer to how many zones are required, and then we'll figure out if we need more teams. I'll get back to you on that.

In the meantime, I'll have the logistic folks work on getting enough weapons to meet your requirements for each team member," Gene told him. "And we'll get the vests. Have a good evening, Jim."

"You too, sir," Jim said before hanging up.

Chapter 50

The following week, after returning from his three-day trip back and forth to El Paso, Jim was watching the local news when the phone rang.

"Hello," he answered, turning down the volume on the television.

"Good morning, Jim," he heard General Barker say. "What's on your agenda today?"

"Wash the car, mow the yard, maybe go get some steaks for dinner tonight," he answered.

"Pretty exciting day ahead of you," Gene replied with a slight chuckle. "You just finished a mundane three-day trip and now house chores. Sounds like you need something to put a spark in your otherwise dull existence."

"I'm not so sure I need the type of spark you've been providing lately," Jim answered. "I've actually enjoyed the mundane, as you call it, lifestyle I've had for the last week or so."

"But I'm sure you didn't just call to discuss the latest episode of Boring Lives of Dallas Husbands," Jim said smiling. "What can I do for you today, General?"

"I have to be in Dallas this afternoon," he answered. "And I thought I'd take you and Jennifer out to dinner if that's all right with both of you."

"I'm sure it will be," Jim answered. "But if you'll remember, Jennifer specifically asked if you'd come over for those 'waggle' steaks."

"I do remember that," Gene told him. "But there's sort of a fly in the ointment that makes me leery about coming to your house this afternoon."

"What could possibly make you unsure about visiting here?" Jim asked. "You know she always enjoys your company."

"There's another person with me," Gene explained. "And last time she was around Jennifer, there was a slight chill in the air."

"You're talking about Debbie, I assume," Jim replied. "Slight chill? Yeah, like a meat locker. Hell, everybody in the restaurant would be running for their overcoats."

"Yes, I'm afraid you could be right," Gene confessed. "I don't want to do something that would make it an uncomfortable evening if I can avoid it. But Debbie and I need to have an hour or two with you to talk about something."

"I can understand your reservations about putting those two together," Jim said. "Especially here at the house. Unless there's an overriding reason for getting together for dinner, I think it would be wiser for just the three of us to meet."

"I don't necessarily disagree with you," Gene said. "But the timing of my trip down there made it conducive to having dinner before I fly back up here."

"I'll be glad to ask her," Jim offered. "But I'm pretty sure what her answer will be. Even if she agreed to the four of us having dinner, it would be in deference to you. And I know how she would be throughout the meal. I think it would be better if the three of us met and you guys have dinner together before you fly back."

"You're probably right," Gene admitted. "You know her better than I."

"Unfortunately, yes," Jim told him. "A rather obstinate lady."

"And Debbie can be a tad bit abrasive herself," Gene said. "So, here's the new plan. Debbie and I will land at Love Field in about four hours. Noon your time. If you can pick us up, we'll go somewhere for lunch and take care of business."

"I'll be there," Jim replied. "Any place in particular you want to have lunch?"

"Nope," Gene answered. "Just somewhere we can have a little privacy to discuss some rather sensitive issues."

"There's a little place called Piasano's that just opened up in the West End area of Dallas," Jim suggested. "Pretty artsy fartsy, but good food."

"What about Venice?" Gene asked. "I'm surprised that you'd go anywhere besides there."

"Oh, I still go there," Jim said. "But this place is a lot closer to Love Field. And they've got a small dining room that I'm sure we can reserve."

"That's fine," Gene said. "I'll be looking forward to it."

As soon as he hung up, he called the restaurant and was assured that the room was available. Checking the time, he saw he had all of his chores finished and showered before he needed to pick up Gene and Debbie.

Three hours later, he jumped in the shower and hastily scrubbed the sweat and grime away. As he was toweling off, he checked the time once again and decided he probably didn't have time to shave before heading to Love.

Arriving at the General Aviation terminal just in time to see Gene's jet pulling in, he stepped out and waited.

"General, welcome back," he said, shaking Gene's hand. "And you too, Debbie. If you're ready, we'll head down to Piasano's and grab something to eat while we discuss whatever you guys traveled halfway across the country to talk about."

Fifteen minutes later, they pulled up to the restaurant and headed inside. "Good morning," came the greeting as they walked in. Welcome to Piasano's. Please, have a seat anywhere."

"Good morning," Jim said. "I called a couple of hours ago requesting a private dining area."

"Yes, yes. It's right back here," he was told. "If you'll just follow me, please. I'm Val, and I'll be taking care of you. If there's anything you need, just ask."

"Thank you, Val," Jim said as they saw a table set for four in the small room.

"What would you like to drink?" she asked as they took their seats.

"Unsweet iced tea for me," Jim said, taking the chair across the table from Gene and Debbie.

"Same," both Gene and Debbie answered.

"I'll be right back with them," Val said. "I'll take your orders when I get back if you're ready."

Chapter 51

As soon as Val brought their dishes and left, Debbie laid a map of El Paso on the table in front of Jim and said, "We ran a program based on what you talked about with the General. We did the same for all of the other locations."

Jim pulled the map closer as she continued, "As you can see, there are definitely areas where MS 13 activities are grouped. There's sporadic activity across the city, but there are definite areas where it's more concentrated."

Jim looked at the numerous groupings and asked, "How much of this is depicting where they live? I would expect to see them at those locations."

"We factored that in by eliminating any location where a target spent a continuous six hours or more," she answered. "These target locations have a mean time of less than one hour but over five minutes."

"Why did you eliminate any target location less than five minutes?" Jim asked. "Is it because I thought we needed to concentrate our teams within a five-minute radius area?"

"Yes and no," Debbie answered. "We actually went back and looked at where the targets were that matched that program parameter and found usually, they were at gas stations and street meetings with other members.

The street meetings were analyzed looking for consistency or any repeat meetings at those locations, and we found them to be completely random," she explained. "Those were all removed from our consideration. The same went for the gas stations. Only a couple of targets consistently used the same one, so we analyzed why. It happens to be the closest one to their homes."

"How did El Paso match data from the other locations?" Jim asked.

"Almost perfectly," Debbie told him. "There were minor variations due to area layout, type of neighborhood, especially areas of apartments, city size, by that I mean how many miles across it, and several other factors that were unique to the specific city."

"Okay," Jim said, sitting back. "This looks like we have a great starting point. "Have you developed a zone system to match these findings?"

"Yes," Debbie said, laying a transparent sheet over the map and matching the four corners. "Each zone is shown within the red lines. There are forty-two zones in El Paso."

As Jim looked at the random shapes comprising each zone, he asked, "These are the zones where you recommend putting teams?"

"Not always," she corrected him. "Some of them will have up to three teams."

"What are you basing that on?" Jim asked as she placed another transparent sheet on top of the first one.

"These are basically zones within the five-minute zones you recommended," she answered. "If we just broke the city down into target concentration within that specific parameter, you would have some areas with three or four times the activity as other zones.

Some of those zones are actually six-minute zones," she added.

Leaning across the table and pointing at one specific zone, she told him, "Take this one. I'm recommending three teams, spread a minute apart, roughly two blocks, to cover this zone because of the number of target locations.

I overlaid the initial system with a map showing how many target locations were in any zone within any five-minute window," she explained.

"What I found were zones where the targets were passing through or congregating for less than five minutes," she continued. "This meant that a single team would probably be tied up on one target while others were transiting the area.

The additional teams are placed in these zones to respond to those situations," she concluded.

"How does this fit the fifty teams we have assigned to El Paso?" Jim asked, looking at Gene.

"We're upping your teams to sixty," Gene responded. "That gives you the coverage Debbie suggested and a couple of teams in reserve back at the convention center."

"Okay," Jim said, looking at the map and the overlays. "This seems good to me. Thanks, Debbie. I do believe this is a good plan."

"You're welcome," she responded. "And one other thing. The phones."

"What about the phones?" Jim asked.

"The members are returning to El Paso much faster than we expected," Gene told him. "I'm busy getting the logistics in line so we can reactivate the operation within the next four days."

"Is it a coincidence that this happens to be the start of my next trip?" Jim asked.

"No, it's definitely planned," Gene answered. "I want you there for the first day of this new strategy to see how it's working and if we need to tweak it a little."

"Another thing about the phones," Debbie chimed in. "Over the last few days, we're seeing an increase in phones that remain in use more than a day or after just one use."

"That must help out your tracking immensely," Jim told her, looking up.

"It does," she admitted. "But it points to what occurred here with your last target."

"What was that?" Jim asked.

"The target kept the phone even though he was told to toss it," she told him. "I'm seeing a dramatic increase in that."

"Is it that the people are holding onto their phones in direct disobedience to the cell leaders, or are they purchasing a phone for personal use, hoping they won't get caught?" Jim asked.

"A little of both," Debbie answered. "But the majority of it seems to be purely personal. Guys are calling their girlfriends, their families, even their friends that aren't members of the gang."

"So now we can track these guys and their normal acquaintances outside the gang," Jim remarked. "That gives us a possible target location if we need to go looking for one of them."

"One other thing," Gene mentioned, laying his fork beside his plate. "I'm going to implement a spotter program using the teams that were there for removal of the targets. They'll be someone who can blend in with the surrounding area and just pass through any store, restaurant, or other location where we suspect there may be more than one target. Basically, they're there to warn the teams if they spot the unknowns."

"How do they know who the unknowns are?" Jim asked.

"They'll have the Bluetooth earpiece and be told where the known targets are in relation to him, just as our teams do," Debbie explained. "But they won't be armed or have any contact other than to pass through the store looking for other people with the MS 13 tattoo."

"That's probably a good use of the recovery teams," Jim agreed, nodding. "Especially since there's not a lot of recovery operations. But why not arm him?"

"These people won't have the training," Gene told him. "As I said, they'll be someone local that we're using purely for information. I want them in and out before the shooting starts."

"Okay," Jim said. "How are the teams supposed to know who's an unknown target or one of these guys?"

"We're tracking them, just like the targets, just like the teams," Debbie explained.

"I think the spotter idea has merit," Jim said as Val came back into the room. "How you manage him is up to you guys. Where are you headed now?"

"Back to Quantico," Gene said, removing his credit card. "You were our last stop."

"How was everything?" Val asked, looking around.

"Excellent," Jim said, smiling at her. "I'll definitely be back."

Chapter 52

The next morning, Jim waited for Jennifer to leave for work and then called Gene. "Good morning, sir," he said after Gene answered. "I have a request."

"What would that be?" Gene asked.

"Could you arrange to have Debbie give me a quick call?" Jim asked. "I have a couple of questions for her."

"Sure," Gene said. "If it's all right with you, I'll make it a conference call so that I'm up to speed on whatever it is that you're interested in."

"Great," Jim told him. "I'll be waiting."

Less than ten minutes later, the phone rang, and Jim answered, "Hello."

"Jim, I have Debbie on the line with me," Gene said. "What do you need to talk about?"

"Good morning, Debbie," Jim said. "I have a nagging little thought, and I'd like to see if you have the data or can get it; that would clear up what's bothering me."

"Good morning, Jim," she answered. "What's bothering you, and how can I help?"

"It has to do with the new phones you said you were seeing and how they were being retained after a call or more than a day," he told her. "Is this still happening?" "Hang on a second," she answered. "I need to take a look at the most recent data."

A few seconds later, she returned and said, "Yes, not by much, but there are more phones showing up in the hands of the MS 13 members, and the majority of them remain in use after we identify them."

"What are you getting at, Jim?" Gene cut in.

"Don't you find it strange that so many of the members are disobeying their cell leaders regarding the phones?" Jim asked. "I mean, I just don't see them putting up with members knowingly jeopardizing their organization. Hell, they'll chop off someone's head for merely insulting them."

"Okay," Debbie agreed. "Exactly what do you want from me?"

"First, let me ask you this," Jim told her. "Are these new phones showing up in areas that match the previous locations you used to develop the zones? And are there some of the same members with multiple phones?"

"I'll have to get back to you on that," she answered. "It might take a little time to go back over the data. Do you just want it for El Paso?"

"No, I need every location," Jim told her.

"Anything else?" she asked.

"Yes, I want you to build me a flip chart, or consecutive overlay chart, to show where the phones are hour by hour," he said. "And I want the new phones, especially the ones that have remained in use, to be highlighted."

"A flip chart?" Debbie asked.

"Take the map of El Paso, Los Angeles, and the others," Jim explained. "Have an overlay starting before the new phones started showing up, then another overlay an hour later, and another for each hour. I want to watch the progression and the locations where these new phones are and move to up until now. And I want you to continue making the overlays for each hour until I ask you to stop."

"What do you think is going on?" Gene asked.

"I'm not sure," Jim answered. "I have my suspicions, but I'd rather look at everything before I say any more. But I'd like to have the recovery teams you were going to use to be spotters start driving by the locations of the new phones a couple of times a day. Make sure to change cars each time. Wouldn't hurt to have different people in the cars either.

Just have them cruise by the location," Jim clarified. "Don't stop or slow down. All I'm looking for is if there are any people in sight at that location."

"And I'm guessing you want this at the other cities as well," Gene said.

"Yes," Jim answered. "If it's happening in El Paso and not the others, I'd be surprised. Let me ask you, what's the progress from Dark Water? Have they managed to complete their operations in El Salvador?"

"Pretty much," Gene answered. "What's that got to do with our operation?"

"Did many of the top tier escape?" Jim asked.

"A couple," Gene admitted.

"Another thing, has there been any leak or evidence that we, Black Water, are behind this?" Jim asked.

"Not that I'm aware of," Gene answered. "What's that got to do with it?"

"If you're correct, these guys don't know who's targeting them." Jim answered. "They may think it's another gang or some upstart MS 13 guys who want to take over some of their cells or maybe the entire city."

"I still don't see the relevance," Gene said.

"If I was the new leader of the top cell in El Paso and a shit load of my guys were being removed, and I didn't have a clue as to who was doing it, I'd start looking internally," Jim offered. "If it's not someone from my city, but maybe from a smaller city that hasn't had the problem. Maybe someone is trying to force a coup."

"And how is the data you've requested from Debbie going to prove or disprove this theory?" Gene asked.

"By the way, I think I can have that data ready within the hour," Debbie interrupted.

"Good," Jim told her. "General, do you think you can have it sent to me today?"

"I think Debbie and I will be on the plane with it as soon as it's ready," Gene answered. "If she's right, we'll be landing at Love Field in about five hours."

"To answer your previous question, I think it's going to show that these MS 13 assholes are smarter than we gave them credit for," Jim answered. "I think these guys are trying to figure out who is killing them and then go after whoever is their leader once they find out who that guy is."

"Exactly how are they going to do that?" Gene asked.

"If it was me, I'd try to set a trap and catch one of the enemies," Jim answered.

Chapter 53

Jim had just finished his lunch of a grilled three-cheese sandwich on sourdough bread and a glass of milk when a message appeared on his company phone. Seeing that Gene was scheduled to land in approximately thirty minutes, he rinsed his plate and stuck it in the dishwasher before going out to his pickup.

Taking the same route that was very familiar now, he arrived at Love Field mere minutes before the plane was due to land. Going into the General Aviation terminal, he asked if there was a conference room he could borrow for an hour or so.

Hearing there was, he went out to watch the small private airplanes vying for space between Southwest Airlines 737s taking off and landing. A few minutes later, he watched Gene's plane smoothly touchdown on the runway about a thousand feet from where he stood.

As soon as they parked, Debbie led Gene coming down the jet's stairs heading for him.

"That was quick," Jim said, shaking her hand. "I really didn't expect anything until tomorrow when I first brought it up."

"Once the data is in the computer, as all of this was," she said, holding up a map case, "it's just a matter of telling the computer how you want to present it.

The thing that took most of the time was doing each location separately so I could make the overlays you wanted," she finished as Gene joined them, heading for the terminal.

"Did you get a chance to look at them?" Jim asked as he shook Gene's hand.

"Yeah, we both studied the maps on the trip down here," Gene answered. "I was certainly surprised about how quickly the dots were growing."

"I think everyone was surprised," Debbie added as Jim held the door open for them.

Leading them down a hall, Jim said, "I've arranged for a conference room where we'll have a little privacy and a table to spread out the maps."

Once in the conference room, Jim said, "Let's look at El Paso first."

As Debbie spread the map in the center of the large table, Jim watched her put the first transparent overlay on it as she explained, "This was the number and locations of all the phones in the El Paso area. It reflects where they were a week ago."

"Not many," Jim said, looking at the widespread dots. "Looks like most of the MS 13 members left town rather hastily."

"I know you wanted an hour-by-hour flip chart, but there weren't sufficient changes at that point," Debbie said, laying the next transparency on the map. "Here's twenty-four hours later."

"I'm going to jump forward two days," she told him, laying the next one on the stack. "Here's the first indication of a major increase. The number of phones doubled overnight.

Here's the next day, again the number of phones doubled," she said. "That happened the following day also.

Now, here's the interesting point," she told him as she tossed on another overlay. "The number of phones is relatively stable but look at the locations."

Jim looked at the dots that were now more or less in four distinct locations. "I'd guess that there are now four cells about to resume operations in El Paso," he said, leaning over and studying the gathering dots.

"I believe you're right," Debbie said as she pulled all of the previous transparencies off the map. "Now, I'm going to put the rest of these on fairly quickly. What's very interesting is how the dots begin to form patterns."

Jim watched as one after another, the transparencies showed similar but varying patterns. By the time she had put the last one in place, Jim said, "The phones are lining up along several roads that lead to the center of each of the four groupings we saw at the start."

"Yes, they are," Debbie agreed, nodding. "And I've confirmed it with Melinda and the other locations. It's the same at all of them."

"Someone is directing this," Gene broke in. "And I'm going to bet it's one of the guys that escaped our people in El Salvador."

"I think you're right," Jim agreed. "I don't see how this could all be coordinated by one of the lower-level members that we didn't get to before they broke ranks and ran."

"We looked at that," Gene added. "On the way here, I contacted the guy running the Dark Water operations, and he confirmed that one of the most senior members of the council of nine evaded our people. They don't know where he disappeared to."

"I'd bet Los Angeles," Jim said. "Since that's where this more or less began, there are probably some pretty strong ties with the members out there."

"You're probably right," Debbie said. "We actually saw this developing almost a day earlier there than in El Paso or the other locations."

"So, how does this fit with your concept of capturing one of the enemies, meaning one of our teams," Gene asked.

"Look how the dots are forming and moving," Jim explained. "Except for one or two, they march inward from the outer boundaries to toward the center and then return back out once they reach the center."

Jim reached over, pulled the transparencies off, and began to put them back on as he pointed out one specific dot. "See how this one moves inward every hour?" he said. "Most of them behave the same way. At all four of these locations."

"And you think they're meant for our guys to follow the phones into the center where these dots meet," Gene mused, looking at the maps.

"Look how they train racing dogs," Jim said. "They put a fake rabbit on a motor that races around the track just ahead of the dogs, and they chase it. Same concept. Except these fake rabbits have weapons."

"What do you think they plan once they lure our team into their kill zone?" Gene asked.

"I'd bet on them having four or five houses up and down each of the roads leading in," Jim answered. "Once a car is within the zone, block it and take care of whoever is inside.”

“So, this is designed to capture just one car?” Debbie asked.

“That’s all they need to capture, just one person,” Jim explained. “Then they can get whatever information they need from him.”

“That’s a lot of people just sitting around in houses,” she said.

“I don’t think it’s that many people,” Jim told her. “You looked at phones that belong to MS 13 members, right?”

“Yes, that’s what we were supposed to do,” she answered.

“But did you look to see which members were buying or using the phones?” Jim asked, looking her in the eye.

“I’m not sure what you’re getting at,” Gene interrupted. “Her voice recognition program only looks for known members. The same members we were targeting.”

“I understand,” Jim said, shaking his head. “What I’m asking is, do you know which member bought or used which phone?”

Seeing the puzzled look on her face, he explained, “I’m betting that there are fewer than five members at each of these locations, or zones. I’m betting that those five members bought all of those phones.

We were surprised at how quickly the members were returning to El Paso,” he continued. “And we were really surprised that so many of the members were disobeying the rules about phone usage.”

Waiting for them to fully understand what he was saying, he concluded with, “That many members didn’t return. Only a select few. And they're using the phones hoping we'll chase them."

"How can we prove that?" Gene asked, looking again at the maps. "How do we know that there aren't members with each phone regardless of who purchased it?"

"First, use the voice recognition program and assign a name to each dot. Then see if the same voice is using different phones," Jim said. "Also, have those spotter teams you were setting up drive through those neighborhoods and look at each supposed location.

I'm going to bet that a lot of the phones are at houses where there aren't any members," he continued. "The phones may be lying in the bushes beside the house. Or in a car parked on the street. But the phones aren't being used by anyone except the few members that are involved with their operation."

"Okay, I understand what you're driving at," Gene said. "Now, how do we prove or disprove it?"

"Pick a phone at each zone," Jim explained. "Have someone go there and check to see if there's an MS 13 guy there."

"You think we should send someone knocking on doors asking if an MS-13 gang member is there?" Gene asked incredulously.

"Send them as Seventh Day Adventists in black suits and white shirts with skinny black ties carrying bibles," Jim answered. "Or have them shave their heads and dress in white robes like Hare Krishna guys while one of them chants and rings a bell. Or maybe have them selling extended auto warranties. It doesn't matter; just get someone to the location to see if the damn phone is being used. I still say we have a small number of MS 13 members at each location trying to breadcrumb one of our teams."

"Breadcrumb?" Debbie asked.

"You know, leave a trail of breadcrumbs for the chickens to follow into the pen?" Jim told her. "Or cookie crumbs like Hansel and Gretel?

Never mind," he said. "But I think you need to get this information to the other locations and have them do the same as I'm planning on doing when I get back to El Paso. By the way, General, I'm going to need three or four good long-range snipers to support my plan to remove our next targets."

"Who are your next targets?" Gene asked as Debbie was rolling up the map and overlays.

"The guys that are dropping the crumbs," Jim said, smiling. "I want to reach out and touch them."

Chapter 54

Jennifer had barely left for work when Jim's phone rang. "Hello," he answered, guessing it was Quantico.

"Good morning, Jim," Gene replied. "I've got some good news for you."

"I won the Virginia State Lottery?" Jim exclaimed. "How many millions of dollars was it?"

"Always the wiseass, even this early in the morning," Gene said. "But this will probably make you just as happy."

"I doubt it, but go ahead," Jim replied.

"You were correct about the bread-crumbing thing," Gene told him. "At all of the locations."

"How many MS 13 members are actually back?" Jim asked.

"Unfortunately, that we don't know," Gene answered. "Unless we get eyes on the ground, we'll never know. The phones were our method of counting."

"I understand," Jim said. "Now, who's running the show?"

"We have good reason to believe that our escapee from El Salvador is in Los Angeles and the mastermind of this operation," Gene answered.

"And you have proof?" Jim asked.

"Enough," Gene replied. "It seems that he had his mistress back in El Salvador use her phone to call the wife of one of the new cell leaders in Los Angeles before he left. The only reason we found out about the phone call was because he unintentionally said something in the background that Debbie's voice recognition program picked up."

"I guess the gods are indeed smiling on us now," Jim observed. "What did he say?"

"He said, and I quote, 'Tell that miserable puta to tell her pimp that I'm on the way and he better be at the airport as directed'," Gene answered.

"And now I'm guessing that Debbie's folks are tracking and recording those two phones," Jim said, nodding.

"Yes, but there hasn't been anything worthwhile since then," Gene told him. "However, those few words in the background told us all we need to know."

"I agree," Jim replied. "Now, do we know any more about who's setting the traps?"

"Yes, we sent random cars through the neighborhoods as well as repositioned a couple of satellites and are reasonably certain that there are four to six people at the end of the trail, so to speak," Gene answered.

"We also looked at rentals or homes for sale in the same areas," he continued. "In particular, we were interested in the blocks where we think they'll try to lure our guys."

"I think they'll try something like we did in Fabens," Jim suggested. "They'll have cars to block us when we enter their zone, and they'll have shooters on each side. Did you look specifically at those houses on both sides of the streets where the phones ended their travel?"

"Yes, and there are usually twelve of them, six on each side of the street, at each zone," Gene answered. "We're trying to get someone to check out who's living there right now, but it may take a little time."

"I'd probably have a house on each side with three or four people in each and then a couple of people in the two blocking cars," Jim told him. "That'd give me a dozen or so shooters. They probably expect only one or two cars, so that's a pretty good ratio of shooters. Worst case, they have a twelve to eight advantage."

"You're assuming that the cell leaders have that many members at their disposal," Gene told him.

"Yes, I'm betting that there were enough low-level guys that weren't important enough to send out of town," Jim answered. "And they most likely never had phones, or at least don't now."

"How do you plan on using your snipers?" Gene asked.

"I need your people to find me at least one house on each block where we think they want us," Jim said. "I'd prefer two, ones close to the ends of the block on opposite sides of the street with a pretty clear view down the street from side windows."

"I'll have our guys get to work on that," Gene told him. "And I'll see if the other locations want the same thing. Anything else?"

"Of course," Jim answered, smiling. "A couple of things. See if you can get some very detailed maps of the area around the traps and have your best people look at ways to infiltrate the area behind the houses on the street we're referring to. I'd very much like to preposition some guns behind the houses we determine are housing the MS 13 guys before we send a car into the trap."

"You're actually going to send a car in there?" Gene asked.

"Yes, I don't know of any other way to get them to come out and play," Jim replied. "And that leads me to the other thing I mentioned. I'll need an armor-plated car. Not something like the Presidential limo, but plates in the doors, bullet resistant tinted windows, and so forth. Put a mannequin or two in the seats and give the driver a vest.

My plan would be for him to enter the zone after we have the backdoors covered, possibly already removing the shooters from the houses, and when he's blocked in, he just drops to the floor of the car," Jim explained. "Then the snipers can take out anyone coming out of the houses or from the cars that are blocking him.

"Who do you expect to be stupid enough to volunteer to be the driver?" Gene asked.

"That would be me," Jim answered. "I certainly can't ask one of my people to do it. And I won't make anyone take the risk."

"I can't allow that," Gene told him. "I'd rather call off the operation."

"It's a little late for that, sir," Jim said. "I've thought this through, and although there's some risk, I believe that it's minimal compared to any other option. We've only got a couple of days to get this done, and I want to use my first night in El Paso to do a dry run with the car."

"What sort of dry run?" Gene asked.

"I want to use the car, cruise the streets where the phones are moving, and slow at each location," Jim told him. "Then, I'll cruise back the same way but never enter where we think they're waiting. Then, the next afternoon, I repeat the process, except I stop at the intersection leading me into the kill zone as if I'm debating whether or not to go in.

I'll sit there as Melinda or whoever's watching us tells me we have our assets in place," he continued. "Then I'll head down the street and let myself get blocked in," he finished. "If this works, there won't be any of the MS 13 guys left to get to my car."

"I'll give it some thought," Gene finally said. "I'm not at all happy about it, but you may be right about any other options. I'll pass this down to the moles in the gaming department and let them have a go at it."

"You should also talk to the other locations and see if this will fit their operation," Jim suggested. "I don't know who the guys are in charge except in Los Angeles, but I'm pretty sure Mike will feel the same way I do. We knew what we were getting into when we joined Black Water. And you wouldn't have recruited us if we weren't ready to take certain risks."

"Like I said, I'll pass this down, and I'll broach it with the other location," Gene said. "I'm not agreeing to it yet, but I'll consider it."

"Good enough for me," Jim told him. "But I'd appreciate it if you'd proceed under the assumption that you will approve it. Have all of the logistical work done and the assets in place when I get to El Paso in two days."

"That I'll do," Gene agreed. "I still have the final decision on final implementation. Just don't forget that."

"I won't," Jim said. "I hope you can come up with a better plan, but I don't think you will. As my great, great, grandfather used to say, 'You have to break a few eggs if you want an omelet'."

Chapter 55

"Hello," Jim said, answering the phone as he finished packing his suitcase for his next trip.

"We ran your proposal, and we believe that we have a major flaw," Gene told him.

"What's that?" Jim asked.

"There are four zones in El Paso," Gene reminded him. "And five in Los Angeles. We tried every scenario, and it can't be done with a single car."

"What about if we don't do the dry run on the first day," Jim suggested. "Or, we have someone else doing it before I get there tomorrow. Then I can probably get the four zones, two the first day and two the next."

"We looked at that," Gene told him. "We think that after the first zone is attacked, the others will run, just like before. Face it, Jim, it won't work."

"What if we have four cars in El Paso?" Jim asked. "And however many they need in each of the other locations. That would allow us to hit them all at once."

"Yes, but I believe you're the one who said you wouldn't ask anyone else to do it," Gene rebutted. "How do you plan on getting drivers for them?"

"Give me an hour," Jim said, checking his watch. "I'll call you back and let you know."

Hanging up, Jim scrolled down his list of contacts on the phone until he came to Nolan. Dialing, he waited until he answered on the third ring.

"Nolan, Jim Lashley," he said.

"Jim, this is sort of a surprise," Nolan replied. "What can I do for you?"

"I have a little problem," Jim told him. "Let me explain what's going on and how I'm trying to resolve it."

Over the next ten minutes, Jim took Nolan through all of the information and planning that he had done with Gene and Debbie. Finally, he said, "The flaw in the plan is that I'll have to be in four places at once or within a very, very short time, or the targets will run, and we'll be right back where we were two weeks ago."

"So, your problem is having drivers, right?" Nolan asked.

"That's the biggest one," Jim admitted. "That and a narrow window of time to accomplish the operation on four fronts."

"You do remember that I taught driving at Quantico before I was assigned to be your chauffeur," he said. "I realize that being your driver was a rather mundane affair, but I am somewhat qualified for what you're describing."

"I'm not doubting your qualifications," Jim quickly told him. "But I'm not going to ask anyone to do something with this much risk."

"This is the risk?" Nolan scoffed. "Having breakfast with you is a risk. Just about every time I was around, you were a risk. I came out to El Paso expecting to be driving some high-level personnel puke who hadn't been in the field for years. And look what a pile of shit I fell into."

"I still can't ask you, or anyone else, to do this," Jim said.

"You don't have to ask," Nolan interrupted. "I want to be part of this. This is why I joined Black Water to start with. And I'll bet that Tim and Brett want in as well."

"I was going to call them," Jim confessed. "You three guys are about the only ones I'd trust in this situation. But I can't ask them either. This is strictly a volunteer operation."

"Tell you what," Nolan said. "I'm supposed to be meeting them in about thirty minutes for a beer. Give me that much time before you make any final decisions. Will you do me that favor?"

"I'll give you thirty minutes," Jim said, checking his watch. "I have to have an answer for Gene in about forty-five. But I want to hear from each of them personally."

"Done," Nolan said. "I'll just explain it to them as you did to me and let them make their own decisions."

"Thanks, Nolan," Jim said before hanging up. "Both for talking to them and for volunteering."

Trying to keep his mind off his plan falling apart, Jim repacked his suitcase, polished his boots, and was counting how many pairs of clean socks were in his dresser drawer when his phone rang.

"Hello," he said, checking his watch.

"Hello, Jim," he heard Tim say. "Understand you used to have a problem."

"Hey, Tim," Jim greeted him. "Sort of. I'm assuming you've talked to Nolan."

"He's sitting right here with me," Tim said. "So is Brett. Hang on, I'll let him say hi."

"Hey, Jim," Brett said, taking the phone from Tim. "Too bad you couldn't be sitting here with us having a cold beer. You did say you liked Heineken, didn't you?"

Laughing, Jim said, "Not a chance. Not even if that was the only way I could have a beer with you guys."

"We might be worth it," Brett said, laughing. "But we're not calling to share stories about what beer we like. Or don't. I just want to assure you that both Tim and I will come force-feed you a twelve-pack of Heineken if you don't include us in this little adventure you have planned."

"He's exactly right," Tim said, taking his phone back. "And just because Nolan was your driver, that doesn't mean he gets any special treatment. We're all in."

"Okay, guys. I hear you," Jim said. "I'll have Melinda brief you in more detail and how it's coming together. If, at any point, you change your mind, just let me know."

"We are in!" Nolan said, grabbing the phone. "You just hold up your end without getting killed. You'll definitely owe us several beers when this is over."

"And it'll be my pleasure," Jim told him. "Thanks, guys. I've got to make a couple of calls really quick, but I'll see you tomorrow afternoon."

After hearing everyone's goodbye, Jim called Gene to give him the news.

"General," Jim said as Gene answered. "I have my four drivers. Do you think you can get all of the other assets in place by tomorrow afternoon?"

"Already working on it," Gene answered. "And all of the other locations have approved your plan and are ready to execute it starting tomorrow."

"Good. Now, could you get Debbie to call Melinda and give her the details so that my guys have the information?" Jim asked.

"Already done," Gene said. "She's set up some sort of computer video, information, sharing system tying all five cities together. She's briefing all of them this evening and will provide constant updates on logistical issues, including shooters and current intelligence on who or where the targets are expected to be. By the time you get to El Paso tomorrow evening, we'll have a nationwide operation timed to the second."

"Seems to me that you've done an extraordinary amount of work on a plan you weren't too sure of only an hour or so ago," Jim observed.

"No, I've done my job to support the plan of someone I trusted would do what I've come to expect of him when shit happens," Gene answered. "I knew the plan was the only way this would work when I first heard it. And I knew that the guys you and the other leaders selected to 'volunteer' would be ready to do so."

"Then I guess all I have to do is sit back and let you and the rest of the folks do your jobs to make this work," Jim said. "Makes my job seem simple compared to yours. All I have to do is kill some bad guys and avoid getting killed."

"Isn't that the way it's always been?" Gene asked, smiling. "From the time you went into the Marines and landed in Vietnam until now. Every assignment was exactly that: Remove someone before they removed you. Now, if you don't mind, I've got to see if we can get everything you'll need in place in the next twenty-four hours."

Chapter 56

Nolan was waiting at the hotel when Jim arrived with the flight crew on the courtesy van from the airport. Telling everyone he'd see them in the morning, he nodded at Nolan and headed to his room to change out of his uniform.

Fifteen minutes later, he stepped off the elevator and joined Nolan heading out of the hotel.

"How are things going here?" Jim asked as he got in the passenger seat.

"Pretty good," Nolan answered, starting the car. "We've got all of the original teams here, and they've been working on their part of taking out the targets who'll be in the houses we've identified.

The long-range shooters have been in their locations since yesterday, figuring out where they want to be and ranging their shots," he continued as they left the hotel parking lot. "I've been sort of watching over your target area and basically just making sure the teams are on track for tomorrow's little adventure.

There's a guy on your team named Michael who seems to be the one who keeps things on track," he added. "He's pretty much a stickler for details and seems to have a bigger picture approach than most of the guys.”

“What’s his background?” Jim asked as they got on I-10.

“Air Force,” Nolan answered, merging with the traffic heading west. “Spent some time as a Forward Air Controller flying OV-10s in Korea before coming to Black Water. Now he’s just another one of you airline pilots who think you own the world.”

“We don’t?” Jim said, laughing. “That’s what the brochure said when I signed up.”

“Be all you can be; aim high, the few, the proud,” Nolan said, shaking his head. “All those old catchphrases the Army, Air Force, and Marines use to lure unsuspecting young men into joining.”

“You forgot the Navy,” Jim reminded him. “‘See the World’ I think is theirs.”

“Yeah, see the world from the bowels of a submarine sitting under the Polar ice cap for six months,” Nolan said as they got to the convention center. “Promises made, promises broken.”

“I owe everything I am to the military,” Jim said as they parked. “They took a small-town country boy and turned him into what you see today.”

“I guess there are exceptions,” Nolan granted, getting out of the car. “Now, if you’ll follow me, I’ll show you your car for the evening.”

Following him to where four rather nondescript well used cars were parked, Jim asked, “Are these the cars we’re using?”

“Yep,” Nolan said, opening the door to a faded blue Ford. “Blends in pretty well and is actually a great car mechanically. Runs like a scalded dog, too.

The mechanics installed sheets of twenty-four ply nylon inside the door panels," he continued tapping on the door. "There're also in the back of the driver's seat, the floorboard, and the firewall behind the engine. All the windows are one-and-a-quarter-inch tempered glass."

"Which one is mine?" Jim asked, looking at what appeared to be the remnants of a used car lot that had gone out of business twenty years ago.

"The beautifully rusted Chevy over there," Nolan answered, pointing to a well-dented car in the row. "We've got your rust red, two almost white, and my faded blue chariots to face the enemy. Very patriotic."

"Have you driven mine?" Jim asked as he walked over and opened the door.

"I checked it out," Nolan answered as Jim got in the driver's seat. "Engine's strong, tires are the run flat variety, and the frame has been strengthened, as have all of them.

Michael, the guy I mentioned, drove it through your target area a couple of times," Nolan told him as Jim looked around the interior. "He didn't have any complaints."

"I see you've had rifle holders installed," Jim mentioned as he saw the cups on the floor and the slots in the part attached to the dash.

"Yeah, same in all of them," Nolan told him. "I know we're not supposed to be shooting, just bait to draw the targets out, but I'll be damned if I'm going into this without some way to protect myself besides my pistol."

"Good idea," Jim agreed. "And I'm guessing you managed to procure a couple of rifles for each car."

"Shotguns," Nolan corrected. "Two long barrel Mossberg 500 twelve gauge modified to hold eight shells. Pistol grips are installed for maneuverability inside the car. One loaded with the RIP 303 slugs you're so fond of, and the other with double-aught."

"Let's keep this a secret," Jim said, climbing out and shutting the door. "Not that I'm trying to conceal anything from the folks up at Quantico, but I'm not going to advertise it either."

"Understood," Nolan replied as they headed for the conference center. "Better to ask for forgiveness than for permission."

"Exactly," Jim said, smiling as they walked into the conference center. "Are the other guys here?"

"Since about noon," Nolan answered, holding the door to their room open. "Everybody's getting pretty anxious to get this over. Even the folks running the computers looking at dots moving around are ready for some action."

"Well, look who finally decided to join us," Tim said, walking over with Brett to meet them. "Just like a Marine, sits back enjoying steak and lobster while we poor schmucks do all of the preparation."

"First in, last out," Jim said, smiling and shaking their hands. "And always ready. US Marines."

"Welcome back," Melinda said, walking up. "Would you like to hear my quick briefing before you guys do your drive-through?"

"You bet," Jim answered. "Let's get this started."

Chapter 57

"This is your zone," Melinda stated, using a laser pointer to denote where Jim's area was.

"How did you determine who had which zone?" he asked, looking at the four areas.

"I assigned each of you numbers based on your first names," she answered. "First was Brett, then you, Jim, then Nolan, and finally Tim. Alphabetically.

I started with the target area furthermost north and rolled a die," she explained. "A one was Brett, a two was you, and so forth. Five or six weren't counted, and the die was rerolled. This was the most random way I could think of."

"That's fine," Jim said. "I was just curious."

"No problem," she replied, going back to the screen. "The snipers that are in each area started watching which houses were being occupied by the targets," she continued using her pointer. "The houses you see here and here in your area have two men inside most of the time. One of them leaves once or twice a day and goes to one of the local grocery stores or fast-food restaurants.

The cars we believe will be used to block the streets are here and here," she said, pointing them out. "There are also two guys in each of the houses where the cars are parked."

"Have there been any changes in the movements of the phones they're using to pull us in?" Jim asked.

"Some," she answered. "After the first drive by, most of them moved to the center of the area we think will be where they try to block you in. My guess is that they'll do that again this evening after you go through the area."

"Have you talked to the other cities?" Jim asked. "Is this the same behavior?"

"Almost identical," she answered. "Debbie had an additional screen installed here so I can watch any city and any zone separately. I can zoom in to any area of interest and quickly compare it to what I'm seeing here."

"That sounds good," Jim told her. "Now, what about the teams that are going to take down the targets in the houses?"

"First, we assigned the teams the same way we did you, a roll of the dice," she informed him. "The team leader rolled a single die, and if it was a one, he was assigned to Brett. And so forth. He then rolled the die to see which house he was assigned."

Waiting to see if he had questions, she continued, "The teams have been given satellite photos that are clear enough to read a newspaper someone sitting on the front steps is holding.

Combined with the sniper's information, building blueprints from the county, and personal observation from other agents, the teams developed their plans for entry," she finished.

"What other agents were used for observation?" Jim asked. "I didn't want too much traffic in the area that could draw attention."

"You'll like this," she answered, smiling. "On your target, Michael persuaded the trash truck driver to let him ride along, pretending to be an inspector from the Health and Sanitization Department. Then one of the team members from the other areas did the same thing."

"Good thinking," Jim replied. "Where is this Mike guy? I need to meet him."

"Right here, sir," a tall, slender guy said, stepping to the front. "And it's Michael. Like the Archangel."

"Michael, I'll remember that," Jim told him. "Anyway, that was smart. Using something they see every day to get close. Did you learn much?"

"They eat a lot of fast food, especially tacos and burritos," he answered. "That and they like Dos Equis beer."

"Yeah, that's important to know," Jim replied sarcastically. "Anything else?"

"Mainly where the gates into the back yards are, if they're locked, any dogs, steps into the back door," he said. "One of the big things was how much crap littered the yards that could make noise during an approach from the rear."

"Good," Jim praised him. "Would you like to ride with me this afternoon and point out anything you think might be important for me to know about my targets?"

"I'd be glad to, sir," Michael answered.

"And if you guys want someone with you this afternoon, let's get it arranged right now," Jim told Nolan, Tim, and Brett.

"We've already done that," Nolan told him. "More because we wanted them to see two people in the car, but we did get a better picture of the area where the teams will be working."

"Melinda, is there anything else we need to cover before we head out?" Jim asked.

"Let's get a quick communications check," she answered, touching her earpiece. "I'd like everyone to answer when I call their name. If you haven't heard anything when you see others talking, check that you've turned yours on. Ready?"

As everyone nodded, she started, "Jim?"

"Here," he answered, looking at her.

Watching her as she read from a list of teams, he was impressed with how the operation was coming together, and everyone seemed to be eager to get to work.

When she finished, Melinda turned to Jim and said, "Everyone's equipment seems to be working as designed. What do you want us to do now?"

"Just keep an eye on us as we drive around," Jim answered. "And I'd like for all of the teams to be in their cars once Brett, Nolan, Tim, and I get close to the target areas. I don't expect anything this evening, but I want the teams to be ready to respond if it does."

"Who's my guardian angel this evening?" Jim asked, looking around.

"I am, Mr. Lashley," Vicki said, holding up her hand.

"Oh yes, Vicki Jean," Jim said, smiling. "Watch me close. I'm prone to many, many mistakes. And remember, I'm just Jim. Mr. Lashley was my great, great grandfather.

And please advise the snipers to keep their eyes on us when we get there, too," Jim said to everyone in the room. "Now, unless anyone has anything to add, let's get on the road."

"Can we stop at a What-a-Burger on the way back?" Nolan asked, following Jim out of the room.

"You bet," Jim answered without turning his head. "Just make sure you get one for everyone. And I'd like fries and a chocolate malt with mine."

Chapter 58

Following Michael's directions, Jim soon entered the neighborhood where their targets were.

"We're about four blocks from the street they'll probably use," Michael said, pointing down the street. "There's usually been a phone about the middle of the next block on the right."

"Vicki, any target phones up ahead?" Jim asked as he started slowing.

"One two blocks ahead on the right," she answered. "Most of them seem to be on the street just past it."

"Let us know when we are beside that phone," Jim told her.

"I've got you in sight," one of the snipers called out. "I'm in the first house on the left on the street if you turn into the killing zone."

Slowing even more, Jim checked his rearview mirror and asked, "Vicki, can you see anything behind me?"

"No, sir," she answered. "Only phones I see are the one you're almost on top of and those down the street."

As he got to the street where the phones seemed to be congregating, Jim eased to a stop and looked down it to see if anything seemed unexpected.

"See anything unusual, Michael?" he asked as he continued to sit at the intersection.

"No, sir," he answered. "This is about the same as when I came through the other day."

Just as Jim started to roll forward slowly, he heard Brett calling over the earpiece, "I think I have someone trailing me."

"Think? Or sure?" Jim asked as he continued past the street.

"Pretty damn sure," Brett answered.

"I agree," came another voice. "I'm in the house at the end of the street, and I saw a car leave just as he passed the street."

"Any changes in the phones at Brett's location?" Jim asked as he accelerated, checking his rearview mirrors again.

"No," Renee answered. "I've been tracking Brett and the phones in his area."

"He's still behind me," Brett said as he pulled his pistol out and laid it in his lap. "What do you want me to do?"

"How far is he from me?" Jim asked Vicki.

"Three miles north," she answered. "And there's still no movement of the phones in your area."

"Brett, how far from I-10 are you?" Jim asked, accelerating away in the direction of I-10.

"He's about half a mile," Renee said. "He can get on I-10 heading south in about a mile. It'll be about a thousand feet after he goes under I-10 on Geronimo."

"Do you know where she's talking about, Vicki?" Jim asked as Michael pointed to where Jim needed to go to get to I-10.

"Yes," she answered. "What do you want me to do?"

"Put me behind him," Jim said.

"I can lead him to you," Brett said. "If we can get either Nolan or Tim, we can trap him somewhere and take care of him."

"No," Jim told them. "Unless he's shooting, we'll try to get him off your ass without him realizing we did it."

"I can join you guys," Nolan said. "I'm just south of both of you."

"I don't think this guy is really after Brett," Jim said as he saw I-10 just ahead. "If they really wanted him, they would have sent at least two cars."

"Hey, shooter," Jim said as he approached the entrance ramp for I-10. "Did any other cars leave the area behind Brett?"

"No, that car was parked in front of the house where we think one of the blocker cars is," he answered. "Both of the blocker cars are still parked, and I haven't seen anything else moving."

"Renee, were any of the phones in that area used while Brett was there?" Jim asked, looking at the upcoming exits.

"There were just a couple of beeps," she answered. "Sort of like when you're dialing a number. It was just as he passed one of the phones on the street leading into the neighborhood."

"Okay, that tells me that they're watching for us," Jim said. "Vicki, did that happen in my area?"

"Yeah, I didn't think much about it either," she answered. "Same thing, a couple of beeps."

"Same with Nolan and Tim," Melinda broke in saying.

"And no other cars trailing any of us?" he asked as he changed lanes to exit. "Where's Brett now?"

"No phones," Melinda said. "Maybe the guy behind Brett isn't part of the gang."

"I doubt that," Jim said. "I don't think they would send one of the phones in the car to follow him. Since they think we're tracking them through the phones, having one would highlight him back there. No, I think he's MS 13, but he's just trying to find out where Brett's going."

"How do you want to play this?" Brett asked. "I'm about to get on I-10. Do you want me to try to lose him?"

"No, that would be too obvious, and they'd know were aware of him," Jim answered. "Vicki, where should I turn around to get either behind or in front of Brett?"

"Take the Hawkins exit just ahead," she answered. "Then head east after you go under the road. You'll be able to reenter I-10 heading east about a thousand feet down."

"Where will Brett be?" Jim asked, taking the exit.

"He'll be about a half mile behind you," Renee answered.

"Let me know when you see me," Jim said, passing beneath I-10.

"I'm on I-10 approaching the Hawkins exit," Brett said. "I should be able to see you as soon as you…..I see you now!"

"Vicki, what's the next exit I can take?" Jim asked as Michael turned to look behind them.

"McRae," she answered. "It's not far ahead, so you may need to slow a little for Brett to catch you."

"What's the guy following you driving?" Jim asked as Michael said he had Brett in sight.

"Little white Honda-looking thing," Brett answered as he closed the gap with Jim. "Got one of those spoiler wing things on the rear."

"Okay, I think I see him," Jim said. "Go ahead and accelerate around me when you think you can jump in front and take McRae. I'll slam on my brakes to make sure he passes me after you do. Hopefully, it'll be too late for him to make the exit behind you."

"What if he makes it?" Brett asked, trying to time his move.

"Stay on the service road and go back under I-10," Jim told him. What road will that be, Vicki?"

"That's Yarbrough," she answered.

"I remember that road," Jim said, tapping his brakes. "That's where the Walmart is that we used earlier to dump our cars."

"That's it," Vicki confirmed.

"If he's still behind you, I can make the exit also," Jim said seeing Brett turn his head looking at him. "You just head for the Walmart, and I'll join you."

Just then, Brett whipped in front, heading for the exit, and Jim slammed on his brakes, forcing the Honda trailing Brett to swerve left to avoid hitting him.

As Brett skidded onto the exit, Jim continued east on I-10, saying, "I'm going to follow this guy to see where he gets off. Brett, stay on the access road until I tell you to head for the conference center. I don't want this guy to spot you if he tries to reverse after he exits."

"Got it," Brett said, stopping at the intersection with Yarbrough.

"He's taking the Lomaland exit," Jim said. "Renee, send Brett somewhere south of the access road. This guy could be back at Yarbrough in time to see him."

"Turn right," Renee directed Brett. "Then take another right in about two hundred feet on Rodeo Avenue. That should keep you hidden."

"I'm going to follow him off the road," Jim said as he took the Lomaland exit. "If he heads back north, I'll follow him to Yarbrough, and then I'll turn toward the Walmart."

A few minutes later, Jim said, "Okay, he did a U-turn and is headed east on the service road. I guess we lost him. Bring me home, Vicki Jean."

"Take Vista del Sol on your right after you pass the Walmart," she said. "Then right on Vista de Oro, then left on Pellicano Drive. That'll bring you to Lomaland; turn right and go down to Rojas. You'll know where you are then."

"On my way," Jim said. "Where are the rest of the guys?"

"Nolan and Tim are here watching," Melinda answered. "What's next?"

"Bring Brett back, and we'll have a quick debrief, and then I have to get back to my hotel for tomorrow's flight," he answered as Michael pointed out Vista del Sol coming up.

"Guess I wasn't much help," Michael said later as they parked at the conference center.

"You did fine," Jim said as they entered the building. "Things just got a little out of control there for a few minutes. But I was glad to have you along. And you knew a lot about our area that I'd never have known if I'd been alone. That'll help out immensely tomorrow when this gets real."

Chapter 59

Jim stepped off the elevator after getting back to the same hotel as last night. After seeing that he got the same room, he wondered why they didn't just book it for two nights instead of one night at a time.

As he'd expected, Nolan was waiting in the lobby to take him to the conference center. "How was the flight?" he asked as Jim headed out the door.

"Gear up, gear down," Jim said, opening the passenger door. "Passengers off, passengers on, passengers off, passengers on. Do over and over and over."

"I figured being an airline pilot would be pretty exciting," Nolan said as they pulled out of the parking lot.

"More like countless hours of sheer boredom punctuated by moments of stark terror," Jim told him. "Sort of reminds me of days in the field back in Vietnam. But without the mud, insects, bullets whizzing by, and those wonderful days during the monsoon."

"Soooooo, pretty cushy job though, right?" Nolan asked, taking a glance at Jim.

"Yeah, cushy," Jim agreed. "But extremely repetitive."

"But all those different cities and airports," Nolan argued.

"Different city, different airport, different hotel, same thing," Jim told him. "Don't get me wrong. It's a great job. But compared to flying a fighter, it's like going from a Le Mans racecar to a city bus. With lots of people who think they need to be catered to and treated like royalty just because they bought a cheap ass ticket from Hillbilly, Georgia, to BFE."

"BFE?" Nolan asked as they pulled into the parking lot at the convention center.

"Bum Fuck Egypt," Jim told him. "The stopping off point of every deployment, TDY, or operation where they need nothing but the brightest and most highly trained to sit countless hours staring at the local residents."

"BFE, I'll have to remember that," Nolan said as they entered the building.

As soon as he entered their room, Jim spotted General Barker at the front talking to Melinda.

Heading directly to him, Jim said, "Good afternoon, General. Down admiring your handiwork?"

"More or less," Gene answered, shaking Jim's hand. "Have you got a second?"

"Of course, sir," Jim answered, nodding at Melinda.

Once they were where no one could hear them, Gene asked, "What's your personal opinion at this point? Is this going to work?"

Without hesitating, Jim replied, "Not a doubt, sir. Our drive-by yesterday had a small snag, but I think that was a fluke. Every other zone worked as planned."

"I heard about that," Gene said, nodding. "You really think that was a fluke?"

"Yes, sir, I do," Jim answered. "I'd like to know where the car went after Brett ditched it, but I'm sure it belonged to the MS 13 members that were in his area."

"What if I told you it had happened at every other location?" Gene asked. "Would that change your mind?"

Thinking for a second, Jim answered, "Okay, maybe it wasn't a fluke. But I still think it was a reconnaissance mission to see if they could tell where we were coming from."

"What it tells me is they may be one step ahead of us," Gene said, voicing his concern.

"They may think they are, sir," Jim argued. "But we've been watching them for almost a week, and I stand by my original assessment. And I think the intelligence we've gathered bears that out.

Have you asked this of the other operations?" Jim asked.

"Of course," Gene answered. "And they all feel the same way you do. I guess I'm just overly concerned that you and the others are walking into a trap that may be more lethal than we think."

"It could be," Jim agreed, nodding. "But, unless you've changed your mind about this being the best solution, I'm prepared to execute the plan as soon as I can get a final briefing with Nolan, Brett, Tim, and Melinda."

"No, I haven't changed my mind," Gene admitted. "Just making sure you and your people are prepared as best you can be for any unpleasant surprises."

"I'm sure we are, sir," Jim told him. "Now, unless there's anything else, I need to get this herd to town."

Seeing Gene looking in his eyes and giving a slight nod, Jim walked over to where Melinda was talking to Nolan and Brett.

Motioning for Tim to join them, Jim waited until they were all together and asked, "Melinda, have you done a communications check with everyone within the last hour?"

Hearing that she had, he then asked Brett, "Are all of your shooters in position? Are the house entry teams standing by their launch points? Have you checked your car and weapons?"

Seeing him nod affirmatively at every question, he repeated the same to both Tim and Nolan. Getting the same response, he then turned to Melinda.

"Are all of the screens working? Are all of the phones, or dots, accounted for? Is our communication with the other locations still operational?" he asked, looking at the number of people waiting for the action to start.

"We've spent the morning rehearsing this, Jim," she told him. "The only thing left is for you to put in your earpiece and turn it on. You're the only one who hasn't checked in."

Smiling slightly, he slipped it in his right ear and asked, "Is there anything I haven't covered or overlooked?"

"I'd tell you that you haven't checked your car and your weapons, sir, except I checked them for you," Nolan told him with a big grin.

"You did?" Brett asked, looking at Nolan. "So did I."

"Me, too," Tim said, grinning.

"So did Michael before he left," Melinda added.

"Then I guess it's time we got this rolling," Jim said, shaking his head. "Good luck to everyone. I'll see all of you back here in a couple of hours."

As Jim turned to leave, he heard several voices softly singing in unison, "Rollin', Rollin', Rollin'. Keep them doggies rollin'. Keep them doggies rollin' Rawhide!"

Shaking his head, he glanced at Gene to see him with a not-so-subtle smile plastered on his face.

Chapter 60

"Hello, Vicki Jean," Jim said as he started his car. "How am I doing?"

"Good, Mr. Lashley," she answered. "I've got you pinpointed and can see the other cars around you."

"How about the zone?" he asked, putting the car in drive. "Anything unusual over there?"

"No, sir," she replied. "Shooters have all said they have clear views, no new cars blocking them. I just heard from the backdoor boys, and they're standing by waiting for you."

"Backdoor boys?" Jim asked, laughing as he crossed under I-10. That's a good description, I guess. What about the target phones? Normal locations?"

"Yes, sir," she answered. "One small exception is the one that was only a couple of blocks from the street where you'll turn is now a block further away."

"Noted," Jim said, merging with the eastbound traffic. "Probably moved him back to give them a little more notice when I pull through."

"Do me a favor and give the guys on the ground a progress report of how close I am," Jim said as he saw the exit he needed to take coming up.

"Done," she replied a second later. "If it's all right with you, I'm going to switch all of you to a common frequency, so you'll have an intercom from this point on."

"Good idea," Jim said, taking the exit that would put him in the neighborhood in about five minutes. "How are Nolan and the others progressing?"

"They're all about five or six minutes out," Vicki answered.

"Okay, folks," Jim said as he turned on the same street he had driven down yesterday. "If anyone sees any reason to abort, say so now."

Not hearing anything, he slowed to make the right turn and said, "Vicki, if the backdoor boys haven't started in, get them going."

"They're going in now," she told him.

Easing forward, Jim saw a car coming around behind him, staying a few feet back. Looking down the street, he saw the faint exhaust of a car in one of the driveways. Knowing he was now committed, he accelerated and said, "If anyone sees a target, take it out."

The car in the driveway suddenly backed out and started toward Jim. As it got about fifty feet away, it slid into a hard turn and blocked the street.

Glancing in his rearview mirror, he saw the car behind him closing the gap quickly. Hitting his rear bumper, it then slid sideways, blocking the road behind him.

Suddenly, the street erupted as smoke grenades were raining down all around his car. Although he couldn't see them, he saw the spider webs where their bullets were hitting his windshield and rear glass.

Knowing that the smoke would block the snipers' view, he accelerated toward the car in front and cut sharply to his left, jumping the curb as he tried to get off the street.

Seeing two forms in the smoke in front, he twisted the steering wheel back to the right and knocked them into the car they'd gotten out of.

The bullets seemed to have slowed and almost stopped as he plowed back through the smoke to the street. Making a fast U-turn, he sat facing the car that had meant to block him.

Taking one of the shotguns from the rack, he checked the load to make sure it was the slugs, opened his door, and stepped out of the car. From the sides, he could hear continuous gunfire from the houses and the yards.

Occasionally, he'd hear the definite sound of a high-powered rifle as the snipers finally found their targets.

As the smoke finally began to dissipate, he saw someone with a compact machine gun about ten feet away coming toward him. Raising his shotgun, he yelled, "Stop!"

As the figure started raising his gun, Jim fired a quick shot at his chest and then another at his head. Seeing the spray of red flying from where the head used to be, Jim took a step toward the car.

Crossing to the right where he had struck the two men, Jim hugged the side of the car and looked at the ground beside the gutter.

As he did, one of the men lying there raised a pistol and tried to point it at him. Holding the shotgun by its pistol grip, Jim swung the barrel up and grabbed the slide as he pulled the trigger.

With the roar of the gun still ringing in his ears, he pumped another shell into the gun and fired it point blank at the other body lying beside the one he had just shot.

Stepping to the sidewalk, he looked through the haze that was all that was left of the smoke. Seeing a body lying on each side of the car that had been behind him, he looked left and right as he approached them.

As a single shot rang out from his left and behind him, Jim ducked and stepped to the car for cover. As he crouched there, waiting to see if there were going to be any more shots from that direction, he felt someone grab his ankle.

Looking down, he brought the barrel of his shotgun to where the arm of the hand that was holding his leg joined the shoulder and pulled the trigger.

Pumping another round into the chamber, he waited a second to see if there was any further movement. Seeing nothing but an ever-widening pool of blood forming, he started to step over the body when a bullet glanced off the pavement under the car.

Rounding the rear of the car, he saw the other man he had seen lying on the pavement with his arm extending under the car.

Looking at the foaming red coming from the man's chest, Jim pointed the shotgun at his face as the man turned to look directly at him.

As he tried to withdraw his arm from beneath the car, Jim shook his head and pulled the trigger.

Knowing that he only had two shells left, Jim started working his way back to his car.

"Vicki, are you still there?" he asked as he tossed the shotgun across the seat and grabbed the other one loaded with double-aught.

"I'm here," she answered. "What's the status?"

"Check with everyone," Jim told her as he looked down the street where he had entered just moments ago. "I'm going to walk back down the street."

Listening to everyone answering when Vicki called their names, Jim slowed as he came to the car that had been behind him. Looking at each house he had passed, he asked, "Which houses were the targets in?"

"The one directly in front of you and the one two doors down on the other side of the street," Vicki answered.

Not seeing anyone in the first house, he crossed the street and saw a body lying on the front steps of the house on that side. Walking up to it, keeping an eye on the other houses, he saw that the lower half of his face was missing.

"All of the phones there have been checked," Vicki told him. "The backdoor guys say they've cleared the houses and want to know what you want them to do."

"What about the single phone on the street before I turned?" Jim asked, crossing back across the street.

"I took him out just as the smoke started," Jim heard someone say. "I've been scoping every house, and there's been no movement."

"All right, everybody, head back before the police get here," Jim said. "Does everyone have a ride?"

"I need one," the guy who had shot the target down the street said. "And the other shooter down by your car probably does also."

"I do," someone said. "I'm on my way to your car. Does it still run?"

"I sure as shit hope so," Jim said, making his way back to the car. "We'll find out in a minute."

As he got to the car, he saw a man with a long rifle and scope standing there, looking at all of the bullet holes.

"Mr. Lashley, I'm Charles," the guy said. "Sorry we couldn't be more help than we were, but the smoke surprised us, and we couldn't get many shots at the guys in the cars we were supposed to take out."

"Let's not worry about that right now," Jim said, getting into the driver's seat. "Let's see if this piece of shit will get us out of here, and we'll grab your partner as we leave."

Pausing just long enough at the end of the street for the other shooter to get in the car, Jim headed back the way he had come and asked, "Vicki, how are the other teams?"

"They're good, Jim," Melinda answered. "They're all on their way back. You're the straggler."

"I need to stay off the main roads," Jim said as he approached the end of the street, leaving the neighborhood. "Give me a turn-by-turn route home."

"Make a left at the next street," Vicki told him. "Then you'll be making another left in two streets. I'll get you back here safely, Mr. Lashley."

Twenty minutes later, Jim pulled into the conference center parking lot. Pulling up beside the other cars, he saw the same damage as had happened to his car.

Following his two passengers into the building, he wondered if there had been any injuries. As they entered their room, Jim saw Gene standing at the front beside Melinda with a smile on his face.

"Well, this may not have been Tombstone, but that was one hell of a shootout," Gene said as Jim reached him. "I think we can call this operation successful and close down shop."

"Anybody get hurt?" Jim asked, looking around the room.

"One of the backdoor guys got cut with some flying glass," Melinda told him. "He's at the hospital for a shot and a couple of stitches."

"What about the other cities?" Jim asked.

"A few minor flesh wounds, some bruises, nothing lethal," Gene answered. "No fatalities."

"That's it?" Jim said in disbelief. "In that case, I think I'd like to have a shot myself."

"Way ahead of you, as usual," Gene said, smiling as Nolan walked in with Tim and Brett carrying three cases of Jack Daniel's.

"First in, last out, and always ready," Gene said as he poured all of the shot glasses full that Melinda was rapidly sitting on the table.

"Then, here's to their blood-in, blood-out lifestyle," Jim said, raising his glass. "At least to their blood out."

Chapter 61

The following morning, Jim was sitting in the lobby having a cup of coffee when Ray came off the elevator with Mary and Susan pulling their luggage.

"Good morning," Ray said, parking his roll-aboard next to Jim's. "How was your evening with the old war buddies?"

"Pretty good," Jim said, standing. "Had a couple of glasses of iced tea, told a few lies, complained about our wives, you know. Standard guy shit."

"I guess you didn't hear about the carnage that happened again last night here in El Paso," Ray said as Paula got off the elevator.

"No, I haven't seen a television since I left home three days ago," Jim confessed. "What happened?"

"Are you talking about all those guys that got shot last night?" Paula asked as she joined the crew.

"I was; Jim doesn't know anything about it," Ray answered as everyone grabbed their suitcases and headed for the exit.

"Really?" Mary asked. "I heard they had to bring in refrigerator trucks because the morgues were full."

"How many people are we talking about?" Paula asked as they waited for the courtesy van to take them to the airport.

"I heard one newscaster say that it was over a hundred," Susan added.

"A hundred, can you imagine that?" Mary asked as their driver started putting their bags in the rear of the van.

"Not only that, but I just heard that the same thing had happened in Los Angeles," Ray said as they got in the van.

"And you didn't hear anything about it?" Mary asked Jim. "You need to start keeping up with the news. I don't think I'll ever bid El Paso layovers again."

"Me neither," Susan chimed in as the van pulled away from the hotel. "Or Los Angeles."

About the Author

Following in his father's footsteps of military aviation and service, Jim joined the US Air Force and flew a variety of aircraft until his retirement. Then joining American Airlines, he finished his flying career and began writing.

With a love for rodeo, ranching, and flying, he spends his time doing those things that bring him pleasure. From bareback riding in his early days to ranching and team roping, he never forgot that the cowboy way was how he wanted to live his life.

Take care of your family. Take care of your friends. Take care of yourself. Everything else will take care of itself.